gatsby

Jane Crowther is the former editor of *Total Film* magazine and is now the editor-in-chief of *Hollywood Authentic* magazine. She is the chair of The London Film Critics' Circle and a member of BAFTA and the Critics' Choice Association. Her debut non-fiction book, *Silver Screens*, was published by HarperCollins in 2025. *Gatsby* is her debut novel.

Praise for *Gatsby*:

'[This] enjoyable debut novel put[s] fresh meat on Fitzgerald's deathless classic' ***Observer***

'A clever, gender-flipped modern-day retelling of the classic' ***Grazia***

'Updating a classic gives it immediacy. Gender-flipping allows for an even more fascinating exploration of beloved characters' ***Sunday Times Style***

'You're pulled along in the tow of this timeless tragedy once more' ***The Times***

'A female perspective adds definite intrigue here, and as aspiring journalist Nic Carraway eases her way into it-girl Jay Gatsby's A-list parties, bartering access to her charming cousin Danny Buchanan, it proves startlingly easy to transplant Jazz Age decadence and obsession to the modern world of influencers and cancel culture' ***Mail on Sunday***

'A glitzy modern-day twist on the much-loved classic' ***The Sunday Post***

'With undertones of romance, jealousy, deceit and tragedy, *Gatsby* has all the glitz, glam and drama of the original'
Sunday Life

'Fans of *The Great Gatsby* are in for a treat' ***The Bookseller***

'In this superb retelling, the author deftly places her Gatsby in the social media age, living an American Dream that promises anybody can fake it. It's stylish and beautifully written, with a cast of the most decadently unhinged characters. I highly recommend joining the party'
James Goodhand, author of *The Day Tripper*

'This timely and unputdownable retelling of the classic tale transports the action to a setting that fascinates and repulses in equal measure. Packed with compelling characters, plenty of intrigue and OTT decadence, it's a seriously impressive debut'
Rosie Mullender, author of *Ghosted*

'A beautifully written reimagining of *The Great Gatsby*... this well-known story is cleverly altered to give a brand-new telling that is equally compelling and atmospheric. *Gatsby* is an addictive read with a heady mix of tension, exquisitely described excess, and a delicious darkness hovering beneath the glittering surface. I loved it'
Amanda Jennings, author of *Beautiful People*

'Smart, stylish and scandalously sexy ... A clever, intoxicating, fresh take on a story that feels made for the influencer era' **Rosamund Dean, author of *Reconstruction***

'A delicious skewering of today's *Polite Society* — *Gatsby* has never felt more relevant!' **Hanna Flint, author of *Strong Female Character***

gatsby

jane crowther

b
THE BOROUGH PRESS

The Borough Press
An imprint of HarperCollins*Publishers* Ltd
1 London Bridge Street
London SE1 9GF

www.harpercollins.co.uk

HarperCollins*Publishers*
Macken House, 39/40 Mayor Street Upper
Dublin 1, D01 C9W8, Ireland

This paperback edition published 2026

26 27 28 29 30 LBC 6 5 4 3 2

First published in Great Britain by HarperCollins*Publishers* 2025

A catalogue record for this book is available from the British Library

ISBN: 978-0-00-867267-6

Printed and bound in the United States of America

For Hal

Fame is a bee.
It has a song—
It has a sting—
Ah, too, it has a wing.

Emily Dickinson

Chapter 1

After a long time weighing up whether to tell the world what actually happened – for reasons of honesty, loyalty and a sense of justice – it was the funeral that finally convinced me to sit down and write. But not the funeral you think. Not the one you imagine you know the sad details of, covered by the tabloids and inaccurately dramatised on Netflix.

Having been asked for my side of the story repeatedly, and advised by healthcare professionals that some sort of journalling might be a good way to make sense of that summer, I eventually found myself questioning what I was so afraid of that prevented me from doing the very thing that had first lured me to the East Coast in the warm months of 2019. In those more innocent days for all of us, before we learnt what regret, grief and reckoning really looked like on a global scale, I had harboured ambitions to dazzle with prose. As a girl, I hoped to manifest a book; as a teen, a following; as a newly graduated scholar, an audience. Now I hope for kinship. There were so many accounts of the ephemeral events in that hot, violent window of time before darker stories knocked this one from the top of the news cycles and the 'think piece' industry. But they don't even scratch at the skin of the truth. I may have only figured in the limited TV show as a composite character, but mine is a voice that truly bears witness – I was there. I am the smoking gun.

As with all things, it's all about perspective. Take the Polaroid photo above my desk where I write. At first glance, it doesn't seem to be anything special. Without context, some might look at the slate-grey channel of water cutting between the watercolour smudge of the shore in the distance – the suggestion of the jade tended lawn, the white of clapboard – and see tranquillity. Others may sense a foreboding in the darker depths closer to the lens where the water looks almost black. Perhaps the value of the real estate on display might be assessed; or maybe the vista simply evokes the taste of salt on the breeze and the delicious chill of the water on such a beautiful day. Those who know the eyes that looked through the viewfinder, always scanning the horizon, the spot just out of focus, might see an act of prayer.

This picture, taken repeatedly by its photographer, is infamous now. Though her feeds were wiped, nothing nowadays is ever truly deleted or really disappears. Images and comments are harvested the minute they appear; stored and saved to be served up later. This one was; the framing of this view given new meaning over the years. A shot that was repeated so many times on her platforms, and copied by others. That she never posted a caption seemed like an invitation to add individual interpretation; fill the empty heart with red. Like, validate, imprint a narrative. When I look up at it from my keyboard, I do the same thing. I start to believe I can decipher the message it's sending out. The manifestation chant of its originator intertwined with the memories of my own misgivings. I cherish and hate it in equal measure because I recall the happiness, the giddiness, the bewilderment and the betrayal I felt being in that very spot looking at the sound so many times that lurid, lush summer. And I wonder if I sensed the tumbling towards an inevitable end even then, felt it like the slip of the angle of repose on a pile of sand – the point at which the heaped grains begin to tremble and slide, no longer able to hold their critical shape.

Even if I did, I likely didn't care. Because Gatsby refracted light when she entered a room – it was often hard to see anything else. Buoyed on hope and romance, she floated, as though in orbit, into any party. Sometimes so brilliant that it felt as though protective glasses were required to view her. And like any beautiful, imperfect thing travelling through space and time, she came into contact with other celestial bodies – knocking her off her centrifugal path. All of that aspect of her life – the fatal collision course – has been written about, picked over with schadenfreude, shared, re-shared, held up as an example of inauthenticity and appropriation. But to me, she represented many other things; chief among them, promise.

The idea of Gatsby thrilled me – her fame, her leverage, her curated life – but I also felt an immediate affinity with her despite our very different existences. Even though her true intentions crystallised after our final meeting, I recognised the dreamer in her. We were both in pursuit of something we imagined would deliver pure happiness. She wanted to resurrect a life she had previously tasted, I wanted to replicate the career of online essayists whose content I devoured. I have since managed to write for money, but not anything personal, truthful, meaningful. I had wanted my name inked in the water-cooler conversation-starters of *Time*, the *Atlantic*, the *New Yorker*, the *New York Times*, *W*, *Vulture*, *Slate*, *Pajiba*, the *Cut*. Then, I didn't capitalise on my time adjacent to a cultural 'moment'. In reality, in the aftermath, I was an invisible copywriter embodying the voice of a famous bread manufacturer, the rallying cry of a

Wall Street broker, the friendly, non-threatening approach of a meds distributor. It has not been what I aspired to.

But if there's one thing I think I know about Gatsby, it's that had she been with me now, she would have championed me to be merciless in my determination, to exploit all the avenues available to me in pursuing the endgame, just as she did. She would have wanted me to use what I have, bow to the insatiable first-person industrial complex, even if it exposed her. She would have wanted the beauty to be revealed as well as the rot. I have long been quiet, respectful, protective, discreet, and nothing good has come from it. My personal growth has only come from psychoanalysis, pressing guilt and the flaying sting of public opinion. Maybe now is the time for some letting go, some public catharsis, some tarnished truths. To write about all the febrile, filthy things my private, respectable parents abhor.

* * *

As the child of educated liberals who were comfortable enough to send me to a college of note without my needing a job or two during my studies, I had been taught all my life to never judge people. 'Be kind', they told me, 'think of others', 'never assume', 'ask questions'. This was a privilege of my economic status; I never had to operate from a position of danger or threat, had no hunger or desperation driving a need to read people fast. I grew up trying to find context in anyone I met, striving to understand their circumstance, applying the benefit of doubt – whether that was a stranger growling obscenities on the subway, the security guard who manned our lobby in a cloud of pungent body odour, the girl with a mean mouth in junior high who bullied me over my flat chest. That's hard to do as a kid when you stand in the shower clawing at uncooperative breasts; harder still, I found, at college in New Haven, where I provoked dorm queen bees' ire as a freshman, for never taking sides. I asked questions and I waited for the answers – and consequently I knew secrets. But I never used them for gain, never felt I needed to, which I suppose is entitled in itself.

My ability to listen and watch was noted by a college professor who suggested that a role in journalism might suit my nascent talents. Having immersed myself in the works of Joan Didion, Gloria Steinem, Barbara Ehrenreich and Susan Sontag, I threw myself into the school paper, reporting on sports fixtures, stage shows and a long-running cafeteria outrage over the relative lack of vegan options. This, I was sure, was the gateway to my brilliant future, and as I amassed college credit and hours in the press room, my scholastic years slid by unremarkably. My experiences were sweet, like the boys I dated. Nothing bad had ever happened to me, and in my final year, I grandly informed my parents when I flew home for the holidays that I intended to move to New York when I had finished my exams. I was going to be a writer.

I know. It sounds pretentious. But the Carraway family were not a people who let logistics or a lack of discernable talent stand in the way of personal glory. They didn't hesitate in supporting me, agreeing to fund a summer on the East Coast to allow me to blog, write and network unrestricted from the end of May until the cooling days of September, in the hope of parsing my content into the actual salary of a paid position. Then, my dad warned me, I would need to stand on my own two feet. It's what Grandpa had done with him, and Great-gramps before that – and look at how well they had done. Sitting around our dining table when he rolled out this plan again to our assembled family as though repetition ensured success, my aunt nodded sagely and assured me that such an enterprise would be 'the making' of me. I liked the sound of this despite rolling my eyes at the cliché. I felt formless and wanted the chafe of something new to reveal the bright edges surely hidden within me.

My dad thought talking about money in numerical terms was vulgar, so I never knew during the last semester of school just what kind of summer I should anticipate. I had saved precisely nothing in the college checking account my parents transferred funds into each semester, yet spent most evenings scrolling through Manhattan apartment rental sites and Instagram accounts detailing cheese plants on sun-dappled windowsills with the curve of a water tower in the background, feet in skates on baking Central Park asphalt, food that looked like art, art that looked like food . . . Though I'd always had Teddy Roosevelt's quote about comparison levelled at me by my parents ('the thief of joy, Nic'), I couldn't help but covet the lives I scrolled through. I wanted the hot noise and vibrations of New York City. I expected that life would happen to me there, experiences sticking to my skin – changing me, moulding me. I would be inspired and create. I would write stirring pieces on culture, fame, the arts, that would be re-shared across platforms and quoted in classes. As it turned out, the rents in Manhattan were alarming when written on the spreadsheet of my father's laptop, the figure in his head not aligned with the cost of a Greenwich Village studio or a Brooklyn loft. I was told to be creative with the cash he offered, to prove my resourcefulness.

When I think back to the girl at that dining room table, I realise that my aunt was right: in the end, that summer did make me. Just not in the way any of us might have imagined. In ways that still prickle me with penitence when I lie awake at night watching the clock instead of my dreams.

Chapter 2

I arrived in New York at the end of May, cash poor but connected enough to call in a favour from one of my cousins when it came to accommodation. Danny and his wife had asked their various WhatsApp groups if anyone had a room for a trustworthy Yale graduate who wanted a place to write after she'd despaired at finding lodging within her price range. Their friendship group were the kind of people who had real estate lying dormant and annexes filled with forgotten sports equipment.

I had chosen to take a later flight out of Minneapolis than my mom had suggested – partly because I wanted to delay leaving my childhood home for what I felt might be the last time as a true resident, and in part because I wanted to prove my own agency to my parents no matter how trivial the point. In actuality, leaving mid-morning didn't lessen the rush or my parents' fussing, it didn't buy me time to sip a leisurely coffee as I strolled to the gate. Instead, I arrived in my seat with minutes to spare, my fingers white around my clutched phone and that familiar creeping sense that something crucial was missing from my luggage. But, I reasoned, as long as I had my laptop, my phone and a credit card, nothing in my stuffed case was invaluable; three hours later when I landed in afternoon sunshine, I had pep-talked myself into feeling on the cusp of an adventure, rather than standing on the edge of a precipice.

In the end I only tasted Manhattan rather than consuming it. Arriving at JFK, I took the AirTrain north to Jamaica Station, dragging a suitcase too heavy to confidently negotiate. There, in my fantasy life, I would have been swapping to the E subway train, my thighs sticking to the plastic bucket seats for the swift half hour it would take to come up gulping for air at Lexington Avenue. But instead, I followed the green signs to the LIRR, picking up the train east, and arriving agitated and heated at Great Neck station. I had not asked New York natives I knew for the fastest route in the self-defeating belief that this was an adventure of my own making. But as the time ticked away and my temperature rose, I felt a rube rather than independent.

At Great Neck station I eschewed a quicker, cooler Uber for the red neighbourhood bus. I wanted to acclimate myself with my new neighbourhood as well as understand the time it would take to commute to Manhattan spending the least amount of money. I also thought it would make an amusing story that displayed my modesty on my social feeds. My sweaty hands grappled to keep my suitcase from skittering across the floor at each lurch and turn as we ribboned towards the edge of Long Island Sound. Within minutes, an elderly woman wearing a vintage hat I longed to take a picture of was jabbing me with questions about how to get to an obscure address and wouldn't take my apologetic word that I wasn't a local. She departed, furiously, before the roads became quieter, the verges more dense with trees. From there we crawled to the tip of the coast and the bus rode the freshly painted yellow centre line of the road to avoid hitting verdant branches. It felt almost rural and, though there was no way I could actually deduce it over the roaring air conditioning and the tang of something familiar and dreadful emanating from the back seat area, I thought I could smell the ocean.

I disembarked at the end of the bus route, next to a large, bottle-green pond, clattering my case down the bus steps and earning a sigh behind me from the only other passenger who had come this far. A heavy-set woman, wearing the unmistakable dress favoured by monied people for their maids, overtook me fast and walked with purpose toward one of the large driveways that led to vast houses perched on the shore.

I wasn't heading for such a palace. My cousin's acquaintance was going through a nasty divorce and wanted to stop her soon to be ex-husband using the ramshackle boathouse squatting at the edge of their acreage on the water.

This is perfect! she'd emailed me. *You get a place to stay and I get a sitting tenant. He'll hate that!*

She asked for a hundred dollars a week in rent, which she quaintly asked to be left in an earthenware jar by the door of the boathouse. She would send one of the children across the huge lawn to collect it as one of their vacation 'chores'. This was also where I'd find the key when I'd arrive. Her rules were succinct: no smoking, drugs, pets or overnight guests. I hoped to break most of these before Labor Day.

A hundred dollars wasn't an inconsiderable sum to me despite my parents' bankrolling, but a steal for accommodation in this neighbourhood, and it would have been inconsequential to my landlady. I wondered what she might spend it on. Would her pampered children be allowed to keep such pin money? Or would she tuck it into her expensive purse each week to use for tips? I had the first six weeks' payment zipped into my bag as I rolled it along the main road, turning off at the narrower lane that led to a turning circle and, at the end, my new home. Google Maps had assured me this was a seven-minute walk from the bus stop but as sweat pooled against the bag jostling at the small of my back and I sensed the ache I'd feel tomorrow, I regretted not taking a taxi and chastised myself for romanticism. This was not a lane that people walked bucolically down. No one but me, housekeeping or criminals would approach these properties on foot. I trudged on, promising myself a shower on completion of my journey, and was relieved to have met no traffic when I arrived at the stone-built driveway pillars of my benefactor's estate. I tapped the code I'd been given into the keypad and watched the heavy gates swing open towards a grand, gravel driveway curving around a manicured lawn to the front steps of the house – and off to the left, a smaller, grassy track leading shoreward. This was my route.

My home for the summer was humble compared to the estates that hulked on either side; a multi-million dollar faux Normandy Hôtel de Ville to my left and my landlady's English manor-style mansion to my right. Both had huge grounds that meant they were neighbours in name only, neither resident troubling the other by interrupting their views. The boathouse was a single-storey 1920s fixture at the end of the track, with high ceilings and a weathered clapboard frontage, a bed in the sitting room and a small galley kitchen with a window overlooking a wild magnolia bush that perfumed the evening as I arrived. The stove was an electric three-ring with an erratic connection, the lights dimmed periodically thanks to the ancient generator in the garden and the shower, as I learned that first evening, toyed between warm and cold in a way that seemed designed to test resilience. But the Wi-Fi was strong and steady, the phone signal adequate and the view . . . well, yes, the view. The bed faced a bow window looking across the sound, water lapping below in the mooring where a small row boat bobbed now, replacing the sailing boat the husband had removed under cover of darkness the night he left. The windowsill had a faded cushion that invited lounging, and at dusk, as I stared out, the lights on the shoreline across the channel blinked on, illuminating patios, jetties, gardens, driveways and ancillary buildings like mine.

Though the land across the water – East Egg – was almost a mirror image of this shoreline and the houses no more opulent, it was considered more desirable. West Egg was the preserve of people with money and merchant marines working or studying at the academy. Those living on the shoreline here were comfortably rich but had worked for it, often nouveau or renters. They were not the truly affluent and connected of the Hamptons, nor the famous faces who blew in for summer. The people of East Egg came from bluestocking families, Mayflower lineage or, at least, could account for wealth in more than two generations. Hollywood and political royalty were welcomed there if the family had long-standing connections with the area, the sale of choice real estate often brokered privately, without ever being offered on the open market. The men of East Egg indulged in pastimes that required investment: sailing, riding, golf. The wives were the kind of unamused women who had grown up knowing they would need extra rooms for staff in any house they eventually lived in, and would require Adirondack chairs in heritage colour washes for gazing at pleasant views.

My second cousin, Danny, had married such a woman. The child of my mom's first cousin, he had always been a favourite of mine at family gatherings where we were customarily pushed together despite his having arrived six years before me. He was always kind when other boys in our clan ridiculed or ignored me during enforced socialising. Our large family insisted on putting all the children on tables together at weddings, funerals, birthdays, cookouts, and Danny never made me feel like a kid. He always took me seriously – treated me as a peer when I was in second grade, like a teen when I was merely nudging up against twelve and desperate to be grown. Though I didn't see him often, we always clicked easily back into a comfortable rapport while we were toasting s'mores on camping trips, jumping about on dance floors or policing the behaviour of the younger kids with us. I adored him.

As he grew taller and his jaw hardened, I had to share him. He matured into a focus for girls in my circle, and I was compelled to become an occasional and reluctant broker of his love life. As a teenager I'd passed messages of admiration to him from friends who glimpsed him in my photos or at my house during national-holiday visits. I was envoy to giggling fellow guests who stared at him over the breakfast buffet as he decorated his plate at a hotel during a Carraway 50th birthday celebration in Michigan. Even in college, I unwittingly gave him to a friend when they were both in New York the same weekend and, wanting to be helpful to Danny, suggested they meet for coffee. I thought that she might be useful to him in landing contacts and cash for his fledgling start-up idea (which he abandoned months later) and that his charm would reflect well on me. I didn't anticipate them stretching a companionable coffee to cocktails and further. Then, when they got serious and began travelling across states to be with each other, I saw Danny more regularly, his golden looks drawing hungry eyes towards us when we drank in bars together waiting for her on the numerous occasions she ran late. I sat ignored while women engaged him in flirtatious banter, his low baritone a purr as he gently rebuffed their advances. Many times they assumed I was the girlfriend, and I knew they wondered why he was with a partner who did not mirror his magnetism. I confess I had wondered if I were not related to him what my feelings towards him might have been. My unconscious self had once deceived me during dreaming as a college student, making me wake mortified and perplexed at the sensual and explicit situations I'd envisaged him in with me. A friend I confided in assured me that this was merely my hormones raging and meaningless; relieved, I went back to watching others admire him.

When he was appraised by women in a naked way I felt protective. Danny was attractive by anyone's measure – tall, with wide shoulders and a narrow waist, a sharp profile that would be described as handsome in any era, cobalt eyes and a mouth that was almost pretty. But he was also affable, tender, empathetic, interested in subjects they couldn't fathom and clearly didn't care about as they watched his loping stride to the bathroom and whispered to each other. That said, I could not have stood up in court and, hand on heart, sworn to know his deepest thoughts, intentions or fears. I didn't know enough to see anything ugly or cruel in him. In that way, like most of us, he kept me at arm's length and his true self hidden.

Tomasina, T to her friends (more derogatory epithets to her enemies), was the friend I had delivered him to like a ribbon-wrapped gift – a Type-A, apex variant of the women of East Egg, who I'd known at Yale. It was quite an achievement to be such a titan in a college full of them. A senior to my freshman, we crossed paths via an amateur off-campus soccer team that met every Saturday for friendlies. Though it was intended as an antidote to the aggressively competitive nature of the official school team, T – as self-appointed captain – took every win and loss personally, barrelling down the field with the muscular thrust of someone playing full-contact football rather than soccer. She considered team tactics mere suggestion and despaired at the notion of indecision. 'Oh Nic, just apply yourself,' she'd say dismissively over post-match drinks to whatever difficulty I might have poured out to her.

T didn't understand giving up, accepting, switching lanes. She was fierce in her pursuit of her goals and didn't allow for weakness. That was true of the way she went about her studies, but also her requirements of service in restaurants; her unsympathetic assessment of classmates who'd become social pariahs thanks to drunken lapses in judgement; and her single-minded selection of a mate. T was assured about her standing in life. What it was and what it should be. Her wealthy family in Chicago had ensured she was never disappointed.

She was athletic, physically and mentally. 'Driven' was how she was diplomatically described. Statuesque and objectively striking, she took up the bandwidth conversationally, exuding an animal power that I could only describe in terms of scent because I didn't know how to put a finger on her MO other than to equate it to the Chanel N° 5 she wore. Like that heavy perfume, she was redolent and lingering. A base layer that demanded attention and wasn't about nuance or delicacy. The sort of smell you could almost taste, that induced a headache after too much exposure and clung to fabrics long after contact. Despite having grown anosmic to her aroma, I'd often wake the day after a team night out and, as much as I'd recall the communal merriment on my furred tongue, I'd also remember the specifics of T's lancing actions or words. I suppose that one of the reasons I remained friends with her was a fear of being the recipient of her criticism within our group. And because, like a lighthouse, she intermittently turned her full beam upon me, expressing interest, solidarity and generosity with laser focus. A cheerleader and protector who displayed fearsome loyalty and support when it suited her. And especially if it benefitted her. Once, I told her offhand about a hurtful spat I was undergoing with a classmate who spread untrue rumours about me. The next day I watched as T cornered her after class to explain in a measured tone how much harder she could return the favour should the girl wish to continue. A guilty flush crept up my neck while I caught snatches of the conversation. The outcome was agreeable to all. The girl never spoke to me, or of me, again.

It was enough emotional breadcrumbs to allow me to overlook the less appealing aspects of her personality. While I'd seen her hurt others, she hadn't yet injured me. It was an adventure to ride or die with her and, for a self-confessed wallflower, I found it exhilarating to be inside her selective court. The sorority feeling of being her friend was something I chased in the early days, as addictive as any romance.

When I inadvertently set her and Danny up on that crisp New York morning, she saw something gleaming in him. Though he lacked direction, he was beautiful, and T wanted that in a man. She had family money and fierce potential, and she liked that while she'd been at an Ivy League college, he had spent a similar number of years trying to start a band in Northern California. It was charming to her that he'd good-naturedly pursued something so patently not within his grasp. He was twenty-six when they met, rangy and aimless – and he was swept off his feet by T's predatory appetite for him, huge post-grad salary as a hedge fund portfolio manager and titanic sense of self.

They ran hot and fast before a small, impeccable wedding that no one in our friendship circle could improve upon. The new Mr and Mrs Buchanan moved from her DUMBO loft space to East Egg within months, to a large estate that reached the water via manicured gardens. They were the youngest couple to own on that coast. An elegant home ornamented with understated European furnishings and covetable art. Danny and T were two more gorgeous things decorating the property.

I'd been to stay during my final semester at school, flying out to visit for a holiday weekend that saluted the dead and tasted of barbecues and beer. They had been welcoming in the way that the wealthy are. Able to offer a sequestered, quiet room with a view of the waves, beautiful bedding, wonderful, plentiful food and drink . . . but it wasn't relaxed. There was an energy in the house that felt like the electric hum before a thunderstorm as the pair of them crackled with sexual tension and something ferocious. They each operated on different registers with me. Danny was warm, teasing and engaged – interested in my world, asking about my dating life, nudging me with his shoulder after causing me to blush. T was distracted and largely disappointed. At twenty-two, she assessed me as she would stock. Should she go long on me when I hadn't yet performed? Having not won a contract at a company that made an impression when dropped into polite conversation, found a covetable romantic partner nor shown any real certainty about my future, T looked at me with amused, patronising eyes over her egg whites and I knew she felt triumphant to be her and not me. I willingly subjected myself to such judgement.

And though it hurts to recall now, I felt nothing out of the ordinary. I wanted T's interest, the possibility of her support, even if that meant an awkward weekend where I felt more child than grown woman.

Later, when the Buchanans offered me a room in their home for the summer after I sent out my pleading group email, I politely declined, saying I wanted to strike out alone without the comfort of family around me. It was no doubt a relief to us all when Danny's friend of a friend threw out her cheating husband and offered a safe haven. In West Egg, I was near enough to visit them and enjoy rationed exposure, but far enough across the sound to feel removed. I'd tried to pick out their lawn and the red-and-white hatching of their tasteful colonial abode while peering through the ancient binoculars left on the windowsill of the boathouse. I had spent so long tracing across the water, alighting on boats to count the sailors aboard, and watching the jetties of neighbouring houses to note the sunbathers, that the cold, heavy metal left an indentation on the bridge of my nose.

In the first of weekly 'wine zooms' with college friends who had also orbited T, I described the area, the homes, the bathing suits of the denizens of West Egg, boasted of the riches of my cousin and supposed that there was surely enough incestuous intrigue and vulgar wealth to write an essay, a blog, a feature for one of the outlets I coveted seeing my byline in. In their framed digital windows scattered across the country, each pursuing proper adulthood with internships, starter jobs or bucket-list travels, the girls teasingly accused me of being a voyeur who was dressing up curtain-twitching as a noble art of reportage. I laughed with them because I knew what they were saying wasn't true; and because I was happy to be underestimated. I thought that being watchful rather than watched wasn't such a bad thing.

Chapter 3

It was nearly two weeks after my arrival when I first made my way around the parabola curve of the bay to Danny and T's house.

I had eventually found a rhythm to my days and filled my cupboards from Great Neck's overpriced delis and grocery stores. I'd found myself starting to wake uncharacteristically early after restful nights of sleep, lulled by the soporific slap of water below my window. My hours consisted of scouring sites and social-media accounts that I followed for inspiration, reading books whose writing style I hoped to emulate and messaging my now scattered friendship circle. I cooked nutritious meals following video tutorials and contemplated swimming, but rarely got further than sunbathing on the small deck that led down to the water. I had fallen asleep numerous times in the bow window, like a sun-toasted cat. It was a beguilingly simple existence and, having been surrounded by people and noise for my academic years, felt like an instructive change of pace. This, I reasoned, was what was needed to then begin the real work. I was dabbling with a blog of essays on movies, literature and celebrity, and populating my social feeds with abstract shots of light dancing on waves, peonies in the rust-mottled metal jug I'd found in the bathroom cupboard, and my painted red toenails wiggling on the shabby-chic wooden floorboards. But I hadn't yet alighted on a project. I felt confident this would come with time, and I told my parents as much when we FaceTimed to complete the *New York Times* crossword together.

But a message soon arrived from Danny, asking me over for Sunday dinner and I knew that we were both aware there was no reason I couldn't make the date. Though he and I had grown up together and fell into easy step, we had not seen each other since my awkward stay in his guest room, and for the first time I felt a distance between us that was more than the body of water separating our homes. He had become fully T's and I no longer knew the secrets of his heart or the details of his latest ventures – a man with no social media is frustratingly difficult to keep track of. Though I was on group chats with T, she rarely contributed more than a one-line update or a reaction emoji to our mutual friends' news, and she hadn't joined the last few digital wine get-togethers due to being too busy with work. I felt, travelling in the Uber towards East Egg that Sunday, as though I was attending a family wedding or a baptism. I was aware of the duty that I attend and though I anticipated that once there I would enjoy myself, I was not particularly motivated by excitement.

When the car stopped with a crunch in the gravel turning circle at the end of their drive, I was directed around the side of the building by one of the staff. It was apparently faster going via the fragrant herb garden than through the labyrinthine house. It was golden hour when I reached the French doors facing the water, opening onto the terracotta patio. The scene was set like an Old Master painting or a curated Instagram post, with a jug of sweating fresh orange juice and a bottle of Dom reclining in an ice-filled bucket on a crisp linen-swathed table, the edges of which fluttered like bunting in the sea breeze. I could almost hear the clink of the beautiful crystal coupes that waited next to covered bowls of fat olives, salt-encrusted nuts and tiny freshly baked cheese twists. My stomach grumbled at the scent of the pastries. I looked around at the garden, down to the shore and into the house for my hosts, but no one was in sight. I wandered onto the grass to take in the view of the waves and sank into a duck-egg blue, pleasingly robust Adirondack chair to await the show.

Within minutes, I heard the approach of footsteps, though not human. I turned towards a handsome black horse, slick with sweat and wild-eyed, T perched on top. I shaded my eyes from the dipping sun to look up at her. She had mentioned in messages that she'd taken up riding but it had not lodged in my brain until this moment when she towered over me, as though charging into battle.

'Quite the beast!' I noted, disguising my fear at the size and power of the creature.

The horse danced on the lawn, churning crescents into the turf that I suspected the gardener would curse later. T gripped her ride with her thighs, pulling the bridle tight against its curled lip.

'I know,' she replied as the horse two-stepped. 'This guy's a fighter! My new obsession. We built stables where the greenhouses were . . .' She indicated in the direction of the hedged horizon at the end of their property. 'Had this fella flown in.'

I knew nothing of equine matters but sensed a horse that

had taken a jet was likely an expensive pedigree, and couldn't conjure a fitting response. I nodded.

'Sorry,' she said, wiping her brow, 'he and I stink. You're early. I'll shower.'

She turned the horse away and urged him around the house as I looked at my phone to assure myself I had arrived exactly on time. She called back over her shoulder, 'Help yourself to anything!' before she disappeared around the corner. I waved in response, wondering if that meant I was allowed to open the bubbles. I decided instead to stand and nudge the disturbed chunks of grass back into the gouged craters with my sandal. I was so engrossed in this endeavour that I didn't hear Danny approach and I jumped as he popped the champagne cork behind me.

'Nic!' he laughed, wrapping a napkin round the bottleneck with the dexterity of someone who'd waited tables, and the practice of a man who owned his own cellar. 'Welcome! *So* good to see you!'

His conviction was charming, reassuring. Clunking the opened bottle back in the ice, he opened his arms, inviting a hug, the pale curtains of the lounge billowing behind him in a rolling breeze that carried the scent of the garden roses with it. He was so real and immediately himself that I realised I had missed seeing him at Christmas. He usually made a fleeting visit to his parents' home and gave out beautifully wrapped, impersonal yet crowd-pleasing gifts when our families united for turkey leftovers, endless cups of coffee and the dads huddled in the den. This year the Buchanans had vacationed in Mustique, T's festive posts showing their sandy legs entwined as they toasted the lens with tropical cocktails.

He was more tanned than I'd ever seen him; his pale blue eyes and white, uniform teeth more dazzling against the nubuck caramel of his skin. His dirty-blond hair was longer than it had previously been, now swept back from his face in an elegant tousled pompadour, and he was wearing understated creams that suggested nautical hobbies, though I knew he couldn't sail a boat to save his life. Still, standing there with the water audible and the wind chime tinkling, I could imagine him at the wheel of a yacht, riding the waves; a poster boy for cologne or Italian shoes.

'C'mere!' he said. We embraced and he beamed at me as he pulled away, turning to pour.

'How's it going, neighbour?'

I laughed and held out my hand for the glass.

'It's going good,' I nodded, the drink fizzing on its surface. I anticipated the tickle of it against my nose. 'Finding my way around, settling in.'

Danny paused while pouring his own glass and looked at me.

'You'd tell me if you needed anything?' he asked quietly, his eyes serious.

His lowered tone suggested a familiarity and concern I found tender and for the first time since I'd arrived in Long Island, I felt the cool pang of loneliness in my gut. I nodded. He smiled then, the slow creep of delight across his face, the one that various girls had told me through the years was the moment they knew they were lost. Whether it was designed or instinctual, it had the effect of making the person receiving it feel valued, as though Danny had discovered a wonderful thing by alighting his gaze on you. Right now, it was a welcome warmth and I felt lifted by the human connection that I realised I'd been without for the last couple of weeks. Though I'd been in constant touch with friends and family, West Egg had so far proved a monastic experience, my nose buried in a book or laptop for the last fortnight. I hadn't realised how much I craved physical interaction.

I smiled back gratefully just as a tall man stepped through the curtains behind my cousin and strode to the table, taking the now full second glass from Danny's hand without a word. While I'd waited to sip from mine until Danny was ready to drink, in one fluid motion the man took the glass and gulped heavily from it, swallowing the expensive champagne as though glugging lemonade. Only then did he make eye contact. He looked at me and jutted his chin upward, then turned his back to look towards the shore. Danny smirked.

'Say hi to Jordan,' he said with a thumb thrown toward the newcomer.

'Hi,' I obliged.

The man didn't respond so I could only observe his proud profile. After a moment it prompted a spike of recognition. Danny had mentioned his friend in passing over the years though the specifics of Jordan escaped me.

'Don't mind him; keeping his mind focused for the tournament,' Danny said, filling another coupe.

I didn't want to ask what tournament – I sensed Jordan would like that – so I inquired instead after Danny and his work. He had found a way to dovetail his love of music with his philanthropic nature and now taught guitar to low-income kids, raising funds for instruments at a charitable trust that T often indulged with crisp cheques. I watched Jordan's erect back, the posture of one on parade, as Danny described the seventh graders he'd formed into a rag-tag band. Jordan's deportment and my sketchy memories pegged him as an athlete but my knowledge of sports only extended as far as watching the Super Bowl to see the halftime act. Jordan simply stood, fully assured in his body, and drained his second glass, comfortable to disregard any polite expectation of him. I admired his lack of self-consciousness.

Just as the sun melted into the waves, T reappeared, smelling opulent and dressed in wide-legged, pale silk trousers and a matching camisole, her hair caught in a top-knot and her wide, high cheekbones glinting with product. As usual she made me regret my own outfit.

'Scrubbed and ready for dinner!' she announced loudly, ceasing the conversation. 'You've met Mr Baker, Nic? Or is he busy "training"?' she asked.

Jordan looked back at her with a frown.

'I *am* in training,' he insisted sharply.

T draped herself over Danny's shoulder and indicated that he should fill a glass for her with a flick of her eyes. He indulged her with a wink.

'Of course you are, J,' she purred. 'Which is why you'll have another,' she paused, 'won't you?'

Jordan outstretched his arm in an exasperated fashion without looking back, his empty glass tilted towards Danny, and T smiled triumphantly.

'Gotta stay focused, right?' she said mockingly, as Danny poured. And then to me, 'How he wins a fucking thing is beyond me.'

Before anyone could respond, T announced that dinner was ready on the west deck. This was a wooden platform to the side of the house that had unparalleled views of the tip of the bay and the bobbing lights of boats on the sound returning home after a day on the ocean. I squinted across the inky water in the dying light to try and see whether I could see the extensive properties that my boathouse was sandwiched between. But before I could trace the shoreline and find points of reference, T pushed me towards the dining table, aglow with candle-lit lanterns and tasteful linen, asking how West Egg was treating me.

'West Egg?' Jordan questioned, turning his face fully to me for the first time. 'Full of poseurs and,' he added an extra layer of distaste, 'the influencers that the Hamptons won't have.'

'Influencers?' I repeated.

'Yeah,' He shrugged. 'People like that Gatsby person.'

I swallowed my champagne with a startled gulp. 'I follow her!'

'Why?' Jordan asked with an approximation to disgust, his forehead creasing.

He wasn't really asking for my thoughts on a lifestyle influencer I had clicked on a year or so ago because her posts were aspirational without being irritating. She, along with a number of others, including actors, musicians, politicians and publications, were now a part of my daily life, like wallpaper. I scrolled her content when I swiped through the tiles and reels on my feed. I had first heard Gatsby's name when my friend Scottie told me about the recipes she posted, and I thought the moniker sounded chic, with the ring of Europe to it. It suggested foggy ancestral piles, walls studded with armour and antiquated weaponry to me. She had an English lilt when she spoke on her posts, but she rarely did – mostly they were soundtracked, sun-dappled videos decorated with stickers and emojis.

I was about to ask where in West Egg this celebrity (to me, at least) lived, but T's housekeeper emerged with a large lobster supper on a tray so ostentatious and impressive it prompted us all to coo.

'Sit, sit!' T commanded us, sinking into a seat at the head of the table. The lobsters throbbed red in the flickers of the candles as the outside lights were extinguished for a more congenial atmosphere. T, sucking on a vape, demanded we eat while she nursed a generous glass of scotch and forked an occasional salad leaf into her bored, puce mouth.

I attacked my lobster, butter dripping irreparably down my chin as I chewed the pale flesh and listened to Jordan – now animated – telling Danny about a new restaurant in Carmel and japes on dark beaches, their hooting, alcohol-loosened voices carrying across the garden. Relaxed, Jordan appeared handsome, his eyes crinkling as he guffawed, his body folding double to cradle a funny memory that he and Danny had evoked. They laughed at vaguely amusing anecdotes with more enthusiasm than the uninitiated to their fraternity could contribute. And they talked of famous people they knew, celebrated venues they'd stayed at, Burning Man festival, surfing spots and great wines of certain vintages that they'd drunk late into the night. I felt parochial listening to them, as though I'd done nothing and been nowhere. Surreptitiously, I googled Jordan under the tablecloth, experiencing the huge relief of recalling something thought lost to memory as I found he was a professional golfer, a rising star and something of a clothes horse. I realised I had been aware of him via the sports pages I left unread in the weekend papers and his appearances at minor celebrity events where I'd swiped over his picture. I had never fitted the jigsaw pieces of Danny's Jordan and Mr Baker together before. And Danny, either through his casual assumption or disinterest in people's public standing, had never been specific about his friend's profile.

I looked at Jordan again across the table. He was used to being observed and measured, on the greens and off. He didn't notice or address my gaze, while those less comfortable with it might have instinctively been aware of being watched. He had innate confidence in his carriage and the way he talked, that chin often raised in what could be interpreted as condescension, arrogance or assessment. On my quick web search, he'd been variously described as cocky, flashy, lucky and I wondered if that terminology would have been used had he not been a good-looking young Black man from Louisville who was unrepentant in enjoying his growing status.

Admittedly, I was more interested in him now that I understood his cachet. I leaned closer in to the table and the men's chatter, positioning myself as part of the conversation rather than withdrawing as T had done, sitting back and furiously typing into her pinging phone, a smile playing across her lips. Jordan was admonishing Danny for not having heard about the Hollywood star who had just died during the shoot of a highly anticipated sequel movie. TMZ predictably had the scoop before the deceased's family were fully informed and mean-spirited theories on her cause of death swirled online alongside virtue-signalling grief.

'Danny, come on,' Jordan said, 'you must have heard this. There's off-grid and there's out of touch.'

Danny shrugged good-naturedly. A proud Luddite, he grudgingly carried an ancient iPhone that he'd removed most of the apps from, and often allowed to die for hours at a time. He had long refused to participate in a digital world if he could help it. Part of this I knew was self preservation – he professed to have an addictive personality and feared he'd lose hours to the device if he really engaged with it. Though he'd never had a significant problem, he'd smoked enough weed at college for his parents to worry, fearing a habit he could not break. And he could become obsessive over certain things: having to own a complete back-catalogue of an artist he adored, seeing certain plays or films multiple times during their run until he could quote the dialogue, baking bread daily for months as he tinkered with different variations, until carb-loathing T insisted he stop.

But part of the revulsion towards social media was also his fondness for anything vintage, manual, artisan. His was one of the few houses on the street that still received a physical newspaper flung on his porch and he used a film camera, fiddling with his exposure length and shutter speed to take pictures he actually had printed and stored in albums, noting that snaps on phones were amassed but never revisited. He favoured physical media over streaming, his recreational room at the back of the house crammed with archived discs and vinyl in floor-to-ceiling shelves, which were lovingly taken down, turned in his hands, and used on a cinema set-up system or a vintage record player he found in a Queens flea market. He read chunky books, getting them crinkled and tattered from consuming them in the bath and he had told me more than once he had no use of social media since his photo appeared enough on the platforms of his nearest and dearest. I was as guilty as anyone of posting his beguiling picture on my own account without ever asking his permission. And I knew never to ask anything urgent of him. He never answered his phone and most of my messages to him sat unread for days before I got a response. Danny could afford to ignore key information; his lifestyle and bank account did not demand his vigilance.

Jordan was storytelling now, recalling a time Danny had missed a job interview because he'd locked his phone in a hotel safe and failed to note all the information relayed to him via email, text and voicemail.

'I just don't want to be a slave to my phone. I don't want the world knowing my business,' Danny reasoned, punching him gently in the shoulder. 'Is that so bad?'

'It is if other people have to pick up your shit,' Jordan said. 'Danny boy, you're going to have to grow up sometime. You don't need to know who's on *Dancing with the Stars* but a little awareness of world affairs . . .'

'Which world affairs do you think I'm not aware of?' he asked. They were still joking, but a slight edge was arriving in his voice.

Jordan threw his hands up in exasperation as though they'd discussed this before.

'Dude, you know.'

For the first time in the evening there was an awkwardness. I wondered if Danny had missed something key in Jordan's career, perhaps an omission of congratulations that had hurt the proud sportsman more than he cared to admit.

'Danny,' I interrupted during this lull, wanting to protect. 'Your caveman tendencies aside, what else is going on with you?'

His eyes flashed across the table and I thought I saw gratitude. He smiled and leaned forward, shortening the gap between us.

'Sorry, Nic, when we get on it, we *get on it*,' he apologised, putting a hand on my arm. 'But you're right. We should talk about something else. Not me. Enough about me. What about you? What have you been doing? What's getting you fired up?'

His tone was genuinely inviting, his head tilted, and when I glanced towards Jordan he appraised me for the first time. I told them that I hoped to be able to find a full-time position writing about culture from a socially responsible point of view, that I was blogging essays in the hope of having enough content to show a prospective employer. They listened and made encouraging noises as I sketched out a couple of pieces on the misogyny of fandoms and ethical complexities of paid influencers versus objective review. I told them grandly that pop culture shone a light on the things that mattered.

'Things that matter?' T interjected from the end of the table.

I had almost forgotten about her. Now, as we all turned towards her, she held her glowing phone in her right hand like a brasserie waiter toting a tray.

'Well,' I responded, warming to my subject as all three watched me. 'It would be nice to contribute to the conversation we should all be having about inequality in this country – whether that's gender, race . . .'

'Oh my god,' T interrupted, 'are we getting woke?'

I frowned at her but detected no sarcasm.

'T gets all her news from *Breitbart* and Twitter these days,' Danny informed the table with a wince.

'Right . . .' I laughed.

'Don't dismiss it like that,' T said, her eyes narrowing on me as I'd seen her do in matches when sizing up the opposition. 'You can't just live in an echo chamber, Nic. You need to listen to everyone's opinion. Not just the liberal ones or the Black Lives Matter ones or the people whining about what sexuality they want to be this week. Honestly, it's a minefield trying to just get through the day without offending *someone*.'

'Yeah, T, when you're pulled over by cops for the colour of your skin, let me know?' Jordan replied lightly, though he frowned.

'You know what I mean,' T said with a dismissive wave of her hand.

'And you know what *I* mean,' he said with a hard look, before Danny squeezed his shoulder.

I didn't know where to start in unpacking this. T had

always been nominally Republican at school but this seemed like a new shift. I felt foolish for everything I had just said within her hearing. She held my gaze as though goading and I opened and then closed my mouth. There was a beat of silence before her phone lit up and buzzed. She glanced at the screen and got to her feet, dropping her napkin on the floor.

'I have to take this,' she said, moving from the table, tapping the screen with her oval nails as she walked towards the open doors.

When she entered the house, I looked at both Danny and Jordan but found nothing in their expressions to suggest any further comment should be made. Danny smiled too brightly and said enthusiastically: 'Man, it's so nice to see you after all this time. We have to do this more regularly. Get the family round the table!'

He glanced towards the house and his mouth hardened.

'I mean, if people actually stayed at the table . . .'

He patted his pocket as if checking for his phone.

'Actually, I just need to . . .' He stood. 'I'm gonna go get . . .'

He scanned the table as though looking for something. It seemed to be an excuse.

'Won't be a sec.'

With three wide strides he too was swallowed by the house. Jordan watched him go and looked back at me with a raised eyebrow.

'Okay,' I said. 'What was all that?'

Jordan leaned closer, his expression glinting between scorn and something more like mischief.

'I thought it was an open secret.'

'Not to me. I didn't know T had turned fascist.'

He shook his head.

'No, no, not that. I mean the affair.'

'Who's having an affair?' I asked quickly, running both possibilities through my head and suspecting it could be either one.

'T. She's got some guy. Well, Danny thinks so. Thought he'd probably told you.'

'I'm not sure he would share that with me,' I said.

'He's co-opted everyone into this conspiracy . . .' He halted as a door slammed inside and distantly we heard raised voices.

We both strained to hear the words. But as quickly as it had begun, the disagreement seemed to evaporate and in minutes both T and Danny appeared back at the table. I watched their shadowed faces, but there was no evidence of a marital implosion, let alone a disagreement.

'Dessert?' Danny offered.

'Depends what it is, dude,' Jordan yawned, tapping his hand against his flat stomach.

'Some sort of pavlova,' T said. 'Light.'

They all looked expectantly at me, the candlelight making masks of their features.

'I'll take some,' I nodded, standing from my chair. 'After I move a bit.'

T turned her face towards the sound.

'I suppose it's too late to take a walk on the shore,' she said. 'Too dark . . . and anyway, Danny's avoiding it since the crab incident.'

She glanced at him teasingly and he smiled wanly.

'Don't remind me,' he shuddered.

'Crab incident? Now you've *got* to tell the story,' Jordan insisted, chasing the ease of earlier.

Danny sat back down in his chair, ceremonially, and sighed.

'Tell them,' T prompted, waving her hand at him.

He blew a breath through his mouth as though mildly aggravated, but he also liked the audience.

'Okay. I was walking down there,' Danny began, motioning towards the shadowy water, 'and I heard the sound of a baby crying. Maybe more than one. Or puppies . . . this crying noise was like . . .' He began to emit a pathetic mewling. 'So I think . . . did someone abandon a puppy or a kid? I started running and when I got to the beach I saw this crate, up-ended on the tide line. I'm thinking awful things as I'm going towards this box. And when I get there, I look in through the gap in the side and it's crabs.'

Jordan and I looked at each other.

'Crabs?' I repeated.

Danny nodded.

'I know. I had no idea they cried, let alone made a noise. They're crying in this box, maybe twenty of them. I didn't know what to do but the crate had a boat name on the side, so I went back to the house and googled the number.' At this, Jordan snorted.

'And this guy, this fisherman, answers and he's all, "Oh yeah, must have fallen overboard on the way back in, I'll come and get them from you."'

His eyes seemed to moisten.

'But they're crying, this desperate *crying*.'

'You just ate a lobster!' Jordan interjected. T laughed.

'Yeah, I know! But I made Juana promise not to show them to me before they were done. I mean, after this . . .'

I asked what he did next, his distress infectious.

'Nic, it was awful,' he appealed to me, leaning forward, his eyes now swimming. 'I asked the guy where they were going, even though I knew already, really. And he says: Daphne's restaurant on the highway. So I said, "How about

I give you what you'll get there and I keep the crabs?" I'm thinking I'll open the box and release them back, right? But the guy can see what I'm thinking and he says, really gentle, "No point doing that, chief – their claws are clipped. Can't feed themselves anyway now." So . . . they're dead either way. They're sitting on this beach, crammed into this box, and nothing can be done for them.'

We sat in a silence suspended like the string of fairy lights above our heads, no one knowing what to say. Danny slumped back in his chair. He pushed his fingers through his hair.

'And that's the story of the crabs,' T crowed.

'Bleak,' said Jordan, shaking his head and giving his friend a light slap on the back. Danny looked back up at me.

'*You* get it, right, Nic?' he asked, almost urgently. The two tender hearts at the table.

I nodded.

'It got me down . . .'

I nodded again, the smell of seafood on my plate transmuting from the scent of decadence and celebration to one of decay. I looked at my picked-over lobster with growing pity and wondered whose idea the shellfish had been.

'And that's why we're never going to Daphne's again!' sing-songed T.

She took up her spouse's story, describing how the fisherman had turned up in a filthy truck and asked to fill his bucket from their garden hose. Had carefully washed sand and seaweed from each crab before putting them back in the box and nailing it closed. Danny had not been able to watch, she reported, and had locked himself in the furthermost bathroom with his headphones on.

'Don't dwell on it, Dan,' T was now saying, rubbing her husband's shoulder as though he were cold.

She crouched down beside him as he turned and looked at her intensely in a moment that seemed embarrassingly intimate.

'It's one bad thing that happened here . . . only one,' she smiled at him, wordlessly transferring comfort and memories to him. Danny's stricken face broke into a huge grin, radiant and uncomplicated, making me wonder if I'd ever seen the sadness a second before. It was like observing a magic trick.

I suddenly felt tired and I wanted to leave. I looked at Jordan, speculating if I could co-opt him into that endeavour. He turned his eyes towards the wine bottle instead.

'Good times coming right up!' he said, picking up the Chenin Blanc.

I resigned myself to another hour at the table, accepting another glass of wine, a few spoonfuls of raspberry and meringue, and dark, bitter coffee in a tiny cup the size of a doll's tea service. Conversation turned to Jordan's next game and, as he discussed the course and his competitors, his proselytising permitted me to slide my eyes all over him. I enjoyed his long, expressive fingers as they conducted a story along with his dismissive voice and the manner in which he slumped so low in his chair in a physical show of disinterest. The way he sneered and disregarded and dissected. I had always liked soft boys, but Jordan was hard, almost brutal.

In the Uber on the way home I followed his social channels, liking posts and adding comments, hoping he'd notice and reply. It was only the combination of the wine and the twisting, womblike roads through the curving trees that forced me to stop. By the time I arrived at the gate to my estate, I realised I had drunk more than I had thought, my supposed sobriety ebbing away from me even as I gulped fresh night air. I despised the feeling, hated the loss of control. I liked the warmth and flexibility of tipsiness, usually monitoring my intake to maintain a bobbing buzz without tipping into the anxiety-inducing stage of double vision, unstable steps and a loose mouth. But as I unintentionally veered off the path to the boathouse, my feet betraying me with a stumble into the weeds, I knew I needed to get myself together.

I took off my shoes and walked away from my home, deciding to breathe in the view and the salty air from the lawn until I felt more steady. The grass was cool and damp under my feet and creatures scuttled in the bushes as I sat down. A breeze blew in from the waves; somewhere over by the road, the jagged cry of someone's night-stalking pet cat. I took a deep breath, determined to focus. The houses along East Egg twinkled like a string of gems, and as I looked along my shoreline another light attracted my attention. On the neighbour's lawn, the unmistakable rectanglular glow of a phone screen.

As my eyes grew more accustomed to the dark I watched a willowy figure casting the phone about her, looking for a signal or filming a video. It was almost a dance as she held the glowing square above her head, to the side, pirouetted with it, flirted with the screen. I felt a jolt of recognition the instant her face turned towards me, ghostly lit. Gatsby. I gasped audibly to myself, a shiver of discovery reverberating through me. The influencer we had only just discussed lived in the turreted, twenties chateau with a balustrade terrace and inclined emerald lawn next door. Seeing her in the flesh and not on my screen thrilled me, and her recent posts suddenly made sense. The rococo details of her large rooms glimpsed in the background, the view of water behind her billowing hair, the boat pictures, the driveway. Of course this was the house. I should have recognised it the minute I saw it. I fumbled for my own phone beside me in the grass.

Gatsby continued to perform for the camera and when it was over she must have pressed a finger to the screen to darken it as she stilled, silhouetted by the lawn lights, the bounce gone from her gait. She walked purposefully to the property's wooden dock at the lapping water, stopping under the lamp there, her device seemingly forgotten as she stared out at the sound. She was barefoot like me, and stood with squared shoulders and a ballerina's poise. Her long, pale hair rippled behind her, making her appear like the figurehead of a ship.

I felt suddenly, keenly, sober as I observed her, the quickening heartbeat of a snoop taking the soft blur off my drunkenness. As I watched, my breath shallow, she raised the phone towards where she gazed, and seemed to snap a photo of the darkness. She kept her arm outstretched long after the image must have been captured. I peered in the direction she'd aimed the lens but could see only the winking far shore, the glow of the houses there and the corresponding pier light blinking green into the gloom. Slowly, she lowered her arm, her face lit from the screen as deft fingers typed. Watching her this way, bowed over her device and oblivious to the fact she was being viewed, she seemed vulnerable.

Then, as if she sensed me, she looked up abruptly in my direction. I froze, not entirely sure what she could see in this unlit portion of the grounds. Her eyes scanned the darkness, passing blindly over me hidden within the contours of my landlady's sloping lawn. She dropped her chin and turned away, walking back to the house, holding the phone above her head again and talking upward to the white light. She seemed to be teasing the screen, confiding, conveying a coquettish happiness that had not been present as she stared across the sound. Her hard silhouette sliced into the light of the bright room, an abductee entering a spaceship, and the slam of the door released me from the sense of enchantment.

With her now gone I doubted myself. Was my booze-fog confusing me? Was it really her? It wasn't too late to send a message, I decided, quickly tapping out a query to my landlady. At the top of our conversation history 'typing' appeared in response and I waited until the answering words appeared below with a chime.

Yes, some wellness influencer, she wrote, with a shrug emoji. *Hoping she doesn't stay long.*

And as I watched, the secondary confirmation that thrilled me:

Jay Gatsby.

Chapter 4

I didn't scour her feeds that night. Maybe because I wanted to preserve the peculiar spell I felt, or because I hardly remember crawling into my bed. But I was alive to the idea the next morning as I chugged Coke from the bottle while standing with the fridge door open, regretting my consumption at T and Danny's table. I watched the video from her lawn repeatedly, studied the way she danced to a track she'd overlayed, a shimmering filter making her appear ethereal.

I had followed her sometime the year before because she intersected my interests in wellness and beauty, one of many aspirational people I swiped through the content of without much thought. Now I pored over her posts and the gossip items I found in searches. Jay Gatsby was twenty-nine years old and a lifestyle influencer who had risen to prominence on social platforms after marrying the actor Dan Cody. Cody was a name thanks to his dynastic New York family (wealth, sleaze, infamy) and his role in a long-running movie franchise about LA cops. He was older, not necessarily wiser, handsome in the way well-dressed men with disposable incomes are. She was a tall, beautiful English girl on a student visa in the

Big Apple and they had met at a fancy Manhattan apartment party where she was waitressing and he was between wives. He proposed fast, they married faster (elegantly at the Plaza) and sold the photos to *Vanity Fair*. Her social profile increased as soon as she began to curate her expensive, ethically sourced new life. Though she was flamingo-limbed and moneyed, her captions betrayed a sense of humour that made her seem genial, self-aware, human. She infrequently revealed beautiful missteps (a bake that wasn't quite perfect, a lost luggage disaster in Cabo, the hair serum she inadvertently forgot to rinse out before a shopping trip) that spoke of sisterhood to me.

Over four years of marriage she had promoted treatments, beauty ranges and luxury retreats, while her husband kept up the family predilection for scandal, culminating in a *New Yorker* exposé detailing years of predatory behaviour towards female staff at his production company and the indiscriminate bullying of almost everyone in his environment. Though he maintained his standing among Manhattan's richest where capital absolved all sins, his film career came to an abrupt halt and his fame soured to notoriety. I recalled seeing reports of him entering rehab for sex addiction, drug abuse and a catalogue of mental health issues a couple of years previously. Gossip websites relayed how his young wife had maintained a 'dignified silence' over the whole affair, immediately filing for divorce, and posting shots of herself burning cleansing sage on a shamanic retreat in Joshua Tree. She had expunged all trace of Cody from her social media and background and lived in various well-appointed apartments in postcard cities over the next few years before moving into the mansion next door within the last six months. There she had seemingly existed entirely online, sharing all her successes with an impressive number of followers, posting introspective and lifestyle content with machine-gun rapidity. She demonstratively supported abuse charities and refused to talk about her marriage, saying that to do so gave Cody power he did not deserve. It was reported that he was more than generous in his parting monetary gift to her.

When I clicked onto Gatsby's social streams I greedily scrolled back through the tiles of her posts, looking for the house next door and, despite myself, drinking in the affluence of her life. I had been taught to disdain ostentatious displays of wealth by my father despite his own family fortune and the impressive salary he commanded as a lawyer. The ethic of working hard to earn privilege rather than taking it for granted had been drummed into me from a young age.

Though my parents ensured my first-class education, they withheld money for extravagances I begged for after coveting my classmates' possessions. Completing my chore list amassed enough cash to buy toys and clothes I wanted, but lines were drawn on certain brands and purchases. I could not have the designer bag I longed for as a teen as it was deemed 'tacky', and when I passed my driving test, Dad and I scoured second-hand dealerships in search of something 'appropriate'. Vanity plates, designer goods with obvious logos, luxe labelled drinks, vacations on yachts, plastic surgery, over-generous tipping were all considered unpalatable status symbols that denoted a lack of good breeding, taste or awareness of others' more humble checking accounts.

So it felt almost clandestine to be admiring Gatsby's feed. Here she was adopting the perfect yoga pose beside a glittering pool, wearing flimsy pants tagged at $1,600. Here, nights in a luxury hotel suite with high-end shopping bags scattered beside the well-stocked wet bar in the background. Here, the buttery leather interior of a private jet. Or lounging in a bikini on a water bungalow deck in Tahiti, her face covered by an impractically large brimmed hat. Diamond facials in LA, lunches at the Dorchester in London, group shots of her beauty squad prepping her for an event in Paris; catalogues of her designer dress fittings, fashion week attendances, expensive sushi dinners, extensive home renovations, champagne at private members clubs, her beaded wrists in namaste pose at a meditation vision quest . . . and earlier in the year, a video of her cartwheeling across that lawn, long legs tracing the clouds above, and the roof of my boathouse visible beyond.

After the post announcing her arrival in her 'forever home', more of the same jet-setting, spending and brand ambassadoring followed, but interspersed were shots of the beautiful view from her dock of the shore beyond – at night, at dusk, at dawn, in mist, in dappled sun. Though she always seemed to prodigiously hashtag her posts, writing about the 'darling' people in her shots or the 'divine' food she'd eaten, these particular missives were left unpopulated. Last night's shot was one of these; an inky square with pinpricks of stars above, the silvered ripples of the sound below and a jade dot in the middle, a light over in East Egg. I smiled, pleased that of all the millions scrolling her feed, I knew the exact location intimately.

I pinched and zoomed, staring at the even tan, the thighs no wider than her knees, the tousled hair caught in a breeze. Noted the layered necklaces glinting around her throat, the gold bangles on her wrist, the tiny waist that accompanied posts on huge dinners and organic chocolate bars, the colours of her nails as she enthusiastically baked cakes in a cavernous white kitchen. The pinkness of her tongue against ice-white teeth as she affected goofy expressions that still showcased the symmetry of her face, the prettiness of freckles sprinkled across her nose. Gatsby re-posted glowing affirmations about her beauty secrets, her house, her view, with winking, kissing and love heart-eyed emojis, promising followers a synergy with her just by pressing the 'like' button.

And then there were the 'weekenders' at her home, the paid-for content produced to look organic. The gong baths, self-care talks, sleep workshops, sunrise yoga sessions attended by throngs of women wanting to ingest whatever secret potion she took, tune in to the frequency she operated at, wanting to believe that creating wildflower aromatherapy sachets for their lingerie drawers would usher in the kind of golden lifestyle she was living. This was the holistic side of her Janus existence, one that pledged clarity, calm and grounding.

But the house next door was also a portal to bacchanalian parties that were loaded with luxury alcohol, food and music, every room a tableau designed to be framed and snapped. Balloons in a shiny mass floating up to the roof of an enormous hall, intricate ice sculptures, exquisite canapés the size of quarters, DJs commanding crowds of orgasmic dances in the period-featured ballroom. Models, musicians and actors were dotted among the revellers, the goodie bags brimmed with merchandise nestling among delicate monogrammed tissue paper and the bunches of fresh flowers dotted around the rooms were so ostentatious I could likely not even encompass them in both arms. Filters were not needed for rooms flooded with flattering, muted light from expensive rigs.

Gatsby displayed the fun, the consumption, the famous faces via reposts of attendees; sometimes seen alongside them, her face and hips always tilted, an enigmatic smile on her lips that suggested neither enjoyment nor ennui. Though she usually held a glass angled sharply from her body with a precise elbow, her lipstick never smeared, her impeccable outfits remained freshly pressed. She appeared like a visitation among the girls with mascara smudges, holding their one shoe – the other clearly lost – and sticking their tongue out at the camera, with grass-stained soles evidence of late-night lawn dancing. Swiping through her social stories, she seemed to hover at the periphery of the maelstrom; swaying to music from a bannister, or handing out fluffy towels to those who'd jumped into the sound at first light and emerged slick and pink-cheeked. The morning-after posts that followed showed her fresh-faced, crisp – a fork poised over a bowl of glistening fruit salad, the detritus of the night being swept and packed by faceless workers in the background.

Tracking back through her feeds, I saw that her high-net-worth soirees had been going on since the start of April. In the last week of May, when I'd just arrived, I had heard one of her events across the grounds, but back then had not known from which of the houses the noise emanated. As a recent graduate I was used to living in close proximity to other people's lives and had grown accustomed to all-hours volume. During my time living at a particularly raucous sophomore sorority house I had developed an ability to switch off from ambient commotion with reasoning that I could do nothing to stop it, nor should I want to. It felt easier to allow it to happen, to fall in step with it, to embrace it even, so that it felt less of an intrusion and more like symbiosis. I had never complained about anyone's behaviour before and I wasn't about to start now. It was simply a soundtrack to my new writer's existence and I had fallen asleep by syncing my breathing to the buzz of the bass coming from the garden.

Now, I tingled with celebrity approximation – that ambient noise had been the party on this post carousel, bright and loud, attended by an international popstar so famous her fans tracked her private jet to determine her location, the entire cast from a smash-hit Netflix show, a Formula One driver, nepo-baby models and reality show wannabes.

She was the most glamorous person I'd ever been in the proximity of and I wasn't immune to the seductive nature of fame. I pressed to add alerts, initially because I wanted to see my own surroundings in her posts. I went about my day, procrastinating while sitting in front of a blank screen and opening additional windows to idly browse jeans I neither needed nor could afford, and revisiting a newsfeed with the alacrity of a sugar-hooked hummingbird. While staring at the blinking cursor in front of me, willing inspiration, I realised I could count on the fingers of a mitten the unique perspective I had on anything cultural that could conceivably be parlayed into an essay. But perhaps Gatsby was my ticket. Observing her consumption across the lawn could surely provide the clay to sculpt a hot take that had a USP. She could be the influencer at the heart of my planned essay on the erosion of true criticism.

The sense of Gatsby providing the answer to my indistinct career plans translated easily into a compulsion to refresh and check in digitally with my neighbour. It would become an itch I needed to scratch more regularly. Soon it was almost the weekend again and the industry had begun anew next door. My phone chimed constantly with alerts, ensuring I missed none of Gatsby's preparation for her next big party, and I willingly invested in it. Would she choose the pale pink or the white flowers? Could the masseur beat the traffic to loosen her muscles before she needed to dress? How did she look this radiant on the boast of only having snagged four hours sleep the night before?

Boredom and loneliness played roles in my growing fascination, but also the idea of existing alongside someone who promised such perfection. Of course I knew sleight of hand and self-mythologising provided an unattainable view of her life. I understood her posts were curated, false versions of reality. But I also felt myself, both subconsciously and consciously, respond to her stories. I read her tags. Followed her links. Zoomed in on the detail of her limited-edition boyfriend-style white shirt. As directed, I coveted items she cooed over. I considered purchasing a serum she used. I had gone down the rabbit hole, drunk the potion. I was hooked.

When the party kicked off on Saturday night I felt a peculiar jealousy. The hashtag 'Gatsby' grew with images and videos that corresponded to the sounds and movements next door and I longed to attend. I boasted to my friends on WhatsApp about my new neighbour and together we conspired to find far-fetched ways to infiltrate. I felt something akin to rage when the music stopped at the peachy flush of dawn, the FOMO almost a physical ache.

I recognised that this was not healthy, that I needed escape from the bubble I had created. When it seemed a civilised hour I called a different moneyed woman whom I knew I could gain access to. T picked up immediately, launching into a complaint: Danny had bought yet another vintage guitar. Her dissatisfaction made me recall Jordan's low voice buzzing about her possible indiscretion across the candlelit table.

'I hope you've got a passion to pour yourself into, like Danny and his music,' I encouraged her, hoping she didn't spot my mining for gossip.

'Nic, you know I do.'

'What are we talking about?'

'What are *you* talking about?'

'Oh, I don't know. Danny's my family but only you know your marriage.'

She paused before she answered.

'Have you heard something?'

I feigned ignorance but told her that women should not feel trapped by circumstance. Bored and spiteful, I talked around what I wanted to know by bringing up and praising a mutual friend who had left a prematurely sexless union after experiencing an epiphany with her personal trainer. T was not drawn. She gossiped about our friend's short-lived husband and moved on to disparaging another acquaintance whose job had recently imploded over an email she had inadvertently replied to 'all'. She gave no indication of the suspected infidelities Jordan had suggested. I found no intrigue and she brought our chatter back to her summer plans with Danny before she ended the call.

Later in the week, as though an afterthought, she invited me for lunch in the city the following Sunday. I leapt at the chance to enjoy a fraction of Gatsby's lifestyle via my rich friend. T would likely choose decadently and pay too.

Wait at the station, she instructed in typically unadorned messaging.

I agreed, enjoying a renewed sense of purpose in having an appointment, sure that the Manhattan skyline and the pulse within its streets would open something up in me after a week of digital obsession. I should have focused on the work I had talked of crafting. But I didn't.

Chapter 5

T pulled up at Great Neck station in a matte black Tesla, too heavy on the brake, bucking her forward in the caramel faux-leather seat. I had assumed she had suggested connecting there so we could take the train into the city together, but she leaned out the window to beckon me over with well-practised impatience.

'Nic! Let's go!' She slapped her hand against the car's bodywork.

I slid in, and before I could utter a word, she stamped on the accelerator. I fumbled with the seatbelt as it pulled taut at an abrupt junction stop, the dashboard pinging to alert us that a passenger was unharnessed.

'Are we late?'

'Kinda . . .' T mumbled, glancing furtively in her side mirror.

I laughed. 'Are we being followed? You're acting like a spy.'

She looked at me then. 'You think I'm acting guilty?'

I couldn't tell if she was challenging me or asking with genuine interest.

'What are you up to?' I asked.

'Oh,' she shrugged. 'You know *me*, Nic . . .'

She smiled at me and punched the music button on the steering wheel. The Rolling Stones blasted out of the speakers.

'Danny,' she tutted at the choice, but didn't change it, keeping it at a volume that discouraged further conversation. As a choir sang the title of the track I submitted to whatever the adventure of her devising was. There was little point in trying to sway things; it expended too much effort, and success was only measured by how much I had compromised on my intention, never hers. I knew her. Understood how she negotiated. Her inability to bend to others' wishes had become a running joke in our friendship group. 'I was thinking of cocktails and then dinner,' one of us would say about their upcoming birthday celebrations, 'but we'll see what T says about that . . .'

Often she would splice two social events togethers, asking an hour before we were due to meet if I'd run across town to a birthday party she was attending. It never occurred to her that the celebrant might not want a stranger tiptoeing into their gathering, or that my needs might have been different from hers. It was the same in the manner with which she ordered off-menu at every restaurant we went to. T always wanted something created just for her – with extra sauce, without the chilli, on the side, to go. It had always seemed to me an affectation. The additional item was often left untouched, the dish without the key ingredient inevitably pushed around the plate and not consumed. But ordering more, differently, with greater difficulty, gilded the story she wanted to tell the world about herself. That she was fearless, with a voracious appetite and the will to ask – and get – things that others wouldn't.

It was hypnotic to watch and bob in the undertow of. I had followed her to new tables from the first or even second we'd been given at eateries, jumped in taxis that took nonsensical detours to allow for her whims, watched her monopolise a friend's date as soon as they entered the bar. But to ride with her was also to end up in unexpectedly exciting places. For someone naturally indecisive and cautious, T was an uninhibited catalyst for gambles and permissiveness. Had she written down where some of our evenings might take us before we set off I'd have likely resisted, but floating in her slipstream, I experienced things I didn't know I'd like.

'I want you to meet someone!' she shouted over the music as she switched lanes without checking her mirrors.

A pickup honked long and low on our flank. I looked at her as she nudged the car along the highway, traffic building as we headed west. She licked her lips and smiled, turning her head to me, inscrutable behind mirrored sunglasses. 'Okay?'

It wasn't really a question. She turned her attention back to the road and we rode without speaking. As we passed the unisphere, a dispiriting metal approximation of the globe left behind from a yesteryear world's fair, a cool pool of mild panic flooded my gut as I suddenly wondered if she was playing matchmaker. Being set up by friends had always been something I loathed. The feeling of being trapped in a design not of my own making was emetic to me, triggered by a teenage New Year's Eve party when I arrived to find the anticipated rowdy soiree was just four of us, and I was expected to play nice with a fleshy boy while my friend lost her virginity in the bathroom. T had more male friends than female and often proffered them as suitable squires, assuming I was unhappy with not having a serious boyfriend. I dated but I rarely kept the boy's number in my phone above six weeks, my interest and attraction waning before any kind of permanence was established. T assumed I failed in my romantic endeavours, when in truth I simply tired of them. When she suggested a date I always said, as I did now – trying to keep the frustration out of my voice – 'you know I hate being set up.'

She jutted her chin towards me in a signal to repeat my statement. I said it louder, reached to touch the volume button on the screen, turning down the music and ensured the message was clear a third time.

'Please don't tell me you've found me a date.'

Even to my own ears it sounded like a tell of weakness. She smiled, pressed the volume button on the wheel and the music climbed back up.

'Not everything is about you,' she told the road ahead of her.

'Are you going to tell me?'

She shook her head, shimmied in her seat to denote excitement.

'Sit tight. You'll see. Anyway, how's the blog coming? Have you met anyone I should know about?'

I trained my eyes on the asphalt ahead as I sorted through what I was willing to give her. I offered up the copywriting assignments I'd picked up through a friend in marketing that would bring in some money while I formulated my own brand. I recalled the goings-on of my neighbours, but I left out Gatsby. She felt like my secret and mine alone. As I talked, winking red tail lights appeared on the freeway ahead. T did not alter her speed, even as the block of stationary cars ahead was evident. I instinctively pressed my hand against the dash in a bracing position just before she hit the brakes. We lurched to a standstill.

'Fuck,' she muttered in annoyance as the seatbelt cinched her neck.

Vehicles pulled alongside us and behind us, locking us in a parking lot suspended above the local roads and squat housing below. T jabbed the satnav, pinching to enlarge our location: Flushing Meadows.

'So close and yet so far away . . .' she groaned, head dropping immediately to scroll on the phone at her crotch.

Above the music I could hear the drone of a helicopter circling overhead. I put down the window and leaned out to look upward. An ABC7-liveried chopper dipped and banked over the freeway like an inquisitive dragonfly.

'Let's see what they say,' I suggested, pressing the window button hard to reseal the car and lock the fumes outside.

The ABC7 traffic feed was mid-report when I clicked on the link on my phone, live pictures from the heavens of toy cars, end to end, as a rapid-fire young woman narrated our particularly mundane traffic disaster. A truck had lost its load exiting a ramp just up ahead and all inbound NY traffic on the 495 was halted. How long would it take to move? Police were estimating thirty minutes or longer but more updates as she had them. But for now, this was TJ Eckleburg signing off . . .

I silenced my phone and looked at T.

'Are we going to be late?'

She shook her head, thumb still stroking her screen.

'No, I never make a time.'

My traitorous bladder sent signals to my brain. I crossed my legs. 'Am I going to need to pee in a cup?'

'I hope not,' she snorted.

I stared out of the car. 'Where even are we?'

'Fun fact,' said T, slipping her phone back between her thighs. 'This is the dump of New York. All this round here used to be this huge trash area where all the ash from the city was dumped. Remember I took that class on city planning for credit? That Robert Moses guy – was he a ruthless fuck or just a guy who got what needed to be done, done? I had to write that paper? They developed it for *this*. Was a dump, still a dump, right?'

I looked out at the neighbourhood below, at the unremarkable streets and brown, blank apartment blocks. Admittedly, it wasn't Long Island, but it seemed like any other blue-collar area on the outskirts of a big metropolis.

'Which was he?' I asked idly. 'Ruthless fuck or get-it-done guy?'

'That depends on who you ask.'

I tried to imagine the ash. Could picture the greyness, the bulk, the acrid dust that must have clung to clothes and lungs. Could almost taste it on my tongue. I thought of Manhattan as a vertical nirvana to those that lived here, looking west to see the taller buildings, but not yet in thrall to twinkling skyscrapers. The Brooklyn Bridge and Lady Liberty, famous markers before competition for the skyline arrived. The island that would become a grid of cloud-piercing needles going through another evolution after tribal fishing and bow-making, the Dutch fur-trading, the revolutionaries, the constitutionalists, the émigrés.

TJ Eckleburg interrupted my thought, headset clamped over her swinging hair, gesticulating as she imparted an update. A word caught my eye on the ticker tape underneath her face: 'clearing'.

'Looks like they sorted it faster than the eye in the sky anticipated,' I said.

'Cool,' T nodded.

'T,' I appealed to her. 'Where are we going? Who are we meeting? I thought this was a girls' lunch?'

'Just go with it.'

'I hate surprises.'

'No, you don't. Not always.'

Ahead, the traffic began to move forward. The domino effect of movement rippled its way towards us and the cars in front nudged ahead. As we crawled along the freeway at a walking pace, I stared out at the buildings alongside the road. At this speed I could peer directly into windows that were usually a blur. I wondered if I might see an inhabitant's face staring back at me and felt a shiver of shame at my voyeurism just as T swerved the car across the lanes towards an exit. She tailgated the car in front of us down the slope to the street with the aggression of someone in a hurry, turning right and driving the network of minor roads without casting her eyes to the satnav. She knew this route, rolled lazily through the stop signs on muscle memory. She sang along to Danny's music despite her apparent dislike of it, balance restored.

'What's around here?' I asked, craning at local ma-and-pa restaurants. 'Lunch?'

'Not *here*.' She patted my knee in a show of reassurance. 'Don't worry, you'll get fed.'

We drove down narrow streets of tall houses, wrought-iron steps leading to upper apartments and driveways filled with trash cans until T lurched the car right and mounted the curb with a wolfish smile. She pulled to an abrupt stop on a forecourt behind a chain-link fence and put the car in park. She turned off the electric motor and we sat for a moment. I took in the peeling car-wash sign and the wonky gas pumps. A new Tesla charging station stood incongruously next to them, the sun dazzling on the white tower, the red-lined lozenge hole through it designed to look futuristic but recalling pornography. In the corner of the forecourt stood a rickety office with meshed windows. Next to that, two hand-wash hoses and a towering pole of tangled power lines, the nest of wire fanning out above us to the buildings surrounding the lot.

T leaned on the horn just as the office door opened and a man stepped out. He raised his hand in greeting and began walking across the space with a loping insouciance, the gold chain at his throat catching the sun. He smiled, his face dipped in what seemed a pose of seduction, or threat. I couldn't tell which. T leaned forward, draped over the steering wheel, beaming out of the windshield.

'What's going on?' I asked, watching the man come closer and pass T's window, his tattooed forearm dipping into his jeans pocket. With a sharp clunk, he opened the back door and slid into the seat behind us, slamming the door behind him. He leaned forward.

'Nic, meet Miguel,' T said in a honeyed tone I wasn't used to.

The man thrust a large hand towards me, the scent of his cologne reaching me. It smelled of oud and orange, extravagant. Instinctively, I took his hand and he crushed mine in a fierce grip.

'Nic,' he said, nodding.

He had an attractive angular face, long dark lashes and looked like one of the groomed personal trainers that appeared in ads on my Instagram. He bulged everywhere. He showed his even teeth and his eyes crinkled.

'Good to meetcha.' He smiled, his greeting accented, lilting.

I nodded back, but his attention was entirely on T, his eyes raking her cleavage. She watched him with an amused expression in the rearview mirror.

She smiled. 'Hey.'

'Hey, beautiful. Beso,' he said low, before plunging between the headrests to kiss her pale neck.

She moved her left hand from the wheel to bury it in his hair, pressing him closer, her lips parting with a breath as she looked across at me.

'Surprise!' she giggled. 'You wanted to know . . .'

'What's going on?' I asked again, even as I realised.

Of course I knew, but my cognitive understanding hadn't quite caught up with my instinct. Who? When? How long? Why? Miguel pulled away, leaving a pink bloom on her skin that might leave a more permanent mark, and I immediately thought of Danny. Sweet, gentle, elegant Danny supplanted by this blunt instrument. Danny, in his pastel cashmere and linen, unaware that a man in sportswear was trying on his life. Miguel sat back in his seat, legs spread wide.

'Ok, let's go,' he said.

T started the car and she glanced over at me.

'What you pictured, Nic?' she asked, pleasure in her voice.

'Turn the car off,' I said.

She obeyed and looked at me, surprised.

'Wait, are you mad?' An uncharacteristic uncertainty danced at the edges of her question.

'Bathroom?' I asked Miguel. A real request but also a stalling tactic to give me space to process.

'In the office,' he said and looked out of the windows of the car as though nervous.

I thanked him and told T I'd be quick as I jumped out of the car and snapped the door shut before she could say anything further. The apex of the day's heat scalded my scalp as I scurried over the yard to the office, hurrying inside and allowing the spring loaded door to slam behind me. Inside, two desks faced each other covered in paperwork.

An air-conditioning unit groaned feebly in the corner and a man slumped over his phone at one of the desks watching a Spanish-language boxing match. He looked up with surprise, a smear of dirt across his cheek.

'Baño?' I asked, and he pointed to the door in the corner.

I nodded thanks and entered, expecting fetid squalor, but while the space was sauna-sultry it was immaculately clean. I sank gratefully on the seat as my phone pinged with T's messages.

Don't be weird.

It's not a big deal.

I'm confiding in you here as my friend. I've told no one. You said you wanted to know.

I sighed. I had asked, not really expecting that she would bestow this special intelligence on me. I had clearly done a better job than I thought during our disingenuous phone call of implying that I would not be affronted on Danny's behalf by any disloyalty on her part. It wasn't true. I had felt immediate outrage when Miguel touched her, my protective love for my cousin flaring bright. But then, as I took my time washing my hands, the fact that the well-built man in the car outside was so diametrically different to Danny strangely calmed me. This was T ordering off-menu again. Paul Newman's quote about infidelity came to mind as I used the sweet-smelling soap in a dainty dish: 'I have steak at home, why go out for hamburger?' T always wanted both. Just as she often ordered two entrees in restaurants, she demanded all the options. And this snack surely wasn't any real threat to Danny. She probably thought as much too. I couldn't imagine her sharing her dirty secret with me if she was thinking long-term. I considered all the hobbies T had taken up and dropped. The racquetball she was obsessed with for a winter, the months-long fevered interest in growing vegetables that died with her failed carrots, the brief flirtation with learning Mandarin. Miguel would be another passing fancy. A trifle.

Not being weird. Just peeing, I typed to T and exited.

I thanked the man in the office as I returned to the white glare of the sun and slipped back in the front seat of the car.

'Let's go, then,' I said lightly.

T frowned a little. I enjoyed that I'd confused her. I rarely did. She punched the start button and piloted us back to the street.

'Okay, let's go somewhere *really* expensive. Yes, baby?' she asked Miguel through the rear-view.

It was the most I'd ever known her to use a mirror while driving. She giggled in a girlish way and pressed the accelerator as we turned towards the vanishing point of Manhattan.

Chapter 6

It was a Midtown restaurant that had been featured in all the right publications, bestowed with stars and celebrity visitors, and so packed – even on a Sunday afternoon – with braying clientele, I felt I was on the stock exchange. We sat at a circular chef's table aside from the main restaurant floor. The table should have seated far more than three, but T had insisted. She waved her hand when they mentioned price, smiling at Miguel and talking about discretion.

I stared at the sea urchin on the delicate turquoise plate in front of me: its texture resembled a tongue. Lipoma yellow and balancing on sushi rice, it was one of the most expensive items on the menu. T had insisted we order the 'uni', beckoning the server with one hand, the other resting in her lover's lap, her fingertips close to what I assumed might be her favoured part of his anatomy.

We had driven from Corona making small talk with T using the light and breezy dissembling voice I knew from college. It was the same timbre she employed when denying she'd worn a garment she was returning to a store or explaining her lateness to a meet-up as the fault of others. She was filibustering her big reveal of how she had entered into an affair with Miguel, a seemingly sweet man with big muscles and limited conversation. He seemed only to speak when agreeing with T and showed no curiosity about me. His voice was low and rasping, a Geiger counter tracing radioactivity.

I wanted to hear the why. I was under no illusion that Danny was a saint – I had seen him flirt with other women in the past – but I had observed Miguel's wedding ring in the car. There were more people involved than just us. I couldn't quite understand why T wanted me to be privy to her extra-curricular activities. I'd known her long enough to expect that no personal information was given without tactical intent. So I bided my time waiting for her play.

She held off an explanation as we drove, valet parking at a garage with alarming hourly rates and popping the trunk to give Miguel a gift bag with a kiss. The bag contained a beautiful jacket that he immediately donned despite the temperature, then crumpled and tossed the cardboard bag towards a trash can on the sidewalk. The restaurant was a short stroll away, but the greenhouse heat of the city was already permeating sidewalks and soles, making the walk feel longer, more tiring. T and Miguel prowled ahead, she leaning on his frame as though already drunk, whispering in his ear. It was only after she'd ordered for all of us without looking at the menu that she began recounting their brief history without prompting, as though at confession. She was correct about me. I did want to know.

She said she hadn't been looking for fun, but they'd met when she had been driving the freeway and her car had alerted her to a change in tyre pressure. Calamitously fearing a blow-out and unsure of the protocol, she'd commanded the satnav to take her to a nearby garage with e-charging. The choices were few, so she'd pulled onto that stark forecourt and begged the woman standing at the gas pumps for help as red lights blinked on the dash screen. That woman had been Georgina (which T pronounced ostentatiously with a Spanish inflection), Miguel's wife, and, by all accounts, the workhorse of the business. The Ortizes did not own the garage but ran everything for a local guy, and lived in a small apartment across the street so they could be on site as early and as late as needed.

On the unseasonably warm day T rolled onto the forecourt, Georgina was sweating in the noon sun and she shooed her new customer inside to the office while she calibrated the tyres and – to further the fee – checked the charge and cleaned the windshield. The office promised coolness, she said. And that was when they first crossed paths. T exploding through the door, sunglasses already sliding down her slick nose and Miguel sitting in front of the feeble AC; his feet on the desk and his eyes on her body. She liked being looked at like that, was surprised by the animal response it prompted in her. In that stifling room they flirted, the hum of their tensile attraction as tangible as that of the vibrating air-conditioning unit. It took precisely seventeen minutes for Georgina to reset the tyres and T to make a rash decision. She'd been continuing to make them for nearly two months since.

They met regularly in the city, away from her domestic life. Sometimes she swung by the garage when she knew Georgina was away from the business, but mostly they grappled in hotel rooms. He raised his eyebrows at this as T leaned closer to me, the drink in her hand tipping towards the table. The sex, she assured me in a low voice, was electric. I reached across to correct her glass, stopping it from spilling, sticky-sweet, on the polished table. It was different from Danny she said: rough, desperate, fast, hot. She might be addicted to it – hooked on the high she got from being pinned, wanted, taken. I glanced at Miguel who was now talking on the phone to someone as T detailed a rush of pleasure, the thrill of discovery, the woozy warmth that buoyed her home afterwards in a conspiratorial hiss. She didn't mention guilt.

'Sometimes you want courteous,' she whispered lasciviously, 'sometimes you don't . . .'

I opened my mouth to form a rebuttal, a question, but she knew what it would be and pulled away slightly.

'It's not serious,' she said.

'Does his wife know?' I looked back at Miguel, preoccupied with his phone's screen.

'I don't think she'd even consider it. All she cares about is that miserable place and trying to save money. Miguel says they don't even sleep together anymore.'

She looked at him with unfettered hunger and back at me.

'More for me!'

Miguel wasn't her usual type. But his lust for her was obvious in the way he watched her through unapologetic, half-closed eyes. Despite the hand-to-mouth existence that T had painted a picture of with something approaching fetishism, he had gold chains at his throat and wrist, a gem glinted in his earlobe. He had pronounced cheekbones and a mouth that I could imagine as both savage and sensual. I could visualise his bruising embraces and the way he might later murmur in her ear. When he gripped the back of her neck and squeezed affectionately as she leaned in to kiss his cheek, I could see the way he might press gasps from her. Ferocious T tamed and grateful. How do you bend a metal bar? You heat it up . . .

I couldn't imagine the same when I thought of Danny, who T had praised during their courting days for his charming appeals for consent at every step. She had always gone for tall, rangy, financially attractive men who dressed impeccably and talked of art or literature. Men who had hobbies that were conversation pieces, like the ex who created ugly abstract sculptures for girlfriends or the one who had competed in the Marathon des Sables and nearly died. The handsome boyfriend before Danny had ties to European royalty and had spent a year before college working in a refugee camp, often tearing up attractively when he talked about the people he'd met there. She liked a partner who exhibited her good taste.

'But Danny,' I interrupted, 'he suspects . . .'

'Nic,' she said with a tone of condescension, 'you're not going to be uptight about this, are you? We're adults. I'm not going to hurt him. Don't make more of this than it is.'

She pulled away and took a long draught of her cocktail.

'And as you said the other day, no one would judge me if I was a guy. Why shouldn't I do, and have, what I want?'

She sat back and looked at Miguel. She had successfully parlayed her own selfish desires into an equality issue. Taken my own words and reflected them back at me. Miguel's arm, with a seeming magnetic pull, reached around her waist as she beckoned the hovering staff, indicating that this conversational thread was over: 'Where's our order?'

As the food arrived we talked of Miguel's interests in baseball, coding and Warcraft – a subject he warmed to with an unselfconscious enthusiasm that made me like him. It was the forgettable chatter of people forced to converse at a social gathering until the point of the party arrived. But there were no candles to blow out, or body to bury. The uni tasted like an unremarkable briny pate, not unpleasant but not something I wanted more of. As a new platter of sushi arrived along with more drinks, Miguel whispered feverishly in T's ear, his lips catching in her hair. She laughed, her body tensed towards him. She looked back at me with blown pupils and they both stood up, hands entwined.

'Excuse us . . .' she said as she swept away towards the bathrooms, following Miguel, fingers trailing down his back.

I hoped this departure was for a coke bump, but as time stretched and more plates arrived it became apparent that they were using the glossy lacquered vanity or the deep sink of the bathroom for more than fleeting recreation. I drank my cocktail and then started on T's, willing the prickle of embarrassment away. The waiting staff were not so discreet that I didn't catch them exchanging hushed information that was clearly about the two diners who had just vacated my table. I watched the time tick away on my phone as I ate sushi and emptied the glass, another appearing immediately, spirited up by a waiter in the black apron uniform of the restaurant that he fashioned with no socks and brogues, his heels rubbed raw. As he whisked my empties away, I smiled apologetically, both for my gluttony and for the actions of my friends.

I imagined the span of Miguel's hands on her, her mouth open, the cool of the porcelain against their heated skin. I could not fathom the need that motivated their urgency. Sex was a foreign country to me where I understood enough of the language to get around, but I wasn't fluent. I'd relinquished my virginity later than most – as a matter of principle rather than passion – and I had yet to meet a man who so consumed me that I'd ever consider a break between courses as an opportunity. I could easily count the number of times I'd undertaken anything sexual outside of a bed, so my thoughts now were not of envy for T's carnal spontaneity, but that I was sitting alone, abandoned, on a huge table.

Despite the amount of rice I'd eaten, the cocktails were beginning to give me a buzz, blurring my anxiety and dulling the introspection. I stopped avoiding eye contact and smiled when staff passed, their faces turned towards me in anticipation of a request. I willed myself to float along with the current of the day, rather than fight it, just as T's distinctive laugh echoed over the din of chatter and crockery.

She sank back into her chair almost purring. Miguel plucked his napkin that staff had refolded from the table and wiped his hands as though he'd just completed an oil change. He smiled without guile.

'All good, Nic?' he asked as he reached out for sushi.

He pinched a piece of dragon roll in his fingertips and dropped it into his mouth. I nodded, telling them I'd consumed their drinks and asking about the hand soap in the bathroom in what I hoped was a cheeky, knowing fashion. Miguel frowned and T ignored me.

'Let's get the check,' she said, rotating her neck until there was an audible click. Her clothing was crumpled now, scrunched where it had been grabbed or crushed.

'To go where?' I asked.

'Miguel's sister's.' She shrugged, producing her black credit card and waving it towards the bar staff impatiently. They were used to rudeness from their patrons.

The remaining untouched platters on the table were dismissed, glasses drained and the check paid within minutes. We were soon back on the sun-scorched sidewalk hailing a taxi and climbing into its dark interior for a ride north, beyond the park and the streets I knew as a tourist. As we chugged towards Harlem, Miguel shouted into his phone, but my high school Spanish failed me as the temperature climbed higher, the cab air conditioning throwing out an aroma of damp fur with its ineffectual cooling. Even though the afternoon was beginning to take the sting from the heat, my thighs suctioned to the plastic seat through my clothing and my arm felt tacky pressed against Miguel's. T leaned against the window cursing the warmth, her fingers languidly tracing patterns on his upper thigh. As I watched the buildings pass I peeled my parched tongue from the roof of my mouth, regretting the soy sauce I had consumed.

It was with some relief that I unfolded myself onto another sidewalk when Miguel indicated that we should stop. As T paid the driver, he jogged up the stairs of a hulking apartment building, pushing a buzzer with an insistent finger. The entrance door hummed and clicked, allowing him to shoulder it open and affect a half-bow toward T and I, like a page ushering a duchess from her carriage. We entered a dingy hall with an indistinct smell and a broken stroller sagging in the corner.

'It's a walk-up, Nicky,' T said, deploying a name I hated and giving me an encouraging squeeze on my shoulders, nudging me towards the staircase that Miguel was taking two at a time. 'You're going to get your steps in today.'

When we'd circled up three flights, my breath was ragged and my armpits damp. T urged us on to the next floor where a woman stood in her open doorway beckoning us in. Miguel kissed her cheek as he passed the threshold, looking over his shoulder to say, 'This is Catalina – this is Nic,' before disappearing into the apartment.

I held out my hand to the woman, which she took in an amused fashion before greeting T with a hug. She was so petite it looked as though T was embracing a child, though her extravagantly long nails disrupted the illusion. Her jean shorts were cut high and she wore platform sandals so vertiginous that her smallest toes had broken for freedom out of the ligature straps across her feet. She threaded a thin arm around

T's waist to pull her through the door, beckoning me to follow. I closed the door behind me and walked down the hallway to the living room where a weed fug hung heavy in the air and various people sat on mismatched furniture swigging from beer bottles. There was tobacco spillage on the glass coffee table, while the kitchenette in the corner of the room was loaded with liquor bottles, bowls of chips and a bag of ice sitting in its own puddle.

A man who looked like a more wiry version of Miguel sat on the sofa, sucking from a roll-up. He raised a hand in greeting that Miguel slapped with a crack. Catalina produced a beer which I chugged to slake my thirst as she introduced me to different people in the room by pointing at them with a talon. T and Miguel seemed to know many of them already, and settled by the kitchen counter talking to a tall, jittery man who blinked constantly. There was a pale couple who were Catalina's neighbours a floor below and produced Patreon content that he conceived and she enacted. I admitted that I had never been on the site and they immediately enthused about the ease of joining and the artistry it allowed him to unburden himself of.

'We only do classy,' the woman insisted, explaining that her spouse's talents were now being sought by more professional outlets and that they both wanted to find a wider audience. What, I questioned, did they actually do? How far? How intimate? Where to draw the line? And this opened up a description of acts, poses and activities so thrillingly debased that I accepted vodka mixed with something, that Catalina put in my hand, without thought. As I sipped, my head swam and I wondered fleetingly if I should drink water. The idea of salvation, of stepping off this train, was momentary though. I drained the red plastic cup and asked for another, giving myself over to the experience with an unfamiliar spontaneity. I wanted to taste recklessness.

As the stereo boomed and the sun sank low I met a woman who seemed constantly on the brink of tears no matter the subject of conversation and two men who spoke of stolen cars with a casualness that felt comedic, before I moved to the sheet-covered couch where T and Miguel had settled. Sitting down heavily I watched Miguel rifle proprietorially through T's purse in search of cash as he growled, 'Ready to party, cariño?'

Catalina appeared next to me, her palm cool when she put a tiny hand on my forearm to enquire if I wanted anything. As though explaining to a tourist, she told me that Miguel had called her friend, a local dealer, who would arrive imminently and furnish everyone with anything they needed.

'Want in on that?' she asked.

I said yes, not necessarily because I did, but because I didn't want to refuse. When he arrived, in a hoodie despite the warmth, Catalina's friend was paid with T's crisp $100 notes as he doled out baggies to different people. Miguel and T snorted white lines off the table so blithely that I followed suit, the tingle in my sinuses sharpening my senses and making me bold. When the dealer slumped between us, I asked with the baldness of an elderly relative how much he made a month. He laughed and told me he couldn't say, but that it was enough.

'You a rich girl,' he stated. 'What do you care?'

I informed him grandly (and dishonestly) that I earned every cent I made, but didn't mention that my pay to date was still in three figures. He asked where I lived, I suppose as a measure of my wealth, and when I told him West Egg, he nodded while inhaling deeply on a blunt.

'You know Gatsby?' he asked, breathing the smoke out.

'She's my neighbour but I don't know her.'

'Oh yeah?' he nodded. 'I know some guys out in Queens who get called to sell up there. They been a couple of times. Big parties, big payout.'

'Wait,' I said, thinking of the bone broths, body brushing and intravenous vitamins I'd seen on Gatsby's socials. 'She's all about a healthy lifestyle.'

He looked at me then as though I was simple.

'Honey, you wanna believe that, believe.' He laughed, getting up to pick through the bottles for a drink.

I turned to Catalina, now sitting on the arm of the couch, daintily holding a lurid liquid in a wine glass imprinted with lipstick marks. She handed me a beer and I asked her all the questions I hadn't been permitted to at lunch.

'They want to get married,' Catalina declared. 'I mean, not so much cos of the lovey-dovey stuff, y'know, but cos of the situation.'

'The situation' was the lack of documentation for Miguel, his wife or her. Having travelled from the Dominican Republic after an unhappy transit through Puerto Rico, they were living under the radar and under the minimum wage. A legal union with a US citizen would help Miguel considerably. I wondered how T aligned her current politics with this fact, but looking across the room at her sitting in Miguel's lap and moving her buttocks against his groin as she talked to the dealer, I could only assume the idea enlivened her. He was like her predilection for dive bars and vacations with day trips to sketchy locations. Places she could always return from.

'But they're both married already,' I noted flatly.

'Yeah. Unhappily,' Catalina said with certainty. 'She has a pre-nup that screws her, otherwise she'd be gone. And him . . . hates his wife. I never liked her neither.'

This at least was seeded in truth. Both T and Danny came

to their union with considerable family wealth; they would have been foolish to marry without legal protection of their individual funds. Nevertheless, the pre-nup sounded like an excuse. There was nothing T couldn't get out of if she wanted to. Catalina went on to detail the type of wedding she imagined for the second Mrs Ortiz, the puppy they hoped to get and rambling stories with no apparent destination as I watched T and Miguel. They touched at all times even as they talked to others. Lust radiated off their skin. He bit gently on her upper arm as he got up to get more drinks. She bent into his touch, returning affection, without breaking conversation. I'd seen her do the same with Danny in the early days, though their mirroring had been more reverential, their greed gentler.

'I'm her husband's cousin,' I said, unsure what point I was making.

Catalina looked at me, again in amusement.

'So? What you gonna do about it? You think he don't know? Miguel sometimes calls the house just to play.'

I thought of the Buchanans' landline phone, another quaint antiquity that Danny had been evangelical about during a recent visit. A retro cream device, it sat in their hallway on a table under the stairs next to the seasonal bouquets in a beautiful glass vase. I thought of it ringing, echoing up the staircase and Danny hearing it. Did he know when he heard the shrill tone that it could be a version of him in T's secret life? Another man, breathing down the wires, asserting ownership through the silence.

'They're gonna wait, find a good time . . .' Catalina was saying. 'It'll be good for all of us.'

I nodded, unable to muster a suitable response. The noise of smashed glass in the kitchen drew Catalina away, scurrying on her heels, her high voice admonishing. I considered that I could message Danny right now, tell him I was assessing his competitor. T counted not only on my friendship to prevent that, but also on my inexperienced heart. She knew me well enough to understand that I would blanch at inflicting injury on Danny. I would struggle to tell him and watch his eyes swim. Especially when this could be over as fast as it started and he could remain safe in his ignorance.

I thought I'd make no protest about the situation but when T knocked my legs as she made her unsteady way past me to the kitchen counter, I grabbed her hand to halt her.

'Having a good time?' she slurred.

'T, I know what I said before,' I began, pulling her closer to me. 'But this isn't fair to Danny.'

The boozy smile slid from her face.

'Oh yeah?'

'He knows, doesn't he?' I asked, uncertain.

'Only if someone tells him,' she said and sank down to sit on the low table opposite me without letting go of my hand. She leaned forward. 'What? You thinking of breaking his heart and being there to pick up the pieces? Letting him cry on your shoulder?'

Her eyes danced and I knew what she referred to in her teasing tone. I flushed at the memory of what I'd told her in confidence a year before she ever met Danny. That I'd dreamt of my cousin in a manner that mortified me. Then, she'd dismissed my squeamishness, told me to stop obsessing over it, that it meant nothing. I forgot about it, and assumed she had too. But later, when she and Danny became an item, she watched me interact with him and then privately joked about him being a 'dream boy', as though pressing a wound. It might have been a minor, fleeting discomfort for others but she knew in me it bloomed like ink on blotting paper.

A silly evocation then, but the instant embarrassment felt like being punched. Just as it did now. My face burned and she smiled, satisfied. She let go of my hand and stood up.

'Want anything?' she asked as she stared down at me. When I shook my head she moved away.

As I swallowed the last sips of tepid beer I knew I'd never tell him. The longer I participated, the more I became complicit. I had already betrayed Danny in a way, and I cared what he thought of me, perhaps more than anyone else at that point in my life. I also knew what it felt like to be on the wrong end of T's displeasure. She had reduced self-assured mutual friends to introverts with her own particular brand of social engineering, designed to alienate, discomfort, denigrate. And her feats of mythomania were truly impressive, convincing all of a certain slant on a story, transposing who was the victim in any given situation. It was best to do nothing.

Hours ticked by until it was dark out and a bone-deep tiredness descended on me, the heavy fatigue of heat and alcohol. I lay my head on the couch and breathed deeply. The sheet on the sofa smelt of outdoor drying, recalling the sheets at my grandma's cabin. As I drifted into the booze-hastened analgesia of pre-sleep, I wondered where Catalina took her laundry. Was it the roof? Did her sheets billow with views of the city skyline, the sun bleaching them stiffly dry, the wind buffeting them like sails?

I was disturbed from my musing by loud, staccato knocking. I opened the eye not pressed to the sofa and watched as Catalina moved to the door, opening it to a robust, angry woman who complained immediately about her baby in broken English. As soon as I saw her exhausted face I became aware of the volume of our music and shouted conversations. Catalina, spiteful and defensive, drew others from the room to the doorway. From my position on the couch I could see the snarl of T's incisors as she threw slurs at the woman that made me recoil, saw the blinking man utter a violent promise as he pushed the complainant back into the corridor. The door was slammed in her face. I sat up straight as the group triumphantly moved back into the room. Everything was wearing off for me now.

'Hey . . .' I implored T as she settled back on the squeaky La-Z-Boy with Miguel. 'Hey, we should go . . .'

She either didn't hear or didn't choose to, kissing him ravenously, palming his crotch. I sat up, then stood, looking at my phone for getaway options. An Uber back to my boathouse would eat heavily into my cash. I felt regret settling on me, cold and dank. It was obvious now that I should have left hours earlier when I could have felt safe walking the city and using the subway. My head was vibrating and a sour taste crept up my throat. Why had I waited for T to determine my destiny again? I made a deal with myself that I would wait ten minutes and hope to feel more myself before departing without announcement, renegotiating the stairs and that sad hallway. I looked out of the window at the street below and watched a couple walk arm in arm from the intersection to a stoop below before parting. I invented a romance for them, caught in the tale just as a woman with a dark red mouth and white-blonde hair joined me at the window.

'Hi.' She smiled. 'Don't jump.'

I laughed. She did too, the long black flicks framing her eyes curving as her teeth showed.

'You okay?' she enquired sincerely, a warm hand on the small of my back, and the kindness almost undid me. I nodded vigorously.

'I'm good,' I insisted. 'I'm Nic.'

Her hand traced its way from my back around my hip and she stuck it out in a formal fashion in front of me.

'Frances,' she said, pushing her hand into mine and shaking gently. 'I assume you're with T?'

I looked over at T throwing back her head with a swallow, an indication she'd taken either a Tylenol or a less legal pharmaceutical. I nodded affirmation as Frances turned, still holding my hand and told me to come with her to find a drink in the kitchen. I allowed myself to be tugged towards the counter, stepping clumsily over feet and banging a shin on the low table. Frances looked back over her shoulder, her silver ponytail swishing against her back and I felt the storm in my gut start to subside. Like a parent with a tear-stained child, she soothed me, putting a drink in my hand and talking gently of things that I knew and understood, warming me with her attention. Emboldened by my narcotic blood, I allowed hidden aspects of myself to rise, considering that if I was T, I would likely contemplate kissing the dark lipstick off her. And then commotion exploded within the room behind us, making me turn back towards T.

She was pushing Miguel's arm away from her as invective poured from her mouth.

'You don't get to say that!' she spat, standing to her full height, in her heels slightly above Miguel. 'You never get to say that!'

I'd seen that look in T's eye many times over the years. It was a glint that told of resolve, of retribution. She was drunk, high and belligerent. And if Miguel had known her longer or understood her type he might have shrunk into an apologetic shell; but instead he challenged her, eyes hardened, spine straight.

'Bitch, I'll say anything I want, okay?!' he challenged and threw his glass down.

It landed on the table with such force it smashed both drinking vessel and surface, icy shards darting in a radius across the rug like a sunburst. At the same time the rapping at the door started again accompanied by triumphant warnings – the cops had been called. There was the sound of tears in the woman's brittle voice now. For a moment there was silence as everyone paused, perhaps no longer than a second. T and Miguel stared at each other with a feral rage that infected the room. Catalina's table was shattered, there were sirens in the distance and the party was certainly over.

It was Catalina who broke the tableau, inserted herself between the duo, trying to shift the weight of her brother while murmuring calming words in his ear. A tiny doll between the two opposing forces. The blinking man and his friends left immediately, grabbing spirit bottles from the counter as they went. They pushed past the shrieking woman in the corridor, whose baby now wailed on her hip. I realised the couple from downstairs had already gone, probably aware of the tide turning earlier than I was.

'We should go,' I called to T but neither she nor Miguel moved.

'Fuck you,' T said low and clear, breathing the insult into his mouth like a kiss.

'Fuck me? Fuck you!' he retorted, bullish.

'You don't get to talk shit about him,' T seethed. 'Don't even say his name.'

Miguel puffed out his chest. Catalina began speaking in feverish Spanish, her tiny hands squeezing his damp shirt. I felt rooted, unable to decide what I should do.

'She called the police. You want to see what happens

to your ass?' T snatched her purse from the couch and rummaged through it, her eyes never leaving his.

He looked furious and defiant. His shoulders flexed and his stance hardened.

'I'll talk about him as much as I like. Danny,' he crowed, and repeated the name, getting louder each time. 'Danny, Danny . . .'

In one movement, T grasped his shoulders and jackknifed hard, bringing her knee in sharp contact with his genitals, folding him. He pitched towards her but she let him fall. He crumpled instantly to the floor like a deflated car-dealership air dancer. He curled immobile on the shattered glass, moaning. Catalina stood frozen for a beat before she turned to block her boyfriend's furious advance towards T. She was deceptively powerful as she leaned her body weight against the man, hissing instructions.

'Self-defence,' T laughed. She leaned over Miguel as the sirens got louder. 'Don't mess with me, Ortiz,' she said in a tone that was almost loving. And then, 'Just go, Nic.'

'But is he okay? Should we . . . ?'

'He's fine,' she interrupted me. 'He'll be fine.'

She crouched over him, unfolded him, planting a leg on either side of his prone body. 'Babe,' she cooed and leaned down to stroke his face. I looked at the smashed apartment, at my shaking hands, at Catalina filling a glass of water and the open door to the dimly lit hallway. The upset woman had now retreated from outside the door. I looked back at T but she was blind to me now, her attention fully on the grunting, clenching man beneath her. I stepped around the glass on the floor to the Bluetooth speaker on a side table, still pumping music at a volume that now hurt. I flipped the switch off and pushed out a breath of relief as silence settled over the apartment, only Miguel's ragged intakes of air and T's soothing whispers now audible. She draped over him, the pose of comfort but also subjugation. She looked like she was riding her horse.

I turned and ran. Through the door; down, down, down the stairs and into the street, still muggy despite the hour. The sirens sounded close and I raced up the block to the nearest corner. Standing under a street light, I ordered an Uber as nimbly as my inebriated fingers could. My gut pitched as I watched the tiny black car icon on the app's map inch down the avenue towards me. Lights blazed from the windows of Catalina's building but nobody came out. Before I could ascertain whether the approaching sirens were destined for Miguel, an anonymous Prius pulled up at the curb.

'For Nic?' I asked gratefully, getting in the back seat and slamming the door on the chaos I'd left.

I looked upwards at the rooftops as we left Manhattan in order to keep a lid on the bile that was now ebbing and flowing with the lurch of the accelerator. If I trained my eyes on the lines against the sky, I could keep the hollow feeling at bay. We drove in silence and not for the first time I wondered why I called T my friend when her greatest contribution to our relationship was disorder. I didn't listen to the ugly, truthful answer that loomed from the deep. I didn't allow myself to think about it when I walked up the drive, shoes in hand, as splinters of the rising sun started raking the sea. And I didn't think about it when I fell into bed fully clothed. There was no point, as my breathing slowed on the pillow, where I admitted an exploitation of my own: that perhaps I used T as much as she did me. I wish I could say the incident forced me to re-examine myself and why I continued to endure her. But it did not.

Chapter 7

Though unsurprised to find no message from T the next morning when I surfaced from a restless sleep, I was nevertheless affronted by the lack of contact from her. I knew she never apologised, but my judiciary sense thought that a simple texted 'sorry' might have been appropriate, or a check-in to ensure my safety. But this was her way. She sent so few messages that each appeared as a gift to the recipient, always ending any exchange to leave the other dissatisfied; and she had an almost psychic ability to reinsert herself into one's consciousness just at the moment that withdrawal from her seemed a real possibility.

As I took a long, scalding shower with the pump's final ice-cold splurge an unannounced insult, I decided this was the moment I was going to be more unavailable to her. I wouldn't send her a message like an eager lapdog, I wouldn't enquire about how she or Miguel were doing. I would not like her social posts, I might even mute her. I chose to blame her for any of my shortcomings. If I had nursed my anger and the sour taste of ignominy into action, perhaps things that came later would have happened differently. Though inaction is still an action, indecision still a decision.

Despite a debilitating hangover, I crouched at my laptop and wrote fruitfully for the first time in weeks. My phone buzzed like a trapped bluebottle, illuminating my desk where it lay face down. Thinking it might be T, I resisted picking the device up until late evening when I spooned comforting mac and cheese into my mouth from a mug. There was nothing from her. But there was a message waiting from my landlady.

Invited to that Gatsby woman's party this weekend. She's clearly trying to keep the neighbours sweet. Good luck, honey ;) I'm out of town – wouldn't go even if I wasn't. You want to?

I put down the mug as though scalded and replied with a thumbs-up emoji. A response followed with an invitation and a QR code to be scanned by security on arrival. With excited blood thumping in my ears, I realised I hadn't looked at Gatsby's feeds for a couple of days. I clicked into one to study the parties that had gone before and remind myself of what I might expect.

Each Saturday soirée began with a Wednesday social dump of prep pictures. Deliveries of crates of limes to fill clear vases, the gluten-free ingredients for canapés arriving at the back door to the kitchen, the staff cleaning crystal glasses and silverware with white gloves. By Thursday, there were shots of a billiards table with blue baize and a glossy frame, a walk-in wardrobe of diaphanous garments, a sauna for the lady of the house to clear her pores. By Friday, Gatsby in a billowing dress, pointing out to caterers where to set up the bar on the lawn and fairy lights being dotted through the trees on her drive by sweat-sodden men wearing event-company T-shirts. Gatsby having a mani and pedi as she answered her phone, her fingers splayed as she held the device to her golden head. By Saturday morning the buffing of floors, the setting out of glasses and the choosing of shoes.

And then the guests arrived. In a wildly different array of outfits from high couture to jeans and flip-flops (though captions told me these were Silicon Valley CEOs who needed to impress no one). A DJ in sunglasses in the shadowy ballroom pointing to a crowd of smiling people, champagne held aloft, faces turned towards him like flowers to the sun. Reposts of people dipping toes into the ornately tiled swimming pool or slurping an oyster from its pearlised shell. Women in heels so impractical they clearly always knew a car awaited them. Young men howling into the night like Neanderthals despite their credit rating.

I was transfixed. I wondered if I could master the flying solo thing that I had never had the guts to pull off in college, always badgering a friend to accompany me, reliant on a plus-one to see me through any festivities. I viewed the invitation as both a challenge and a boast. I wanted to experiment and see how I would fare, arriving at an exclusive event without a wingman. I would casually drop evidence of attending onto my socials the next day and wait for my scattered friendship group to react in different time zones.

I scoured my meagre wardrobe for an outfit that would work and decided on all black (meritocratic, classic, invisible), then counted down the days to Saturday as I observed the flurry of activity over the fence. By Saturday afternoon I was no longer peeking politely from behind my magnolia, but sitting in prime position on the grass on one of my landlady's rusty lawn chairs found in the wardrobe. PB&J sandwich and beer in hand, I watched four-poster loungers being erected by the jetty with sheer curtains that puffed like jellyfish when the wind changed direction, a stage appearing by the glass doors to the house and a cavalcade of trucks arriving bearing food and drink as they made their doleful crescent turn, up to the rear entrance and retreating to the city. Gatsby wasn't seen as her minions crawled all over the grass and pebbles, the flags and the pool. Inside the house the same industry was no doubt also at work.

By 5 p.m. she stopped posting the progress of the shellfish bar and the taco van, a lull in informing her followers of her every move. This, I assumed, was in order to ensure the maximum impact of her appearance at this event. Having scrolled through the last few parties, I noted that Gatsby always materialised in the midst of the merriment, when guests were already glassy-eyed and loose-limbed, the dance floor messy, the toilet selfies messier. Her look impeccable, the hashtags copious. The most dazzling of the stars in a firmament of them, her light reaching Earth in a more pronounced way having been hidden.

It was past 6 p.m. now and, as the last of the vans disappeared through Gatsby's gates and the sky began to bruise with the possible threat of rain, I drank the dregs of my beer and collapsed the chair, ready to fuse her digital world with my corporeal one. I dressed and stared at my reflection in the mirror as though preparing for a date as the noise from next door built. My phone alarm informed me, mid mascara slick, that now was the time I had set myself to cross the lawn. I looked around my abode as though anticipating what came before and what came after would be two diametrically different things. Picking up my shoes, I walked across the grass barefoot to the boundary line between my landlady's grounds and Gatsby's dominion.

Though a formidable fence separated the properties near the road and buildings to provide privacy, the gardens that petered out to the sand and then the water were open. Proprietous borders were most certainly drawn on deeds, but the impression of the houses here was that the access to and from the sound was egalitarian, organic. One could theoretically walk along the entire shore without impediment, the dwellings of the wealthy unrestricted by such coarse signifiers of ownership. Predictably, as I approached the point at which my grass ended and Gatsby's began, a figure moved from the shadows of the house towards me, gathering pace as I turned toward the blazing windows and the thumping bass. The man approached with his headset crackling and an unwelcoming smile on his face.

'Help you?' he barked, blocking my progress.

I held out my phone, the code glowing in my palm. 'I was invited,' I said and gestured behind me to the boathouse. 'I live just there.'

He looked over my shoulder, perplexed, and back at the screen. His expression returned to blankness as he pulled a scanner from a holster which read the code with a cheerful chime, and then clamped a pale ribboned band on my wrist. He pulled it tight and nodded. 'Enjoy your evening,' he said without inflection.

As I approached the house, the guests who had arrived at the front entrance unspooled through the property to flood out from the glass-panelled doors onto the rear patio. They were silhouetted by pastel lighting rigged around the space, bathing them in a golden haze or a pool of soft blush. The music that had begun as I showered was louder now that the doors were thrown open, the ballroom beyond already a throng, shouted conversations overlapping and escalating, sounding like an exotic birdhouse. I walked at a leisurely pace, wanting to take in the whole scene, both deliciously thrilled I was about to step into this sought-after event and also putting off the moment I would have to join the crowd. I climbed the stone stairs as though ascending a dais to receive a prize.

When I slipped on my shoes and stepped onto the patio, I bobbed and weaved my way through animated groups to the bar I'd seen built in a time-lapse TikTok video the day before. Glasses covered the surface, grouped into different coloured cocktails, lined up in rows like flower beds. An easel in the corner told me the ingredients of each but I allowed my eyes to guide my choice, passing over the tall icy highball of apple-green, the pale martini, the thimble of scarlet. I reached for the cut-glass saucer of fizzing amber from France that I associated with red carpets, and turned to watch the dancing, swaying, laughing, whispering bodies. Floating islands of candles and flowers bobbed on the azure water of Gatsby's pool like tiny atolls. Even at this early hour, guests had removed their shoes and were sitting on the side, drifting their submerged calves back and forth as they chattered.

I felt curiously unashamed of staring as I watched each new batch of people who appeared, disgorged from taxis, town cars and limousines. They crowded around me at the bar and plucked at trays of gem-like canapés that passed on gloved hands. I caught snatches of conversations: about the considerable schlepp from the city, boasted recollections of previous parties, luxurious plans for summer vacations and savage assessments of other guests. As I stood sipping my second champagne, another woman, also alone, stopped at the bar while hurriedly typing into her phone. She leaned backwards against the structure, causing glasses to wobble and spill, one toppling and smashing to the floor at our feet. The bar was not as sturdy as it looked, a temporary structure not designed to outlive the evening.

'So sorry!' she shout-apologised as white gloves

immediately swept the crystal up and dabbed at the sticky puddle near my foot. She stepped closer. 'Did I get you?'

I looked down and shook my head.

'I don't think that will be the first or the last tonight.'

She nodded with a conspiratorial smile.

'Been to one of these before?'

Over the music I shouted back that I had not, but that as an immediate neighbour I had seen plenty of build-up and aftermath. This seemed to pique her interest, her dark eyebrows raising slightly. She asked my name and told me she was Lily Shield, suggesting that we were both outliers here – what with me being a local when most of the influencer crowd came from Manhattan, and because she had lied her way in with bribes and subterfuge.

'Why?' I asked, allowing my empty glass to be refilled by an anticipatory server.

'Come on,' she scoffed, her accent tinged with something I couldn't place. 'Everyone wants to know what goes on here, right?'

She told me that she ran a celebrity lifestyle site that was gaining traction, Gold Shield, which denoted both her surname and the quality of her sources and gossip. That she'd 'taken down' a couple of famous people with blind items and was fighting the good fight against celebrity hypocrisy from her keyboard. She'd been in London first, then LA and now New York, and this was by far the juiciest location.

'So much filth hidden away,' she practically drooled. 'The worst people, the dirtiest secrets, seriously. Proper sleazy.'

She pointed into the house.

'Did you see the goody bags? Most people here could buy the state but they love a free face serum.'

She quizzed me on my name, what I knew of Gatsby – who

visited, what she did on her downtime, whether I talked to her? Had I received any of her famous gift baskets? Did I see any of a string of famous men stand on this spot in the mornings? I had nothing to give her that any of Gatsby's followers couldn't have offered. Our nighttime interlude was my only offline experience of her and I felt strangely protective of that moment. I shook my head.

'I don't know her at all,' I admitted.

'Well, I guess I'll mingle,' Lily said finally. 'I want to nosy around . . . look me up online if you get anything, yeah? Good or bad. Especially bad!'

'Sure,' I replied, certain that I'd google her website but not that I'd contact her. Though I fancied myself a journalist I didn't consider us as comrades. I didn't trade in rumour and smut. I watched as she walked up to a group of barely dressed women who had starred in a popular reality show and inserted herself into their chatter. Soon she was enveloped by the hordes. I decided to do the same, slide into the undertow and let it take me. I had no one to find among the faces and no agenda apart from seeing our host in the flesh.

I put down my glass and allowed the syncopated movement of the dance floor to jostle me towards the doors, into the ballroom and past a sushi station manned by two industrious chefs, beyond a mountainous shellfish bar. The eddies of human movement bore me around the perimeter past dainty cheese boards and a gourmet popcorn cart, through double doors to a quieter place where heads bowed in hushed chatter over flickering candles on tiny tables. I walked the length of the room inhaling the scents being burnt, through to a corridor leading to a cinema with plush leather seats where a studious group of young men watched a classic James Dean movie while drinking scotch, frowning as I broke their concentration by entering.

Moving down more corridors and passing giggling actresses who had famously formed a friendship on a recent horror franchise, I found the spa area where a sauna, steam room and ice-cold plunge bath were primed but not in use, the artisan wooden benches around them full of people drinking and conversing, their voices bouncing off the tiles. Through a heavy glass door, I came upon a smaller indoor pool, a myriad of dancing lights playing across its domed ceiling like a baby's nursery projector. An unseen speaker diffused singing bowl sounds over the water, and fluffy oatmeal robes hung from bronze hooks on cedarwood walls.

Retracing my steps I found a Polaroid photo booth dispensing monochrome ticker-tapes of hard-copy photos, a treatment room full of equipment sitting silent covered in plastic wrap and a pebbled courtyard where food trucks beckoned smokers and booze-hungry scavengers outside with greasy smells and bright interior bulbs. As I returned to the outside patio and pool area, I finally saw a familiar face.

'Jordan!' I called out as I made my way towards where he was standing, holding the attention of a circle of pink-cheeked girls.

He was dressed in a beautiful burgundy suit and sneakers, and he glanced in my direction with wariness, perhaps anticipating a zealous fan. His frown melted in a way that gave me a fizzing feeling deep in my belly. He jutted his chin up in his familiar, cool greeting.

'Hey, Danny's cousin.'

I pushed eagerly towards him, ignoring the territorial stares of his coterie, the smile widening even further on my face at the thrill of seeing someone I could place outside this environment.

'Nic,' I corrected him. 'I thought you hated influencers?'

He shrugged. 'Not enough to miss a party. How come you're here?'

The question's true meaning was implicit.

'I'm famous in my own way,' I joked.

He looked over my head towards the darkness of my landlady's property. 'Oh yeah, you live nearby, right?'

'Just there.' I pointed towards the water.

His eyes rested on mine with a jocularity and interest that hadn't previously been present.

'Mmn huh,' he hummed and took a step away from the group. 'I bet you've seen some things?'

I wobbled my head in a way that was neither negative nor affirmative. I wanted to detain him.

'You know Gatsby?' he asked, turning his body towards mine.

'Not yet . . .' I looked around the room again, hoping that she might appear. 'It's weird to have a party and not be at it. I feel like we've all broken in here.'

He shrugged again, whether to convey a lack of worry or knowledge of Gatsby's whereabouts I couldn't tell, and then tilted his head towards the bar.

'Drink?'

Leaving the group without a backward glance, he beckoned me to follow. I might have considered this rude had he not now been directing his attention at me. I would come to learn that this was his way; an abrupt disengagement from anyone or anything that no longer interested him. He moved through the crowd with the gait of a man who knew people enjoyed watching him walk away. I appreciated his swagger as I trailed in the wake he carved through huddled groups.

'So,' I shouted above the music as he turned and handed

me a long-stemmed glass brimming with an orange mixture of spirits, 'how did the tournament go?'

He grimaced, shook his head and looked out over the pool, closing that line of questioning.

'Have you been for a snoop?' he asked.

I told him of the rooms I'd discovered, the opulence of the fixtures, the number of people crammed in each space; he described an impressive library which seemed to be the only place quiet enough to make a phone call.

'Someone told me she has a seaplane,' he chuckled, 'parked down there with the yacht and the jet skis.'

'Does she?' I asked, mentally scrolling through her social posts for reference. I had never noticed a seaplane but that didn't mean it didn't exist.

'Who knows?' He shrugged and started bobbing his head to a new bass-heavy track.

I followed suit, dipping my chin to the beat while watching the sea of rippling bodies lit by the now full moon. We stayed like that, the music moving us, feet almost touching, for several songs. I liked the idea that people who passed by, recognised him and said hello, thought we were together. Why not? I mused. Though I wasn't wearing something as obviously expensive as many of the women here, I could be every bit as mysterious. Unlike many of the people gathered in the room whose lives were lived via social posts or through gossip sites, I was a civilian with an undocumented existence, and therefore a lacuna. I wanted to be that to Jordan; I wanted his curiosity. He swallowed the last of his drink and slid the glass onto a passing tray. He leaned towards me, his jaw brushing mine for an instant, his words buzzing against my ear.

'Gotta go say hi to a couple of people. See you later?'

I nodded and he smiled, dazzlingly, a hand on my shoulder as he moved up the stairs to the house behind me. He turned part-way up, knowing I'd be watching, and called, 'I'll come find you!' before he was gone. I shivered in delight at the idea of him gliding back through the room, his eyes like an alligator above water, sweeping the area to locate me.

The drinks I'd consumed gave me a mission to fill the time before Mr Baker sought me out again and I found a bathroom labelled 'Ladies' with a gilt signpost, resignedly joining the line snaking along the wall outside. It was quieter here and conversation thrummed among the women as they toyed with their phones and makeup, reapplying colour to their faces in tiny shards of mirrors produced from bags and pockets. A pair of famous blonde twins in front of me swiped through their social feeds, checking reactions and murmuring to each other in the low, bored cadence of the West Coast.

'I mean, this much traffic for this?' one exclaimed scornfully to the other, her final word crackling in her throat like a death rattle.

'Notoriety. You think she *didn't* know what her ex was doing? No way. I swear she's dark,' the other commented. 'There's shit to come out and I'll be here for it.'

'Dude, she'd never get the sponcon if there was serious tea,' said the first. 'Gatsby has stuff on other people, for sure. Bad stuff. That British thing lets you get away with serious crap.'

Her sister rolled her eyes and thrust her phone deep in her pocket.

'Hate her.' She paused for a beat. 'Still want a picture with her.'

They both cackled, their heads tilted together, like poppies. They moved on to eviscerate another competitor, bloviating about the party as we shuffled slowly closer to the bathrooms. I tuned in to other discussions speculating on the cost of the party ('At least half a mill, right? And most weeks!') or trying to place famous faces who passed (an ex-Nickelodeon moppet, a baseball player or a bit-part indie actor?). By the time I got into a stall my liquor buzz was beginning to wear off and I felt as though I'd toured a fan convention without seeing the star; a curiously depleting experience. When I'd reapplied my lipstick in the mirror alongside an assembly line of open-mouthed faces doing the same, I returned to my wandering; drinking mindlessly from various glasses, consulting my phone if self-consciousness came over me and picking my way through a dessert buffet. As midnight came and went, there was still no sign of the host but this didn't seem to trouble the guests as the liquor and food continued to be replenished by ghostly staff who slipped past tables refreshing platters and glasses.

As I swayed on the patio and considered dipping my feet in the pool, a splash at one end made me turn my head. Under the water, moving like a mermaid, her hair streaming behind her, swam a girl in a full evening dress. Her high heels waited neatly on the side of the pool where she'd executed the perfect dive that was now shooting her beneath the undisturbed floating candles towards the other end. Although the music still boomed, it felt as if the crowd held a collective breath watching her arch her arms in a wide stroke, no air bubbles rising to the surface, her sequin dress twinkling, phosphorescent, as she glided over the floor tiles. With one more pull she crested the surface at the opposite end of the pool, and in a fluid movement burst from the water and pushed herself up on the side. She stood, the heavy dress clinging to her skin and affected a Lady Liberty pose to applause, her hair a wet serpent down her back. It was one of the most elegant things I had seen someone do.

A man wrapped his jacket and then his arms around her shoulders, pressing an admiring kiss to her glistening cheek. She folded into his embrace. I decided to find Jordan, this time not letting him slip from my grasp. I wound back through the house the way I had come, holding my glass like a tour guide with a flag, scanning faces, hoping that he meant what he had said about tracking me down.

When I arrived at the library, I saw him sitting with a long, lean woman who had draped one leg possessively over his knee. Hoping to repeat the trick of our previous meeting, I uttered his name as I approached. He looked up sharply before his eyes softened, a hand raising in salute.

'Nic!'

'What happened to finding me?' I chided teasingly, shifting one hand to my hip. 'I don't think you can be trusted.'

He stood up, the woman's calf sliding unceremoniously from his straightening legs, his focus now firmly on me. Neither of us glanced at her as we mimicked each other's stance.

'I was on my way.' He smiled, smoothing down his shirt and tucking it into his trousers, drawing my attention to his waistband and my thoughts irrevocably to his body. It was probably the point.

'I was looking for Gatsby,' I said.

His eyebrows raised. 'Oh yeah? Find her?'

I shook my head. 'Want to look together?' I held his gaze longer than I usually dared. I turned away, looking back at him with a challenge. 'Coming?'

The woman tutted with annoyance in her seat but he didn't look at her, just continued smiling at me. I wondered what magic I'd suddenly harnessed. The exhilaration of pulling the focus of such an imperious man vibrated through me.

'Yeah,' he said, stepping forward and slipping a light hand around my waist, his fingers resting on my ribcage, a whisper away from my breast. 'Lead on . . . you seem to be having more fun than me.'

We began to walk in step towards the door.

'So now you've seen how the influencer lives, you're interested?' I asked archly.

'Intrigued,' he whispered into my ear and I felt, as he obviously intended, that he might have been talking about Gatsby or me.

'She seems sweet.'

'For a scammer.' We paused at the door, his palm on the handle. 'I heard she pays for followers. And that accent . . .' He rolled his eyes.

'I like it,' I said.

'I'm sure you do.' Jordan smiled, exerting pressure on my waist as he opened the door, moving us both to the next room. 'That's the idea.'

'Oh, but what if she has a seaplane?' I teased. 'Would that change things?'

He glanced sideways with amusement. 'Did you find it?'

'Wouldn't you like to know?' I shrugged in his circling arm, thrilling to the coquettishness he conjured in me.

He brought his mouth close to my ear again, his lips moving against my skin.

'Proceed with caution,' he warned, merriment in his tone – but the messaging seemed earnest.

I turned to ask for more reasons for his dislike just as a famous DJ was announced and took to the stage, greeted by cheers from sweating guests. He was married to a more famous pop star and the exact figure in dollars it took to have him perform at a billionaire's birthday party popped into my head directly from the pages of a gossip website. Jordan nodded in surprised approval and whooped himself.

When the mass of bodies began to move with a new beat, I glanced to my right, as though drawn by her aura, to see Gatsby finally emerge into the room at the top of the stairs. She looked like polished onyx in a sleek, black-sequinned column that twinkled as she exhaled. She seemed regal as she gazed around the room at dancers lost in the tempo. With her high cheekbones and a slice of buttery hair hanging over one eye, she appeared timeless to me, Veronica Lake in a modern world; only the phone in her hand, resting against her thigh, denoted her era.

She smiled as she surveyed the room, a slight dimple forming in one cheek. I hadn't noticed it before, and wondered if she edited it out of her pictures as it conveyed too much homespun charm. She started scanning the room, looking for something or someone. Her eyes seemed to stop on me and I felt a blush of pleasure at my throat before I realised she was actually looking at Jordan beside me, her head then quickly dipping to tap something briskly into her phone. She looked back at us and, with the instinct of a fan, I raised my hand to wave, but thought better of it. Instead I pressed my fingers over Jordan's hand, still resting on my body, pulling his attention towards me. He curled inward to hear.

'Gatsby . . .' I began, intending to point out our host just as a girl with a clipboard and headset pulled his other elbow, demanding attention. He leaned towards her instead as she conveyed an urgent message from behind her hand. He nodded at her and she disappeared as quickly as she'd arrived.

'What?' I shouted.

He pulled me flush with him and I felt my body respond in a wanton way that startled me.

'Gatsby wants to see me.'

I looked at him in confusion, jealousy prickling me. He pulled a face, conveying his own consternation. His hand fell from me leaving a heated imprint and he peeled himself away. He smiled as though he could read my thoughts. My face burned.

'Message me!' he called as he left me for a second time, and when I tore my eyes from him, I noted that Gatsby had gone from the room as well. Both of my quarries had slipped through my fingers.

Immediately, I opened my phone contacts and scrolled for Danny's name, punching in an abrupt missive asking for Jordan's details. I added an 'X' to soften the shortness of the demand, but I wanted to make good on the promise of the last few minutes immediately. Despite his disavowal of his cell he was online for once – Danny slept poorly and was often up in the small hours – and I let out a relieved breath when the three dots appeared denoting a reply incoming.

Nic, you sly dog! he wrote with a dog emoji. More dots. *Sending now . . . x*

As soon as the contact appeared, I saved it and began to compose a message to Jordan. The first three attempts were deleted for their transparent eagerness, their thirst.

So . . . ? I ended up sending.

I pocketed the phone and looked out at the sea of strangers, enjoying observing with no pull to join them. Like the lulling pleasure of watching waves break on a shore, I followed the movement of the crowd as the DJ commanded the floor, driving the rhythm, setting the pace until his set came to a triumphant end. He was hurried from the stage by a huddle of bodyguards and I realised that considerable time had passed. I had been suspended in this moment, transfixed, thinking of nothing – a state I congratulated myself on as a habitual over-analyser. But just as a sense of contentment settled over me, my eye was drawn to frenzied movement in the crowd. A fight was beginning in the centre of the floor; a pushing spiral like a cotton-candy swab bumping around a spinning bowl. The idea of violence immediately recalled the anxiety of my recent trip to Manhattan.

I hurried from the room, arriving back outside at the pool area, away from the shouts and the jackdaw shrieks of women intervening. Here the party was naturally thinning out, stumbling guests who had been down on the shore wearily climbing the stairs back to the house, the first fingers of dawn strobing the sky to the east. I took off my heels, enjoying the cool, flat plane of the pool deck and looked towards the purple-shadowed gardens and the siren light of my bedroom window beyond the trees. I'd left a lamp on to pull me home through the darkness. I no longer felt the alcohol in my blood but my tongue was heavy in my mouth and, without looking at the time or my message app, I drew a line under this event. It was time to go. Swinging the shoes in my hand, I walked back down the steps to the sprinkler-dampened lawn and crossed it towards the perimeter. A security guard facing the water called out that there was no exit in this direction.

'I live just there,' I pointed without slowing my approach and he nodded, less concerned with those getting away than those getting in. As I passed him, the static hiss of grave voices conveyed emergency over his radio. We both turned back towards the house, him setting off at a loping jog, me watching the building.

Perhaps it was the fight, perhaps the late hour and affronted neighbours that brought them, but winking police lights were soon visible, flashing off the front walls and gate. I had extricated myself at precisely the right minute, as all the music suddenly ceased and the pretty, dancing lights on the patio shut off. Silhouettes around the pool and through the windows began to move in one direction, becoming a huddled mass. In my pocket my phone illuminated.

I left, Jordan wrote. *Sounds like it went to shit. You still there?*

I didn't open the message, left it sitting on my home screen so he wouldn't know I'd seen it. If he liked intrigue, I decided to give it to him. I continued to my bed. I was learning.

Chapter 8

I managed to resist Jordan's message for longer than I expected I could hold out. But after a WhatsApp chat with my girl group the next afternoon I was convinced not to be too unavailable to the handsome golfer. There was, I was counselled, cool-girl poise, and there was haughtiness that lost a potential prize.

Saw Gatsby. Wouldn't you like to know . . . ? he had written at 5.09 a.m., deliberately repeating my words back to me – a tease I struggled to decipher. Was he enticing, or joshing with Danny's kid cousin? As I composed, deleted, composed, deleted a response, an Instagram notification flashed onto my screen. @MissJayGatsby was now following me. Before I could inform my friends of this turn of events, I watched as my meagre follower number ticked upward in real time, over thirty people in minutes. My hands sweated. I was simultaneously delighted and terrified. I had to put the device down. My heart raced. I took a deep breath looking at the water. Perhaps Jordan had told her my name. She had been eager to meet with him and might think I was a way to a second meeting. But then why would either of them need to involve me in their flirtation? I stared at my screen bewildered. Then a businesslike knock at my front door startled me as a card dropped through the letterbox, snapping the flap with a clank.

It was a rich cream envelope, looping cursive spelling out my full name in old-fashioned ink. It exuded a perfume even in my hand. When I pressed it to my nose I detected roses and something earthy, exotic. I flung the door open to find its sender. On the brow of the slope was the retreating figure of the headset girl from the previous night. I ripped the beautiful stationery to get to the message in the same large handwritten script.

Hey neighbour, so sorry we didn't meet this weekend. Would adore it if you could swing by next Saturday? The theme is 'Heavenly Bodies'. My assistant will be in touch. X

I messaged Jordan first.

I'm going back to Gatsby's next weekend. Will I see you? #OperationSeaPlane.

Maybe, he replied immediately.

I waited but there were no further dots. I stood in my kitchen, my coffee forgotten and my thoughts tumbling. If he wanted her, he'd have surely shown more interest. If he wanted me, the same was true. Or maybe this was how they behaved. Much as I wanted to be a clinical observer of celebrity, I was reverberating with the idea of abutting it. There was an undeniable sense of anointment, a charge from being recognised by those who are known.

My week fell away, marked only by DMs from Gatsby's assistant sending my digital entry to her palace, and the like that Jordan bestowed on my post of my feet paddling at the water's edge of the estate. Any planned productivity was torpedoed by the promise of the weekend. I went through the motions of work, calls with my parents and friends, restless sleep. But I was riding a rotating carousel and Saturday was the opportunity to grasp the golden ring.

This time I waited until much later to cross the lawn, aware that Gatsby wouldn't appear until the Cinderella hour, and that catching Jordan's attention required a lack of eagerness. I arrived at my neighbour's home after midnight and retraced my steps through this week's extravagances, feeling less imposter syndrome and remembering this time to document my progress via photos. Elegant notices throughout the house posted the WiFi password to ensure ease in uploading. Wandering through the rooms, I looked for both their faces among the plumped lips, stretched brows and fluttering lashes, weaving through rocking bodies and the hooting conversations of competition. Despite drinking as I walked, my mouth felt dry.

After stumbling through the shadowy library where couples melted into one another I found myself in the cathedral-like hallway at the front of the house where the spiral staircase was entwined with white, perfumed flowers and the marble floor so polished my shoes squeaked on it. Here the music was less insistent, the bodies passing me cooler and the air less charged. The front door was open and guarded by black-clad security with headsets, the driveway beyond still producing guests. They came up the front doorsteps in a gaggle, surging forward with meerkat heads, assessing the pleasures ahead. The stairs to the rooms above were denoted off limits by a velvet rope and a totemic security guard. As I stood at the foot of them, a woman in silver silk pushed against those arriving, like a salmon wriggling upstream, and took an exasperated intake of breath as she paused a moment next to me. She looked at me briefly before barking, 'Sweetie, take this,' and passing me her empty glass.

As she sashayed to the exit, I looked down at my unremarkable black dress and realised with a mixture of amusement and embarrassment that she had mistaken me for wait staff. I cast around for somewhere to discard it but there was no tray, no hurrying waiter. I slunk to the side of the stairs and surreptitiously slid the glass through the bannister onto the smooth surface of the tenth or eleventh step. It almost collided with a shoe as the owner descended. I glanced up just as a woman leaned quizzically over the railings to look down at me, her hair falling forward around her face in honey waves, her earrings swinging like chandeliers. She wore white and feathers, diamonds glistened at her tanned throat. She smirked.

'Well, hello!' she said crisply, her accent elongating the vowels of the greeting, 'I'm Gatsby.' She smiled over the bannister, 'and you, my love, must be my neighbour.'

She descended the stairs as though transported by escalator, all but twirling around the bottom step so that the feathers around her neck fluttered. She stood before me, arms open, her pale wrists exposed, revealing her pearly canines as the corners of her mouth lifted.

'Nic Carraway?' she asked as her eyes crinkled at the corners; the delight of her gaze warming my bones. She looked at me with the fondness of family, as though our positions were reversed and this was my party, and she was merely a guest pleased by her famous host. Dazzled by her stature – both physical and social – I felt the rush I recalled when shaking the hand of a famous actor who had taken time to meet the audience after a campus Q&A.

She seemed less angular than her social-media image and I enjoyed seeing the smile I'd seen in Paris, London, Dubai on her grid directed at me.

I accepted her proffered hug, moved forward and placed my hands lightly against her narrow back as she bowed her head to meet mine and breathed 'lovely to meet you' in my ear. She smelt of warm summer citrus fruit and a tropical flower I couldn't identify. A feather tickled my neck when she pulled away, her face still registering resolute interest in me.

'Oh gosh,' she laughed, 'so pleased you could make it!'

I nodded dumbly in assent as her joyful focus made my cheeks pink with pleasure and self-consciousness. She held a hand up to her mouth in a mock-whisper pose and said with a narrowing of her eyes, 'You're the only neighbour I invited that I hoped would come.'

'Oh?' I was surprised to be so valued. Did she socially compartmentalise her neighbours in the way they did her?

She grabbed my warm hand with her cool one and asked earnestly; 'Tell me, are you being looked after? I see your glass is empty . . .' she gestured to the abandoned glassware on the stair with a tilt of her head.

'That's not mine,' I replied foolishly.

She swept past me, pulling me behind her as she looked through mink lashes back at me.

'Come with me,' she said over her shoulder, the clipped vowels of her English background surfacing through the sort of transatlantic accent I usually couldn't bear. 'Let's get a drink. I want to know all about you . . .'

I allowed myself to be pulled through the crowd to the next room where Gatsby summoned staff to her side with the raising of her free hand. Her narrow gold bangles slid down her arm to jangle at rest as her fingers beckoned, then raced back to her wrist when she reached out to take a saucer of champagne from a mirrored tray and offered it to me. She did not let go of my fingers as I accepted. With an almost imperceptible shake of her head she rejected a glass for herself, allowing the waiter to merge with the crowd again.

We were standing at the top of the couple of stairs leading to the dance floor and for a moment, she gazed across the room at nodding heads, gyrating bodies and glasses held up like offerings with the satisfied expression of a denizen of Mount Olympus looking down on mankind. She turned back to me and dropped my hand.

'Did Jordan make it?' she asked.

I shrugged and she looked away as though the answer displeased her. I sipped champagne, anticipating that she would imminently excuse herself from me to circulate the room in pursuit of a better conversationalist. I wondered if I could ask for a photo with her before she slipped away.

'How are you liking West Egg?' she asked suddenly, her face bright and turned back towards me. 'I know it's hard to move somewhere new.'

I told her I liked it just fine and admired her dress. She looked down and smiled before thanking me with such sincerity that I was taken aback by the idea that perhaps she didn't hear compliments as often as I assumed. She enquired about my work and asked questions as though she actually wanted to hear my replies, and as we talked of nothing I felt the adrenaline hit dissipate and the halo of her fame shrink around her so that I felt less that I was conversing with a media ideal, more of a real person. I liked her almost immediately because she was everything I was not, and because she seemed remarkably unguarded for someone who was being judged by everyone in the room. It made me honest as I answered her queries in the manner of a patient sketching their feelings and thoughts to a therapist. She nodded and congratulated, expressed interest and agreement. It was almost dizzying to feel so heard, accepted.

'We really should get together – not just like this,' she said, suddenly sweeping her hand across the room. 'It would be nice to have a new friend.'

She scanned the space as though searching for something and when she turned back to me her mouth was open and forming a question, but something distracted her. Abruptly her eyes dropped and she produced a phone from the folds of her gown. A small frown appeared on her tight forehead as she glanced at the screen, the light from it dancing in her irises.

'I have to take this,' she said with regret, one hand squeezing my shoulder, the other waving the phone. 'Chicago.'

She smiled again and mouthed 'sorry' as she pressed the call to her ear. She turned and disappeared into the hallway again, leaving me feeling as though a cloud had just tempered midday sun. I might have even physically shivered. Momentarily disoriented, I spun slowly on my heels in a full circle surveying the party, a diorama of guests captured in my gaze like a zoetrope as I turned. I felt emotionally adrift, excitement bubbling, a strange euphoria charging my veins. I didn't understand how Gatsby could be so thrilling, a person I really knew nothing about. But as I twirled, everything had shifted. This was the liminal moment at which I became what could only be described as infatuated.

The glow of meeting her was offset by the disappointment of not finding Jordan among the increasingly damp bodies. I was attracted to him in an aggressive way I wasn't familiar with. I had fantasised about different scenarios of meeting him again within Gatsby's walls all week, my fingers working below my waistband. Even if his brown eyes were fixed on her, I wanted his attention. But the only way I could reach him tonight was by painting a picture on social media of what he'd missed and hoping he saw. I spent longer bowed over my phone than I did at the party that night, crafting casual captions to carefully staged photos and edited videos. I added attractive filters to hollow and streamline my face, augmented my lashes, my lips. It was not an accurate representation of my evening, it was a tool. I was reaching out to one by reaching out to many.

Chapter 9

My fish bit the next morning. My bright lure had given Jordan pause, prompted him to send a message at an hour that took no consideration for my late night.

How was it? he asked.

I sipped my coffee and considered whether I should let him flounder a while. Instead of replying, I direct-messaged Gatsby, expressing my gratitude at being invited to her home and hoping that she hadn't had too much aftermath to deal with. When I'd sunk into my deliciously cool pillow hours earlier, I'd been aware of the clear-up sounds next door before sleep took me. As expected, I heard nothing back.

Danny had also been in touch, probing for dirt; where had I been last night? What was going on between Jordan and me? Did he need to play the protective cousin? And then later, around noon, a message from T after the long radio silence since Miguel.

Hey you. What's new? and an eggplant emoji.

I might have known Danny would tell her I liked Jordan. And equally predictable that it wasn't guilt, an apology or a sense of care that had prompted her to get in touch. Rather the possibility that she, of all people, might have missed out on something. Daringly, I ignored them all and opened a pristine paperback with a pleasing new-print smell instead. I put my phone in a kitchen drawer that held a ball of twine, some batteries of indeterminable charge and various water-damaged plant seed packets.

I couldn't evade their world for long. In the late afternoon the drawer buzzed, Danny calling me, his playful voice insisting he needed to know how I was doing. After assessing my general wellbeing, he moved smoothly into asking why I had not responded to Jordan's messages, betraying his friend's interest. Why, I questioned, did he need my version of events when he clearly already seemed to have a comprehensive narrative?

'Awww, Nic . . .' he said appeasingly in the husky tone that I could never stay mad at. 'Come on . . .'

Loquacious as ever, he talked me into an agreement to respond to his friend. And so after a restorative shower I found myself re-threading the needle with Jordan and, feeling magnanimous, with T too; though we never touched upon that night in the city. I assumed she and Miguel were still together but I didn't ask in our message exchange. She likely didn't even consider it worth mentioning. She sent a bored voice note asking how I was and detailing a dreary get-together she'd attended where the hostess had cried in the middle of an afternoon botox party. More concerned with the weakness displayed by the woman than the cause of her pain, T recounted the embarrassment she felt on her behalf and criticised the quality of her catering.

'You would have laughed, it was impossible.' She chuckled. And then, as an afterthought, 'And how was your party?' before signing off with a promise to meet up soon.

When I finally responded to Jordan I told him Gatsby had asked after him and that I was surprised that he hadn't appeared given his apparent interest in her.

Intrigued. Not interested, he replied.

What's the difference?

I think you know, he typed.

It seemed like everything he said was loaded with alternate meaning if one looked for it. Right now, I wanted to believe he was suggesting I understood his intent, and it was the same as mine. I asked again about Gatsby – why had she whisked him away for privacy last week?

Jealous? he asked.

I was. Of her. But also of him. Before I could respond he sent a flurry of voice notes, his words laced with unmistakable flirtation. He told me that Gatsby had secrets, but that he would feel less caddish if he told me in person. As he hadn't so far exhibited a concern about the way he appeared to others, I took this to mean that he was guarding against incriminating screenshots or recordings while also aware, via my gossip-site scrolling, that he did not have a reputation for fidelity. If it meant meeting up with him again, I was happy to engage in a performative show of manners. I couldn't deny that I enjoyed his insolence and strut, the way women looked at him when he entered a room. He was so different from tender, sweet Danny that I could hardly believe they were friends. But equally, I could see that they both inspired the same reaction in their intended target via their very different approaches: a want. And even though I was fully aware of it, I was not inoculated against it.

When I claimed no covetousness fuelled my enquiries, Jordan called me a tease.

Say that to my face, I challenged him.

Gladly. Name the date, he parried, a delicious dual meaning.

Later, my landlady called me from her Sandy Lane sun lounger to let me know her housekeeper had alerted her that a parcel was waiting for me at the front gate. Pulling on some clothes, I wandered up the path where a distressed wicker basket sat overflowing with tasteful tissue paper. The basket was heavy and I struggled to carry it without reassessing my grip on the way back to my kitchen. The rustling paper was vintage in design and smelt heavenly. Nestled among its folds were artisan soaps, organic face creams, small-batch olive oil, a pot of caviar, a bottle of biodynamic wine, a sumptuous cashmere throw. On top of it all lay a cream envelope addressed to me in that same beautiful, sloping cursive. Inside, on thick card, the handwritten note apologised for the lateness of the welcome hamper.

Please, she wrote, *use my grounds all you want and let's try to get together. J*

In opening my social channels to post pictures of the gift and give public thanks, I lost hours scrolling through the plethora of pictures from the party, noting who the various guests were and the hashtags they used. As my coffee grew cold by the sink, Gatsby liked my post and commented that I was a 'darling', earning me immediate new followers and beginning a digital conversation that felt as freighted as the chat with Mr Baker.

As it turned out, Jordan was busy with events much of that week, so our meet-up was delayed, succoured by teasing messaging and a couple of late night FaceTime chats. We swapped memes and snarky comments, an ongoing interaction that kept me up at night as he travelled through time zones, and made me check my screen as soon as I woke. Finally, on the longest day of the year, his schedule cleared and we arranged to meet up. He pulled up outside the gates of the estate in a suitably conspicuous car, spraying gravel as he stopped. It was not a date but also not something else.

He drove us, fast, to the Garden Of Allah, an exquisite restaurant on the water where we ate rosy seafood, drank expensive wine and shared a dessert, taking turns to lick a single spoon. Whatever Gatsby had said during her meeting with Jordan was now lost, the enticement of it merely a device to further something that had begun between us in the library. As the sun turned orange Jordan relaxed, his chin lowered and his sharpness softened – and I allowed myself to believe in a romance. I was not unattractive, I was sincere, and I offered him a view on the world he didn't often see in his merry-go-round of unchallenging promotional events, tournaments and parties where people habitually praised and shielded him. I told him he was a snob and he liked it.

'You want to kiss me?' I asked. He tasted of coffee and the sweet fruit flavour of his vape pen.

We left the restaurant holding hands and for forty-eight hours after that I willingly suffocated myself with him; any thought of writing, of earning, dropped from my priority list along with a boy I'd been keeping in email touch with from college. I went straight from the dinner date to Jordan's Brooklyn apartment and only came up for air when we drove over to Danny and T's for Sunday lunch, our new bond betrayed by me wearing one of his T-shirts and him caressing the small of my back as we passed over the threshold. Danny, barefoot and leaning against the front door, a welcoming martini in hand (a Gibson of course, not the more common twist or with a crude olive), read us immediately; azure eyes dancing in delight.

'Oh, guys . . .' He laughed, moving his other hand to cover his heart in a show of sincerity. 'I love it.'

I was surprised Jordan hadn't told him already and his secrecy gave me reason to hope that he perhaps cherished our time together. Danny closed the door behind us, pressed the glass in my hand and called for T, excitement ringing in his tone. Slinging an arm round both our shoulders and squeezing, he walked us through the house towards the deck.

'Babe,' he hooted when T appeared at the foot of the stairs. 'These two!'

She looked between us and I couldn't help but grin. I felt jubilant. She would not have considered me for him.

'Nic, you never cease to surprise me,' she said finally.

'Let's celebrate!' Danny whooped and rubbed my back as he propelled us onward, towards another feast, making fun when he caught Jordan's fingers intertwined with mine under the tablecloth. T smiled and asked nothing. Though Danny detected our lust as the evening drew to a late close and offered us the guest room, we left Jordan's car at theirs while we Ubered back to my place and tangled ourselves in my mismatched sheets. His touch spoke to me of danger, and when he coaxed a gasp from me I shuddered in his arms with triumphant thoughts of what Danny, T and Gatsby might think of us.

Chapter 10

By the end of June I had two famous names in my contacts, both in my favourites. Gatsby followed up the house-warming gift with an invitation to dinner and she stood at the top of the steps to her patio waving as I crossed the property line, the sunset tinging her wedding-cake house a soft peach. She was as warm as the day had been, using any conversation topic to ask about me, my interests, my aspirations. She exuded a calming stillness, with an ability to listen like Danny did. Her silences gave space to my thoughts, made my every utterance feel profound as she nodded and spooned a beautiful salad onto my plate; offering no solutions, suggestions, or stories of her own. As an overlooked child in a family of clever, charming and sporty people, I blossomed under her radiated empathy.

She made a point of turning off her phone and leaving it at the very end of the table. It was a courtesy I hadn't had from anyone else and one that I regretfully never employed myself. She spoke of dynamic breathing and manifesting, told me I had untapped potential and suggested books that had helped her navigate a life that had been, by turns, traumatic and blessed. I asked about the seaplane after Jordan reminded me of it during a playful message before I left the boathouse, then felt guilty of gossiping when Gatsby admitted that she had heard this several times at the party I'd attended and didn't know where it had come from. She leaned back in her chair as the plates were cleared by her housekeeper and declared that a seaplane was the least practical of airborne vehicles and really, why would she have one of those if one could have a Lear?

Her dark sunglasses hid her eyes from me so I wasn't sure if I was being made fun of, but it was a pivotal moment where I realised that any false notes in our relationship would come from allowing the discourse conducted over threads by anonymous commentators to inform our real conversation. As we drank bittersweet coffee martinis, I found myself telling her things I didn't divulge to my mother and certainly not my friends, exposing the soft, pink flesh beneath my self-protective shell. I confessed the surprise of the clawing, biting passion I felt with Jordan, told her how I feared I had no real career ambition, that the shameful thought of marrying well and not having to work wasn't wholly anathema to me.

I told her because her soothing European tone encouraged me, because I wanted to impress her with my openness and because I knew she conversed with no one in my social sphere who could use the information against me. Whatever spell she put on us that evening, I felt close to her in a supernaturally fast fashion, as though some sort of fate played a part in our connection. Perhaps we were meant to meet here and now, to cling to each other in the firestorm of our twenties, as she left hers and I fully entered mine. Even looking back at this enchanted evening, I can't see the delicate path Gatsby must have been navigating to get to where she really wanted to be. It was elegantly done. Like a pickpocket so skilled that their marks register no loss until later.

Though I didn't see her use her phone, she must have. Photos of our dinner appeared on her grid later that night – I recognised my silhouette in the image of the sunset and the table laid with artisan bowls. It thrilled me to see myself inside her frame. After that she messaged me often, indulged me when I dropped her a line with an amusing thought or sent her a link to something I thought would interest her. I still have the messages we shared over the summer, her enthusiasm and affection shining through, the silly sense of humour she hid from her followers. Her missives could be dismissed as a campaign of flattery, but I interpret them differently. I think she was trying to forge real attachment, be the friend I so clearly needed. She wanted me to feel whole, powerful, loved – and hoped that, in turn, I would want that for someone else. That if she gave that to me, I would choose it for her.

Another evening we had a movie night in her cinema room and watched *Roman Holiday* while slouching on the pillowy chocolate leather seats that slid our bodies horizontal. We saw very little of the movie; by the time Audrey Hepburn was placing her hand into the stone opening we were discussing romance and its past disasters. For Gatsby, who embraced most things, love seemed to be one of the few things she was wary of. She talked about it being complicated, compartmentalised.

The child of air-force parents, she told me how she'd moved around the world as a kid and never felt as though she belonged anywhere. That was why, when she crossed the line to adulthood, she'd left for university in Oxford. Once there, amid the ancient buildings and green meadows, she found that she didn't fit there either. An enrolment at Columbia for a year on a course I hadn't heard of followed. This is what had brought her into the orbit of her future husband. Dan Cody was handsome, connected. His matinee looks were those that might have been crafted in a lab. It was clear he'd loved many women before her. A force that devoured everything around him, she'd found him powerful and impressive. He'd pursued her, wooed her with a certainty that was indefatigable, and she had allowed herself to succumb.

'It's hard not to get swept up in something that intense,' she said, staring at the ceiling, her hair a halo on the headrest. 'Especially when you kinda want an escape.'

She rolled her head on the leather so she was looking at me.

'I thought he'd be a distraction, but then he became a habit.'

She told me how she couldn't have known what he'd become, stressing that as she morphed from his girlfriend into his wife, he had kept her entirely separate from his darker life, his needs. When his infidelities and abuse were laid bare, she had been as appalled as everyone else. She had turned away from him immediately, and the chasm of cancellation had consumed him.

She must have anticipated that every new relationship she began would be saddled with the context of the numerous articles written about her suspected culpability in his behaviour. She assumed that I had knowledge of his misdemeanours and the scent it left on her; expected that a person getting to know her wanted the answer to the unspoken question. Did she know? Could she have stopped it? I hadn't asked but I wanted to. And now she shook her head insistently. She had been horrified. She couldn't fathom the hurt he'd caused, how he'd destroyed so many lives, including hers.

'That's not what love is,' she said simply and, as though surprised by how much she'd revealed, she shivered. It had made her stronger, but also more vulnerable, she concluded. And then she changed her posture and switched to asking about my family, where they called home. Her Britishisms slid into a tired drawl.

I told her about my parents at length and noted a slight frown, as though a dish had been delivered that hadn't been ordered, and I suggested we continue watching the film instead. Gatsby sniffled in the final moments as Gregory Peck's handsome newspaper reporter did the noble thing. When I returned home she sent a video message of herself in a white bathrobe, her hair pulled back tight, her face scrubbed bright and clean.

'I loved spending time with you.' She smiled at the end, blew a kiss and waved a sign-off before the screen clicked to black. I still watch it sometimes to hear her voice and think how I fell more quickly, more willingly, with less suspicion for Gatsby than I did for Jordan.

* * *

Before Jordan visited me again he had an expensive coffee maker delivered to my kitchen with a cocky note that read, *For the next morning after.* Operating it felt like trying to understand the workings of a steam train. I couldn't fathom how to use the thing as it squatted on my counter like a gleaming Buick and stuck to the simple French press that had left him so unimpressed. At the very end of June he took me to a house party upstate and called me his 'girl' to his friends; a maddening term that didn't seem to conclusively denote fidelity, yet suggested a certain fondness. Jordan enjoyed dirty talk over FaceTime and called late at night from events he was attending, liking the idea of me sleep-flushed and barely dressed as he shrugged out of an expensive suit in a hotel suite bathroom, propping his phone on the side of marble sinks to leave his hands free. His unapologetic voracity kept me off-balance, breathless in a way I found exciting and by the Fourth of July weekend, we were attending another party over the fence together. A couple by definition, if not by name.

When he arrived at the boathouse dressed impeccably in black he brought a designer gown and a pair of scarlet-soled shoes for me. The fact that he'd judged my sizing so accurately pulled at something in my stomach. He watched me dress and when I prepared to leave the house barefoot, carrying the shoes in readiness to pad across the still-damp grass from that afternoon's storm, he shook his head and tutted. We should arrive at the front gate like everyone else, he reasoned, why were we sneaking in like criminals? Or second-class citizens? He didn't need to expand on his fear of a misunderstanding happening more easily between him and security if it seemed as though he was trespassing or worse. I stroked his cheek and protested that Gatsby's gravel drive was no surface for my new shoes, but he sat me down on the bed and pressed the stilettos onto my feet before pulling me to a standing position like a doll.

'There are ways round that,' he whispered.

After I'd stepped out of the house and locked up, I turned on the step and he swooped me into his arms, bridal style, laughing at my surprised wriggling. He carried me easily up the slope. That's how I arrived at Gatsby's for a third time, deposited on the stone flags, my skirt brushed down by Jordan's decorous palms and my hand taken to walk the final steps to the open door. I felt different.

We walked the now familiar corridor to the dance space, this time as the people I'd previously observed – pausing at the top of the stairs to survey the room and allow ourselves to be seen by the throng. Jordan passed a possessive arm round my waist as he looked across the room.

'Shall we?' he asked when his roving eyes landed back on my face.

I felt a dopamine hit as he steered me down the stairs towards the bar and before long I was booze-buzzed and swaying in his arms. Every time we decided to leave the room, traverse the house, another tune began that made us look at each other and want to stay. It felt as though the universe was granting my wishes in both setlist and scenario, imbuing me with new courage. Jordan, loose with tequila, clowned as I reached to tip some of the drink we were sharing into his open mouth causing it to spill out of the corner. He tried to catch it with his hand but a drip rolled down his chin and traced the line of his jugular. I leaned forward and licked the rivulet up his throat to his jaw with a flat, licentious tongue. He quirked an eyebrow as I stepped back, took a greedy swig from the glass myself and smiled at him, my own lips glazed. He pulled me closer, his hands in my hair, slightly tugging as he kissed below my ear.

'Let's go . . .' he whispered and pulled me through the crowd, past red, white and blue cocktails and a lobster bar, past the doors to the library, beyond an area lined with stars and stripes and glowing candles, casting his eyes about, appraising spaces for his need. At the north end of the house he tried a couple of door handles until he found one that opened, to a stairwell that presumably wound towards Gatsby's off-limits upper rooms.

'Oops, that should have been locked.' He chuckled looking up the stairs. 'Should we?'

He didn't wait for an answer, towing me up the steps after him, the door behind us clicking closed, the party muffled as we climbed. At the top, a dark corridor led to another door and I faltered.

'We shouldn't.'

'Scaredy cat,' he taunted me.

'She keeps this private,' I reasoned, yanking at his hand to stop.

'Come on, Nic, she keeps nothing private,' he said dismissively, turning back. He smiled then, the slow one. 'It's quiet though,' he said, eyes dipping to my lips.

'Yes,' I murmured, both agreeing and granting permission.

The sense of transgression heightened the thrill of his kiss when he leaned down, pushed me against the wall and hummed appreciatively into my mouth. I felt powerful as he unspooled something in me, his thigh pressing between mine, his urgent hands pulling a moan from me. I grabbed at his shirt, fisting it loose, encouraging, feeling like a different me. We froze when a voice cut through the moment.

'Hello, lovers!'

I snapped my head towards the now open door and Gatsby silhouetted within it as Jordan turned his back to her, leaning against the wall, shielding both of our dishevelment. He looked back at her over his shoulder with undisguised annoyance.

'Hey,' he acknowledged her gruffly.

She laughed. 'I don't want to break up this particular party . . . but I'm glad to see you.'

She flicked a light on, making both of us blink, his hand falling from my hip as he looked back at me, biting his lower lip like a naughty child. I kissed his cheek, chastely, and looked towards Gatsby. She was wearing red everything, and an amused expression.

'Sorry,' I began, slipping my strap back onto my shoulder, stepping away from the wall and around Jordan. Gatsby held up a hand.

'Please,' she purred, 'don't be. But this is fortuitous.' The formal word hung in the air. 'I was hoping to see you tonight, Nic.' She held out her hand to me. 'Jordan, can you spare her?'

He and I exchanged glances at the dismissal. He was not used to being sidelined in any situation.

'Sure,' he said tightly. 'Find you later?'

'Be good!' she called, her voice like a wind chime, as he retreated down the stairs with a glance backwards. He was frowning.

'That door really should be locked,' she noted as she hugged me, manoeuvring me towards her sanctum.

I wondered if I would be scolded for our trespassing as I walked into a cosy sitting room. It glowed cocoon-like with dim lights that recalled a spa ante-room, a gardenia scent perfuming the air from a huge, squat candle flickering in the corner.

'I'm sorry . . .' I began.

'So much calmer in here,' she interrupted as she walked around me to sit on the soft, caramel sofa, patting the seat next to her. She looked up with doe eyes.

'Nic, you look *amazing*,' she exclaimed, activating her ability to flatter without seeming phoney. The sensation of having been called into a principal's office dissipated under her rays. I smiled back.

'Thanks, so do you,' I said, plopping into the cushions. She immediately turned her whole body towards me to show her full attention, and stroked my arm as if I was cold.

'I so wanted to have a natter,' she said, the vowels of the English colloquialism bending. 'But it's so hard to do down there.'

I nodded.

'I swear I don't invite half these people . . .' She laughed and wrinkled her nose in a charming way. 'Hey, I want you to come to my yoga weekend – it's going to be on the lawn, looking at the ocean, we'll do a gong bath – super cleansing. Will you?'

Before I could answer, she apologised for not letting me talk; asked me how I was, what she'd missed. Though we'd only swapped digital thoughts the day before, she leant forward, her phone hanging in her lowered hand untouched, her eyes attentive. I relayed that my parents had called to say they wanted me back home at the end of the summer if I hadn't found a 'real' job. They wanted monthly paychecks, benefits, a pension, the trappings of security for me. Plus the ability to say I worked for a publication their friends actually recognised.

'What's a real job anyway.' She smiled. 'There are so many ways to make money.'

'Like you?' I asked.

'Sure.' She twinkled. 'I could help you. Build your brand.'

'I don't have any kind of brand to build. I feel like I either need to be perfect or just really, really messy . . .'

She dropped her eyes to the floor. 'Messy,' she repeated, as though rolling a marble around her mouth.

'Jay,' I said, using her name for the first time. I liked the taste of it. 'I didn't mean . . .'

She stood then, talking quickly, with a heat I hadn't seen before. She spoke of the latest man she'd been linked to, a married podcast host whose self-billed hard truths enraged liberal commentators and feminists. Did having her picture taken with someone mean she was sleeping with them? She must be sleeping with half of New York if that was the case. And since when did being polite in someone's company mean you shared their views? I watched as she expelled her frustration: the thrill the media took in making her life look like a wreck so they could be sanctimonious about its tidying. As she paced the room, her hand alighted on items as she spoke. She turned a vase here, traced a finger along a table there; the acts reminding me of my brother's method of stemming a panic attack by grounding himself in his surroundings. Though I knew the narrative well enough already from her socials, she added new details that had me swinging wildly from believing every word to doubting all of it. Then she talked of Dan Cody again, using such similar phrasing to what she'd whispered in the cinema room I felt the pinch of suspicion. For the first time her words felt rehearsed.

I shifted in my seat, slight discomfort prickling me. Before, I had delighted at being confided in by a celebrity, but I now wondered if I was naïve to have not considered an ulterior motive. My imposter syndrome flared; the idea began to metabolise in me that I had been a dolt to believe the love-bombing approach of someone as golden as her. I was a nobody with no influence. Just as I thought I might interject and baldly ask what was really happening, she put her hand over mine and paused.

'I want us to be honest with each other,' she whispered. 'I feel like you understand me, that we're the same.'

She looked at me so appealingly that I was newly fascinated, felt an affirmation, as she squeezed my fingers. She inhaled deeply as if bracing herself and her hair fell over her face hiding her expression for a moment.

'I wanted this to be more . . . organic,' she faltered. 'But I admit, I've become impatient.'

'What is it? Is everything ok?'

She shook her hair away and looked up shyly through her lashes.

'I haven't been completely honest,' she said and I felt a hot thrill at the prospect of hearing something Lily Shield might actually want to know for her gossip website. 'I'm sorry . . .'

'You can tell me anything,' I assured her.

Her palms were now warm. If I knew her better, I might have suspected she felt nervous. I waited, sensing something was about to shift.

'I wonder,' she said, almost timidly, 'if Jordan spoke to you?'

I frowned. 'About what?'

'About me? He didn't?'

I shook my head, feeling wheels turn and dynamics transpose. Had I been a fool? She blushed. It made her look younger, uncertain.

'I knew Jordan before,' she said and stared at the floor.

I thought of their limbs entwined as I waited for more, despondency flooding my synapses. They fit together.

'When I saw him at the party, I wanted to say hi and I wanted . . .' She searched for words, her fingers tightening around my limp, now dejected hand. 'I wanted to talk to him about Danny.'

The way she said his name was with reverence, hushed.

'Danny?' I repeated. 'My Danny?'

She looked up and met my eyes, blinking assent.

'But Jordan didn't seem open to that,' Gatsby continued. 'And when he told me who he was with, I thought this was too serendipitous. Too magical. Danny's cousin living next door. You.' She breathed this. 'You – such a lovely, compassionate, wonderful person.'

I pulled my hand away.

'You know Danny? How? When?'

'I wanted to tell you so many times, but I didn't want you to think . . .' She left the sentence open, understanding I was already filling it in. Her heartbeat fluttered at her throat. Again, I waited.

'We were together years ago,' she said. 'How crazy is that? We were kids. At school. I was very different then . . .' She waved the words away with a wafting hand as though they were nothing. She smiled brightly. 'And I guess, everything that's happened to me recently has made me reconsider the kindness of people I knew in my past. I supposed it'd be nice just to see an old friend again.'

'He's married,' I replied flatly.

'Oh, not like that!' she said, her cheeks pinking further, her eyes sliding away from mine.

'So, you want his number . . .' I began but she interrupted.

'Oh no,' she said quickly. 'You understand my position more than anyone. I've told you things I've told no one. Things a lot of people might pass along.' Gatsby paused, and in the gap I wondered about those confessions. About her patience, her planning. If perhaps she had tested me with false tales, waiting to see if any of her planted seeds had taken root on gossip sites. Though Lily and I had remained in touch as she scrabbled for dirt, I had told her nothing.

'I can't reach out to him myself. That could be misinterpreted. I need discretion.'

I might have been insulted. I wasn't. I liked that I had passed an assessment and she considered me discreet. That she considered me one of her trusted few, I liked even more. It made me feel protective of her. I melted.

'You want me to . . . ?'

'I couldn't possibly ask, Nic,' she murmured and I was unsure of whether she couldn't ask Danny for a meeting or couldn't ask me. 'I wouldn't want you or him to feel uncomfortable. I'd just love if we could . . . run into each other.'

I stared at her beautiful, hopeful face and felt my ethical pendulum swing. I shouldn't. But I could. I wouldn't. I might. I saw sadness reach her eyes as she took my silence for refusal.

'I'm so sorry,' she said in sudden rush, 'can we forget this?'

A brisk knock at the door stopped any further discussion. The young woman with the headset walked straight in, dipping to Gatsby's ear to whisper urgently. I watched my host's spine lengthen as she listened, the softness in her evaporate. Her armour returned.

'Okay.' Gatsby nodded. 'Tell him I'm coming.'

She turned back to me as she stood.

'The cops. Always trying to shut us down early, but I've been to too many parties with the commissioner.' She towered above me now. 'Nic, this is my assistant – she'll give you her number in case you need anything. Any help at all.'

The girl smiled tightly and held out her hand.

'Chloe Klipspringer,' she snapped as we shook. 'I have your details.'

'Chloe,' cooed Gatsby, 'bring me the iPad.'

Chloe disappeared through the door as efficiently as she'd arrived. Gatsby continued to stand over me. She shuddered as though shaking off a feeling.

'Look, this is really not important.' She smiled, and fiddled with the gold ring on her finger. 'I just . . .'

She looked towards the door and, as if she willed it, Chloe returned with the requested device in hand. Gatsby stepped eagerly towards her, taking it from her and swiping as she began to speak again in a brisk, businesslike tone.

'I don't want to keep you from the party, Nic,' she said. 'There's fireworks soon and I know you'll want to find Jordan.' She squinted at the screen. 'Let me see if I can find him for you . . .'

Whatever she'd been about to ask had shrunk back inside her. I realised that she was scrolling through the rooms in her house on CCTV. No wonder she appeared like an apparition next to various people at the perfect time. Gatsby was like me. She liked to watch.

'Ah!' she said, triumphant, 'the library.' And she passed the tablet to me.

I took it with curiosity and watched as Jordan passed from the corridor into the room. Pressing the lozenge marked 'library' to switch cameras and perspective, I watched as he crossed the threshold following a woman, their hands connected and a familiar look on his face. I peered closer at the monochrome images as she tugged him towards the sheltering bookshelves and turned into him. With exaggerated paleness, her hand glimmering on his chest. His head bowed towards her, exposing his neck . . . I snapped my arm outward, holding the pad back towards Chloe as my ears roared with an adrenal spike. I saw, rather than heard, Gatsby ask if everything was fine. I nodded, sidestepping towards the door and found my voice to tell her I'd see her around. I slipped from the room.

In the corridor I took a deep breath and pressed my palm to my chest, willing the panic away, hoping for the creep of uncertainty. But I was sure. I wanted to wait a minute more before moving, but my feet carried me down the stairs fast, clumsily. I burst out of the door and dodged partygoers along the now familiar route to the library – the only quiet place in the house, where Jordan and I had first clicked. He wanted quiet again now, and I knew what I would find. As I turned the corner to the corridor leading to the heavy door, he exited the room. His face brightened immediately on seeing me and made my weak heart doubt.

'So?' He strode towards me, confident, without conflict.

'Let's talk about you, not Gatsby,' I said, and noted the slight line that marked his forehead as confusion passed over his face.

'Okay . . .' he replied slowly.

'Did you forget about me?'

His eyes narrowed fractionally, his hand reaching out as he asked gently, 'What's this about?'

I wanted to not care. 'Did you forget that you came here with me?'

The meaning wasn't lost on him. He pulled me closer towards him.

'No, I did not.'

'There are so many women here . . .'

'And I haven't talked to one of them.' He lied, easily, fluently. He held my shoulders to still me. 'I've been waiting for you.'

Though I couldn't know whether he had truly betrayed me in the minutes I walked from Gatsby to him, the way the untruth dropped so effortlessly from his lips stung, and my face must have been unable to disguise it. My reaction seemed to amuse him all the more. Jordan slid a soothing hand round my waist. 'Are we having our first fight?'

I stared at him, unsure, feeling the pull of his words that suggested intimacy, a building history, the spectre of fidelity. He smiled and I felt foolish.

'Let's not,' he said lightly, 'especially when I know you'd much rather talk about your obsession.'

'My what?'

'Gatsby.'

'I'm not obsessed,' I scoffed, and he smirked. 'You seem to know her better than me.'

'Ah, she told you.'

'Not enough,' I snapped. 'Just like you.'

'Nic, it's not a big deal.'

The conversation I wanted to have was escaping me. He began to walk us away from the library towards the patio, every step a moment away from a threatened confrontation. We passed under a camera and I wondered if Gatsby was watching. His hand against the small of my back propelled me through the bar and the dancers, and we arrived outside at the balustrade overlooking the grounds. A couple argued on the lawn beneath us, the girl scratching at her partner's chest in rage, his voice high and hurt. Jordan waited for my signal to continue, his palm stroking my waist. A sportsman's patience to see what his challenger would do.

I squared my shoulders as I watched the lovers fight and considered that both Jordan and Gatsby had sought to deceive me within the same hour. She had wanted to reveal, he had been exposed. They were connected by a hazy past that she wanted me to know and perhaps he did not. And that they both now waited for me to react to their actions.

I didn't want to unpick the loose seams on either relationship, I wanted to tighten them. I was greedy for more of each and their specific validation. I could tamp down the suspicion in my gut and tell myself I had no proof of Jordan's betrayal. I could reason that Gatsby's selective honesty was a protection mechanism when feeling out those drawn to her celebrity. Like many things that summer, I was prepared to let things slide. To discover more about both of them was to advance; socially, emotionally, sexually. Knowledge was power.

'Tell me everything,' I demanded, and he did.

Chapter 11

Danny and Jordan had been high-school acquaintances back in Louisville but only became close when they attended the same West Coast college, UC Santa Cruz; both sent by parents who could well afford the fees and were indulgent enough to send them to a Californian institution that prized lived experience over hot-housed academia. In a low-roofed campus among the redwoods on the hill above the hippy coastal town, they had found their people. Kids who preferred toking Humboldt County's finest bud and surfing to the frenetic, scholastic pace offered by Berkeley further north. A school that was apocryphally 'clothing optional' and still lived by the vibe of its establishing year of 1965, where moonlit drum circles and spiritual retreats were common; burnout was not. There, the two boys from the same hometown far away from an ocean found their twin in each other. They bonded over music and movies as Jordan focused on his golf at Pebble Beach. Though he'd considered turning pro at eighteen, he'd decided to live a little before committing, something his father approved of and his mother was overridden on.

Santa Cruz, with its nostalgic wooden boardwalk on the sand, treacherous two-lane switchback highway through the trees, foggy mornings and occasional earthquake tremors, felt like a quaint escape. A place that Danny – with his long, tanned limbs, bohemian bent and lack of ambition – seemed built for. Both of them spent longer outside of class than they did in; Jordan finding joy on the greens and Danny embracing the surfer lifestyle before falling headlong into heart-stopping romance in the last summer of his teens.

According to Jordan, my cousin's university career spun emotionally out of control over breakfast in Zachary's, Pacific Avenue's laid-back diner frequented by locals and students alike. He enjoyed eating there alone while reading a book – so regularly that his order was brought out without consulting the menu. After one such visit Danny had been breathless as he'd arrived at Jordan's student house to tell him about a lone girl on the next table who had interrupted his meal to inquire if the mountainous plate of the establishment's famous 'Mike's Mess' was the thing to have. He had offered her a bite of his and by the time the waitstaff changed shifts, he and she were still sharing a table, drifting into the lunch menu and making plans for the weekend.

Jordan assumed this would be another of his friend's hot, fast flings but Danny was soon in a love affair that burned wild and bright, ultimately smothering all his other interests. He missed the weekly poker and keg night, reneged on a weekend hiking in Yosemite, became a physical vacuum in Jordan's life. As the weeks slipped into months and through a semester, Danny was looking ahead for the first time in his life.

For as long as Jordan had known him Danny had never planned any part of his world more than a week in advance.

But as he turned twenty he began talking of the future, even speaking of marriage; a concept that alarmed Jordan but entirely petrified Danny's parents. This girl was from an unknown family and town, not someone Danny should be thinking about in such permanent terms. While Jordan had met her briefly, the Buchanans had not and did not intend to, despite Danny's enthusiasm. He was summoned home where his father had told him that his lifestyle was funded by loving parents who only wanted the best for him. And that if the best for him was to allow him to learn to pay his own way, then that's what they were prepared to do. There was, he was advised, plenty of time for such impulsiveness, without starting off his adulthood with such folly.

Though Danny baulked at the suggestion that his heart could be compromised by cash, there was a change in him when he returned to Santa Cruz. As the fog began to drift in from the bay, marking the turn to autumn, Danny also cooled. He still clung to the idea of twinned destinies but he tamped down his acceleration instincts. When the girl left the country for several months, Danny's fidelity eventually frayed with a few meaningless hook-ups. He told Jordan that he felt guilty, but also that he'd promised nothing. They both knew that wasn't true. When Jordan dropped out of school to turn pro (a decision hastened as much by the school's concern over his attendance as his talent), Danny transferred to another university town in another state with a vague idea about pursuing entrepreneurship. The plans with the girl were left behind like the textbooks he never cleared from his shelf in his student house.

For the girl, the fade in interest was more than confusing. It was destructive. She had built her future around getting back to Northern California but to the relief of Mr and Mrs

Buchanan – and possibly to Danny himself – the bright, perspicuous connection between the lovers was easily muddled, made indistinct. Her pain was evident in her bewildered voice messages that Danny played Jordan with an expression that suggested he had no choice, deleting them immediately in an attempt to be clean, incisive – a cruel kindness on his part. He built a new collegiate life and he forgot the girl in the diner. Until he didn't.

After graduation he had decided to wait tables in a beautiful Big Sur restaurant high on the cliffs while he played intermittently in a local band. He was a decent guitar player as rich people with hobbies are, but the year he spent hoping for recognition was fruitless. He earned more in tips and made more connections charming the tables of diners visiting from San Francisco or LA than he did through his gigs. It was a lifestyle that his parents hadn't dreamed of for him, and when the music carried him nowhere he tried to start his own company with their relieved investment – travelling to Manhattan to pull strings and favours, connecting with T in a Greenwich Village coffee house. Things were already getting serious with her some months later when he met Jordan for drinks in New York in between golf commitments. By the time Jordan arrived at the bar at the hour they'd arranged, Danny was already coked up, torn down and deep into what was about to become a bender.

It seemed the girl from California had reappeared in his notifications. She was about to be married, and she wasn't certain. Danny knew she hoped he would be certain for her, but he hadn't been willing or able to be – pulled between the appetite for the fantasy and the comfort of reality. She wanted him to stop her; he didn't. The tearful phone call between the two had tipped him into a self pity so blinding that he'd called his dealer before messaging his friend. While their night was bawdy and tinged with an unspoken sadness, Danny woke the next day on Jordan's hotel-suite sofa only voicing regret for the amount he'd imbibed. He'd never spoken of her again; it simply became another part of their shared history.

It was only at Gatsby's party that Jordan had formally met the woman he considered unworthy of the title 'celebrity'. Though they'd attended events together he'd never been in close proximity to her, but as they stood feet apart at her party she had casually reminded him of their previous connection, her face suddenly making sense to him. She hadn't gone by Gatsby back in their student days and he hadn't thought of her for an instant in the years since. He couldn't recall her actual given name but the glow-up from her travelling days and her conceit of using her mononymous moniker now had prevented him from realising who she was earlier. His intuition made him leery of motive.

'Did you tell Danny?' I asked. 'Did you tell him you'd seen her?'

Jordan rubbed his cheek and looked into the distance.

'No.'

His conciseness enraged me.

'That's it? Just no? Why not?'

His chin floated upward. He was already tiring of this conversation.

'Because it's nothing. If I told Danny about every ex of his I meet . . .'

'I thought guys always told each other this stuff – "that chick you banged in college has done really well" . . .'

The corners of his mouth quirked in mirth and he tried to take my hand. 'Why are you so pissed about this?'

'Why did Danny never tell me any of this? Why didn't you?' I was unable to keep a certain petulance from my voice.

'I don't tell other people's secrets,' he replied, a note of condescension on his tongue. 'And it's not my business. Or your business.'

'But it is now,' I pointed out peevishly. 'She just asked me to arrange for Danny and her to run into each other. At least I think that's what she wanted.'

'Okay,' he said and looked at me. 'Maybe she's a romantic.' His hand crept over mine on the balcony and as much I wanted to move it to make a point, I didn't.

'Maybe she thinks *you're* a romantic,' he added. He raised his brows as though he agreed.

'You can't just dismiss everyone as that.' I tried to pull my fingers from his, but he gripped them to prevent me.

'I don't. I admire you soft-hearted people.'

He was smirking again and I couldn't be certain if it was at me or the situation.

'Come on, Nic,' he whispered with his most seductive look. 'Don't give me a hard time over this. What do you want to do about it?'

'What would you do about it?' I felt torn.

Jordan shrugged. It was a noncommittal, indifferent gesture that he often used and it was beginning to grate.

'Jesus, I don't know,' he sighed. 'It's drama. I'm no fan of T, and she could use some competition. But I guess he's married . . .'

'Yeah,' I said stiffly, 'he *is* married.'

He nodded with a neutral face.

I stared out towards the water, over the heads of the couple who were now holding each other as though winter had come. I contemplated Jordan's question and I didn't know the answer. I felt played but also tempted by the intrigue. How could two people who intersected my life in entirely different ways have once shared the same reality? As I tracked the line of the reflected shore across the sound, I could pick out the green lights of the docks that belonged to the houses there. One of these would be the Buchanans'.

Suddenly, it made sense to me why Gatsby continually posted this view to her accounts. She wasn't simply admiring the curve of the bay – she was trying to send a signal, a flare, attempting to will something into existence. A ritual designed to catch the attention of the gods. She could have simply reached out to him herself, made an overture that demanded a betrayal from him. Perhaps it might have reduced something treasured to transactional. Instead, she wanted him to rediscover her, to marvel at her anew. That struck me as curiously out of step, fallible; and yes, romantic.

There was movement on the beach and suddenly, in syncopated unison, a line of rockets launched towards the sky, bursting into constellations as they crested. The Independence Day fireworks had begun. I held my hand up towards the explosions as if I could touch them and looked at Jordan, lit red, blue, orange, green by their starbursts.

'Isn't this Pandora's box?' I shouted above the explosions and the delighted whoops of people now spilling from the doors to admire the spectacle. 'This could be a terrible idea.'

'She's the one who asked. It's not on you,' he shouted back.

'What if it gets out of control?' I argued, and Jordan raised an eyebrow.

'It would be worth it to know T doesn't control everything. And besides, it'd be kinda fun to see what happens.'

I looked at him sharply. 'What if it isn't fun?'

He didn't respond, just smiled conspiratorially, began to nod his head to push my consent.

I huffed out a breath and looked back at the imploding heavens raining multi-coloured embers down on us. His words burrowed deep into me, finding a home despite my ambition to be ethical. I wondered why I cared about trampling relationships if no one else did. T didn't adhere to her vows so why should she expect her husband to? And Jordan was right to mention her control if he wanted to persuade me. As I looked across at East Egg's shoreline and the Buchanans' green dock light, it was hard not to recall Miguel's sister's apartment. The bile rose in me, demanding a retribution, a punishment of T for making me feel that way. This seemed a gift – revenge delivered easily via Gatsby.

I considered that I might also like making a bad decision. I had enjoyed giving in to impetuousness with Jordan, surprised myself with the pleasures of carnality when I stopped trying to ascribe to being a 'good girl'. I might like to instigate, allow, submit here as much as I had under Jordan's practiced touch. I felt like lighting the touchpaper on this whole situation and standing back to watch.

Chapter 12

I resisted immediately messaging either Gatsby or Danny. I told myself I was still morally wrestling with whether to be complicit in this fantasy, but in reality I'd become part of their story the night Gatsby asked me. My admiration for her, my love for Danny, my desire to prove to T that I was not insignificant stilled any misgivings. Besides, I thought I could remain blameless if I played it right. It only took until Monday for my machinations to begin.

I asked Danny over for lunch on a weekday when I knew T would be at the office in Manhattan. Though he nominally worked, we all knew his job was little more than a hobby. He would enjoy the opportunity to break the sweltering, unending heat with a new activity. When he agreed to the next Thursday, I informed Gatsby in a casual message and received a flurry of gratitude and heart emojis. It distracted me all through the week. Though I pretended to myself that I was not invested – busying myself with a native-content job, messaging Jordan and swimming in the sea – I knew I was. My mind kept returning to their reunion; I wanted to see the moment they reclaimed each other. Jordan, away in Georgia, asked nothing. He had stepped back, either to allow himself the alibi of ignorance or because he truly cared so little for the fallout.

I cleaned the boathouse in the morning of the lunch and watched the time tick to 1 p.m., changing self-consciously from my usual attire of cut-offs and T-shirt into something smarter, trying to allay my own nerves. I had bought the ingredients for lunch, but I knew they would remain in the refrigerator no matter how this went. If it was awkward, I would suggest Danny and I go out; if it wasn't, I assumed I wouldn't be eating at all.

Danny arrived characteristically late, calling from the gate to ask for the entry code. When he appeared on the track, he was riding a gleaming motorbike and wearing a battered leather jacket, the type that should have looked a cliché but on him appeared artless. He grinned as he came to a halt by the door and dismounted, pulling off his helmet and warmly calling my name.

'New?' I asked, pointing to the bike, and he blushed slightly as he raked a hand through his hair.

'I bought it,' he admitted, pocketing his sunglasses. 'Triumph TR6 Trophy. McQueen model.' He pulled me into a crushing hug. 'Nice place.'

He smelt expensive, and I wondered how close Gatsby would get to catching his citrusy, woody scent. When we entered the boathouse he poked around, complimenting some of my furnishings, admiring Jordan's coffee contraption and shrugging off his jacket.

'It's cosy.' He smiled at me as he ran a finger along the coffee machine.

'If you want a coffee, you'll have to do it,' I told him. 'This thing . . .'

He laughed and put a hand on my arm. 'Excuse me, allow the expert to work . . .'

While he ground beans, tamped the granules, flicked switches and poured milk into a jug with the skill of a barista, he asked for detailed updates on my life. It felt quaint to tell him when everyone else in my life simply liked my posts and presumably forgot about them shortly thereafter. As I watched him work, I tried to view him through Gatsby's eyes. Had he changed since they last spoke? T carefully guarded her social media so Gatsby couldn't have digitally stalked him there, but I had pictures of him grinning into the camera all over my grid. Had she pinched and zoomed on his flexed bicep as he shaded his eyes last summer in Maine? Did she linger on his tongue poked out cheekily at a birthday party? I recalled that he had longer hair in college, the affectation of surfer style that required wearing hair ties around his wrists. Was he much different from then?

He was still lean and rangy, but his style was no longer from the beach, it was bought from boutiques. The white T-shirt he wore as he moved around my kitchen appeared generic, but I knew it probably cost more than my weekly rent. He had a confidence about him that seemed to change the molecules of a room just as Gatsby did, his ability to train attention towards him effortless. Danny had almost old-fashioned manners and a deferent way of listening that made everyone who met him describe him as 'sweet'. As he chatted and poured frothed milk into the artisan cups Jordan had also bought, there was a knock at the door. I felt a giddiness as he stopped mid-sentence, looking quizzical.

'Who's that?' he asked, elbow hovering, steel jug in hand.

I made a pretence of surprise and scurried to swing the door open. There was Gatsby, carrying an enormous wicker basket overflowing with gifts and flowers, looking ashen on the step. The open door prevented Danny from seeing my guest immediately and he continued with his task as I glanced over my shoulder at him. I turned back to Gatsby as though cueing her.

'Hey, neighbour!' she trilled with unconvincing brightness. 'Hope I'm not interrupting. I just wanted to give you this . . .'

I moved aside and waved her into the room.

'Come in,' I offered, watching Danny as she stepped up and inside.

'Danny, this is my neighbour, Jay . . .' I said as he looked up from the counter. She paused just as he did. 'Jay, my cousin, Danny.'

The moment hung suspended like a water drop from the faucet. I became keenly aware of the sound of a mower on the lawn outside. The tissue paper in the basket in Gatsby's arms rustled as she seemed to tremble, staring at him, all charm sapped from her. I watched his friendly, anticipatory smile at the introduction falter as his eyes scanned her, thoughts racing across his features. Recognition. Confusion. He slowly lowered the coffee cup to the counter, the warm jug still in his hand, and cleared his throat. Suspicion.

'Jay?' he repeated. A question that seemed to ask for clarification as well as seek confirmation. His eyes were huge.

'As in, Gatsby,' I added unnecessarily.

I almost didn't know where to look as they observed each other, the seconds elongating to discomfort. I thought about saying something else when Danny nodded, breaking the spell, and put the jug down with a bump.

'We know each other,' he said simply, with no emotion.

'Yes,' Gatsby said.

She licked her lips nervously and took a shaky breath. I looked back at Danny and regretted the whole thing immediately as his blue gaze shifted to me and I saw the realisation of entrapment there. His jaw flexed as his eyes slid back to our guest.

'It's been a while . . .' he said with a little more kindness.

'Yes,' Gatsby said again, standing stiffly, blinking rapidly.

Danny looked down at the cups in front of him and then back up at her.

'Want a coffee?'

'You still need your caffeine fix then?' she asked, trying to load a shared history together into her nervous tone.

He smiled at the counter as though a memory played in his mind.

'I do,' he nodded. He pushed the cups towards both of us.

'You two have it,' I said quickly, turning to take the basket from Gatsby, pulling it from her arms before she dropped it. 'This is so lovely, thank you.'

She looked at me then with panic in her eyes.

'Well, I can't stay . . .'

'What? You can.'

I frowned and leaned around her to slam the door shut, blocking her escape. She startled a little at the sound and I wondered how to draw her out of herself. She looked pale, insubstantial compared to her usual persona. I willed her to flower.

'Was this the intention?' Danny asked quietly.

His arms were crossed now, but he didn't appear to be angry or upset. I could do nothing but nod, the smell of a gardenia candle wafting up from the ostentatious packaging. He continued to regard me, wanting more.

'You wouldn't have come if I told you,' I said. 'Would you?'

He raised his shoulders and looked back at Gatsby with more softness than before.

'I'm here now . . .' he said, and it seemed only directed at her.

'Can we talk?' she practically whispered.

It almost sounded as though she was on the verge of tears. The voyeur in me wanted to stay, watch. Instead I saw the opportunity being presented and didn't wait for his response, turning to put the basket on the table as I played director.

'Look, I'm going down to the beach for half an hour. You guys catch up and call me when you're done. I think I'm only making things weird being here.'

They both stared as I picked up my book from the sofa and walked to the door, placing my hand on the door handle.

'Okay?' I asked, but as more of an instruction.

They looked like negotiators, divided by the counter, both in defensive poses. I nodded encouragingly at them and disappeared before they could reply, slamming the door behind me and jogging to the beach in front of the mansion. I had no intention of reading as I sat down in the sand and watched the boathouse, fully expecting Danny to hurry out after me and kickstart his bike. But there was no movement, the quiet lapping of the waves the only sound as I waited for something to happen.

By three o'clock I was hungry, thirsty and aware I was burning in the sun, but neither one of my guests had contacted me. I had read no more of my book, the pages bent and gritty from the beach. A return to the boathouse was required, but I wondered if it would shatter the delicate bubble they had formed inside. I brushed the sand from my thighs and began to retrace my steps, typing a message to both that I was coming back. It remained unread, so I stomped on the gravel in pantomime fashion as I approached, hitting the steps heavily and taking my time twisting the door handle. I peered round the door as I entered and found them both standing in the living area, too close for strangers, their faces furtive. I noted that the bed that I changed and smoothed that morning was dented, the coffee untouched.

'Sorry,' I mumbled as Danny's face broke into a huge grin. He knew there was no hiding it. Gatsby, her lipstick faded, radiated joy as she echoed his expression. 'It's three o'clock,' I announced pointlessly.

Danny put a hand to his mouth. 'Lunch, Nic,' he apologised. 'We forgot.'

'Want me to get something made?' Gatsby asked, sliding her hand on his shoulder with a touch that spoke of renewed intimacy. 'Come over and I'll get . . .'

Danny pulled away, his arm reaching out for his jacket as he shook his head. 'Next time.' He walked to the door and stood in front of me, his brows knitted together.

'So sneaky,' he marvelled, as though he couldn't believe I was capable of it.

'Sorry,' I said again. 'But is it okay?'

He smiled forgiveness. 'It's cool.'

He looked back at Gatsby and gave her his full wattage beam. 'Want to walk me out?' he asked, using the register I'd heard him employ on T in happier times. She crossed the room and linked his arm without hesitation.

'Well,' he said to me, his eyes glittering with play. 'This was an education. Next time, let's actually do lunch.'

And he was pulling her away, like a dance partner, murmuring something in her ear as they descended the steps in unison. It was clear I had been dismissed and I closed the door quietly behind them as they talked in low, private voices. I watched from the window as he moved the bike off its stand and began to push it along the track back to the gate. Gatsby walked alongside so that she brushed his body with every step, her arm waving down to the beach and towards the house as she told him secrets. I watched as they moved out of view, beyond the curve of the slope. No longer able to follow their progress, I immediately turned to my phone.

I want to know EVERYTHING! I wrote to Danny and hit send.

Chapter 13

Danny was uncharacteristically coy in his response, which naturally took several hours. He said, vaguely, how glad he was to see an old friend after so long and that he'd be over to visit me again soon. When I pressed for details, he simply replied that he'd tell me when he saw me and I wondered if he was protecting himself. I could imagine that T checked his phone and that, despite her own indiscretions, would be fuelled by both jealousy and vengeance. Curiously, I felt no fear of T discovering my involvement, testing the sensation of her finding out as though weighing an object in my hand. She could not complain of complicity when she had visited the same upon me only weeks earlier. Gatsby only replied to my questions with enigmatic and infuriating emojis that provided no context.

Instead of receiving intelligence from either party I had to content myself with reading meaning into Gatsby's social updates. The post of the view now with a blue heart emoji attached, an inspirational quote about happiness, a GIF of a romantic film where the lovers reunite after years apart. I asked Jordan if Danny had confided in him but he knew no more than I had told him.

I felt I was owed something, so the following week after a night out with friends visiting New York, I contacted Klipspringer and asked to use the terrace pool at my neighbour's house. I told her that my landlady had banned me from the cool respite of hers, despite the heat. This was only partially true. She had forbidden me from the pool during certain hours when she took a siesta, the sound of slapping water disturbing her fragile peace. Klipspringer informed me that fresh towels and refreshments would be at my disposal whenever I wanted, and so I wasted no time in crossing the lawn to climb the steps and sink into an oatmeal sun lounger. Without the lights and paraphernalia of a party, the pool looked smaller, less grand. As I lay there, I watched idly as perspiration collected in my navel and the jug of ice water sweated next to slices of lemon and lime. I baked and waited, hoping for an appearance from the lady of the house.

But as I watched the windows surrounding the patio, they remained impassive. No one passed through the long doors to join me or flitted past the glass. My curiosity remained unsated and, as I plunged into the cool depths of chlorine, I momentarily forgot my fascination as I sank to the Moroccan-tiled subterranean floor. Not everything had to be blazing and urgent, I told myself. I needed to get out of town, see more of my friends, stop my fascination with other people's stories. The dark coolness of the depths soothed me and I held my breath as long as possible before surging for the surface, exploding out of the water with a gasping suck of air. Of course, Gatsby now awaited me on the side of the pool. Dressed in all white, dark glasses covering her eyes and a playful expression on her face.

'Nic, darling,' she said as I exclaimed, pushing my sodden hair from my eyes. 'I did wonder if I needed to call for help.'

I laughed and swam to the side of the pool, squinting up at her as she stood in direct sunlight.

'Were you about to jump in and save me?' I asked.

'God no! I know it's crazy, but I can't swim. I'd only be contributing to the body count.'

I frowned. 'You have two pools.'

She laughed, tipping her face back attractively and I could imagine snapping a picture and posting it. 'Like I said, I know . . . I'm happy dipping my toes, and that's it.'

She began to walk to the tray sitting next to the lounger I'd been inhabiting.

'Do you have everything you need?' she asked, tracing a finger against the condensation on the jug.

I thanked her and told her how grateful I was and she told me to use the phone secreted in the cupboard near the door to call the staff if I wanted anything, anything at all. Then she began to turn back towards the house.

'Jay,' I said in a tone that meant 'stop'.

She paused, the glossy ponytail high on her head swishing and glinting gold in the light. With her eyes hidden by black lenses I couldn't decipher her expression, but the tension in her body suggested a certain wariness. I folded my arms on the poolside, pulling myself higher out of the water.

'Have you seen Danny again?'

She smiled, one of secrecy. 'Perhaps . . .'

Locked out of something I'd been invited into – manipulated into – and instrumental in pushing forward annoyed me, gnawing at my sense of entitlement.

'Whatever,' I said with the finesse of a teenager, sliding back into the water. The tone was juvenile and immediately regrettable but I felt I couldn't claw it back. 'Thanks again for the pool,' I added stiffly as I sculled in place and she continued to watch me, giving nothing away.

'Whenever you want,' she replied airily, stalking towards the doors. The conversation was closed. 'Use it as your own,' she called as the house swallowed her again, leaving me treading water.

As I look back now, I wonder that I didn't have more pressing conundrums to fill my summer minutes and hours. But I had isolated myself on Long Island – a decision that left me bored, lonely and without counsel in the moments that were not consumed by Jordan, Gatsby or my relatives on the other shore. As the sun glittered on the water I felt the sharp stab of jealousy; over Danny or Gatsby, or both – I couldn't determine. After I'd clambered out and towelled my pruning fingers dry, I sent an invitation for T to visit.

She expressed measured enthusiasm in hearing from me and a scolding response that she had been waiting for her lunch date, especially as Danny had been over a couple of times already. Evidently he was using me as cover. Armed with this information, I messaged him with false concern that I might say something wrong when T arrived for lunch the next week if he didn't keep me up to date with his activities. I knew the risk of T's ire would galvanise him into action. As I arranged a time for her arrival, Danny's uncharacteristic urgency made my phone shiver and vibrate on the table, first asking me to delete my message then sending a series of rapid-fire replies, arranging to swing by that evening before dinner with a bottle of wine. I felt satisfied. For good measure, I sent a flirtatious voice message to Jordan, suggesting he call me later as I was running hot on such a muggy day. I put down the phone and lay back on the lounger, deciding to sun-dry myself to the point of discomfort before returning home.

Chapter 14

Danny arrived at 8.30 p.m., the wrong side of anyone's idea of before dinner time. I heard the bike on the gravel just as I sat down to eat, having given up waiting. When I opened the door he offered a beautiful pinot noir and a truant's smile. As he moved round the kitchen opening drawers and cupboards in search of a corkscrew and glasses he asked how much I knew about him and Jay, pouring with both glasses balanced in his fingers. He listened to my pretence at being uninformed as though he believed it.

'Tell me . . .' I said. I wanted to hear the story from his vantage point, rather than diffused through Jordan's lens.

The wine, I noted, was an expensive small-vineyard pinot from the Santa Lucia Highlands, evoking the twisting coastline roads and mist of Northern California before he even started painting me a picture of his past. His version of his and Gatsby's meeting was much the same as Jordan's account, a meet-cute over eggs, but Danny sketched images of the two of them fused in a romance that tasted of sea salt and the smoky dampness of the redwoods. He said he'd fallen hard for Jay, her things bundled into the cupboards of his student room within a week, time spent together daily – other commitments curtailed to allow for more moments spent sitting on beaches, fingers laced, or driving his beat-up Toyota to postcard viewpoints. They drank in beautiful vistas with the belief that they held in their hands something as impressive as the Golden Gate Bridge glowing at night; something as new and pristine as the dawn-strobed dunes in Death Valley, the sand freshly imprinted with the tracks of nocturnal animals. He smiled softly, moving his expressive hands to trace the lines of the places they visited. He remembered thinking that no one had felt like this before.

He knew he was in real trouble, he said, when they visited the Mystery Spot in Santa Cruz, an area that boasted a supposed gravitational anomaly that twisted trees in peculiar shapes and made balls roll uphill, a shack on an incline allowing visitors to appear to defy logic in the angles they could lean. An Americana sideshow attraction that couldn't be taken seriously but nonetheless amused them both, Danny looked at Jay as they balanced on opposite ends of a sloping plank and knew that she had tilted his world on its axis. That, drunk on her, he no longer knew which was north or what laws of science applied. She threw him, catapulted him into a state of frenzy, dizziness that he hadn't known before. As they walked back to the car hand in hand, he confessed his desire to never sober up. She'd returned his feelings and floated an interest in permanence, something that usually scared him off but now exhilarated him. They had flirted with ideas of shared homes and babies that might come later. He still had the yellow bumper sticker they got that day.

In his recollection, Danny, with his serious ocean eyes and earnest tone, even had me convinced that this love had been unique. He nearly had me believing it was thwarted by unseen circumstances, rather than his own withdrawal.

She had left the country and been unable to return to the States, he said. He'd been transferred to another school, their desperate transatlantic conversations becoming tense and fraught. The gaps between their shared experience lengthened and loosened until they couldn't summon that sense of staring at each other in the redwoods. It hadn't been his fault, he insisted, it was just something that happened. He omitted the conversation with his parents and the story of his and Gatsby's reconnection on the eve of her nuptials to the actor. He either forgot it or I suspected he felt it did him a disservice in the retelling.

He shrugged; he had moved on, patched up, distracted himself with T. And in practising feeling for someone else had found a softer, quieter passion that reverberated with practicality and assurance. Against all expectation, T had been the safe harbour, not the storm.

'And now?' I asked, sipping the wine.

He swirled his glass, spinning the pinot in a vortex, a clandestine smile creeping across his face. I thought he might not continue as he watched the drink in his hand, his wedding band silver against the red. But after a sigh he nodded, as if making a decision, and described his marriage as one of miscommunication, of suspicion and biting conversations conducted where the staff could not hear. He admitted that he did not recognise that version of himself and seeing Jay standing in my kitchen had been like time travel. She was even more beautiful than the picture he'd kept in his mind and certainly more successful – everything about her more polished, gilded. She was intimidating despite the shiver in her voice. And then, in talking and touching, that golden carapace around her had fallen away. She made him feel like that giddy young man full of promise again, and his world had tilted anew. For a man who felt insubstantial within his own house, the sensation was now an opioid to him.

After they had reconnected as I fretted on the beach, Gatsby had urged him to visit her. They had arranged to meet days later when she dismissed most of her staff to ensure secrecy and greeted him at the door. She walked him through the rooms I had explored, allowing him to marvel at the life she had built for herself. They had pulled books that they'd both previously enjoyed off the shelves in the library, trailed fingers over the keys of the grand piano, dipped hands in the spa pools, ascended to the private quarters and peered into tastefully designed room after room until they arrived at Gatsby's ultimate sanctuary. He detailed the richness of her furnishings, the scale of her walk-in closet.

With a prime view of the shoreline (and my boathouse), she pointed out the speck on the horizon that was his house and turned him toward her California king bed. He'd left newly addicted, returning the following day to sneak in a prearranged side entrance for a stolen hour. And he continued to do so when his schedule allowed. Though he didn't say it, I could interpret his renewed attraction. Danny chased his uncomplicated teenage existence in many aspects of his life. In T that sometimes transmuted into her treating him like a boy. With Gatsby, he was worshipped for it.

'So now you know,' he said, sitting back and tracing a finger around his lip line. 'Do you think I'm a bad person?'

'I don't think anything,' I assured him, topping up our glasses, not yet fixed on what I actually thought.

'You won't tell T?' he asked lightly, but I knew that this was the locus of his visit.

I shook my head, holding eye contact.

'But do you know what this is yet?' I pressed. 'Are you

having an affair?' The term sounded antiquated, but I knew of no other way to say it.

He pushed a hand through his hair, a tell that he was nervous, and looked towards the window.

'Nic, I don't know . . .'

'What does Gatsby think it is?' I asked, knowing how I might feel in her shoes.

He stood up and walked towards the window to look out across the water, cradling the wine and allowing the question to pull like molten glass.

'I don't know,' he repeated quietly.

'Don't you think you should know? Before . . .'

I stopped myself short of detailing cataclysmic situations, of people being hurt as I heard the voice of my mother in my tone. He was a grown man and could decide for himself. He had not asked for advice. He turned from the window and back to me.

'She wants to throw a party for us,' he said, his voice bright. It was a line drawn under any further thought of consequences.

'For us?' I pointed between him and me, pleasure beginning to bubble in me at the idea of a Gatsby soiree in my honour.

'For me and her,' he clarified. 'To celebrate getting back in touch. She says it's a way to show the world, without showing the world. She says her events are epic, she wants me to see.'

'They are,' I agreed.

'Jay wants us all to go – you, me, Jordan, T . . .'

Her name crackled in the room and he laughed almost nervously, as though he understood the danger implicit in such a suggestion. I nodded and held his gaze. It was steady.

'Isn't that weird?'

He swallowed the last of his wine, pushing the glass back across the table with a scraping sound.

'More weird not to invite her. Suspicious,' he shrugged, checking his watch. 'It'll be fun.'

That word again. A careless syllable that he and Jordan used for so many things. He stood and swiped the bike's ignition key off the table with a flourish.

'Want to stay and drink this whole thing with you but I have to get going,' he grinned, 'T will have dinner waiting.'

He held his arms open for a hug and I walked into them. He squeezed me like he was comforting or congratulating me.

'We should hang out more,' he noted before he was striding across the room and flinging the door open. He stopped and looked back at me.

'So . . .' He elongated the vowel. 'Our secret?'

Like a kid I mimed zipping my lips, locking and tossing a key, which prompted a guffaw of laughter, his eyes crinkling as he mimicked a salute and slipped outside. As his bike roared to life, I wondered how cold my dinner had got and messaged Jordan to tell him to be available to talk in a half hour.

Eager, he wrote back.

It prompted the pooling feel of need in me and I ignored my plate of food in favour of changing clothes and applying lipstick. I wanted to feel disoriented and lost, craved an abandonment of logic like my cousin and my neighbour. But when Jordan's face appeared on my screen and I told him, almost breathlessly, of Danny's latest adventures he chided me for getting too involved. He was marginally enthused about the idea of a party but urged me to sweep my excitement for others aside to be present with him as he leaned his phone up against his hotel room lamp. I thought of Gatsby's California king bed as the light dimmed across the sound and Jordan talked low and encouragingly through the speaker.

Chapter 15

Predictably, T shirked coming to my side of the shore for lunch, relaying that Danny had described my accommodation as 'quaint'. Why not take advantage of her chef instead, she asked when she called the day before we'd planned to meet. She managed to sound both seductive and insulting as she reasoned that her air conditioning was more aggressive than mine against such hot weather. Besides, she'd get to see my place when she came over for the upcoming party at my neighbour's house on the last weekend of August. At the mention of Gatsby her voice turned playful.

'God, Nic, this woman,' she breathed. 'Danny knew her vaguely at school but I've been digging and apparently it's common knowledge she hired women she knew her husband would like and then just turned a blind eye. She likes that stuff.' There was relish in her tone. 'And those parties are just a front for darker things.'

'What kind of darker things?'

'I heard trafficking. Sex rings. Who knows.'

'You heard?' I scoffed. 'From QAnon?'

She allowed the dig, skimmed over it. 'What do you know? What's going on over there? You must see it all . . .'

Of course I had read the rumours, noted the blind items that pointed so obviously to Gatsby – 'the NY-environs ex' and other less flattering descriptors – tracking the theories across social media. Lily Shield had been my constant narrator of rumour via her DMs, voraciously scrabbling for purchase on a fact or a certainty that I might provide. Social threads and blogs claimed that Gatsby's line of cosmetics seemed to be a fallacy, a product bought by thousands and, more often than not, never received. She was being chased down by the IRS. She had connections to criminal characters and was part of underworld circles. There was no money, there was too much money; she was a lie, she was a liability. I had dismissed it all as the standard noise surrounding anyone who required a security escort when they walked through an airport. Gatsby attracted gossip just as she did camera flashes. It served me, as well as her, to disregard it as the fabrications of the jealous, the pernicious, the avaricious.

At the beginning of the summer I might have wanted to show T that I had access where she did not, and would have taken pleasure in being privy to a secret that I could dangle in front of Lily Shield like a prize. But now I sat on the knowledge I had like a satisfied hen on a golden egg. I made a show of changing the subject in the hope of implying unspoken mysteries, switching to ask her about Miguel. The mention of him didn't prompt her to reflect on the last time we'd been with him but did elicit a conspiratorial tone and complaints about his 'bitch of a wife'. Her voice lowered slightly when she described her last assignation in a suite at the Plaza Hotel. The detail was almost pornographic.

That both Danny and T felt comfortable telling me intimate details of their sex lives, assured that I wouldn't tell their spouse of their infidelities, fascinated me. As I sweltered on the porch of the boathouse, I listened to T talk and agreed to travel to the cool sanctity of the Buchanan property.

At lunch the next day T, heated and pungent from riding, pressed for more information as she used her linen napkin to dab her upper lip and then laid it on the cushioned seat of her chair to protect the upholstery from her dampness. She told me how she had met Gatsby recently, and fleetingly, at a charity event chaired by a girlfriend.

They crossed paths at the buffet table. The influencer had been, she noted, fiddling with tiny sandwiches with lacquered fingers, overly friendly to the point of ridicule. T impersonated the accent, stuttering between two continents. Gatsby had gushed in English idioms, mentioned Danny and attempted to orchestrate a bar visit after the party.

'She was so *keen*,' T hissed as she yanked off her boots and slung them under the dining table. 'Embarrassingly so.'

T had agreed to go for the drink after the event then pulled a French exit with her friends, sneaking away to head to a nearby hotel bar where they could laugh at the newcomer over cocktails. They imagined her consternation to find herself left behind, congratulated themselves on the social slight. I could imagine it all too well. Gatsby morbidly curious about who Danny had replaced her with and twinkling bright over the finger food and fruit platters. I wondered at T being so immune to her charm.

'She just wants to make friends,' I appealed to her, as freshly baked bread appeared from the kitchen smelling delicious. T waved it away.

'Friends like you?' She smiled with something approaching pity, then turned to call to the retreating housekeeper, 'Just bring the salad!'

I shrugged. 'Yeah, why not?'

'Why not?' she repeated and nodded as though contemplating a crossword conundrum.

Gatsby had called me a friend after all. She had taken me to Trimalchio's the previous week, a luxurious shoreline establishment with billowing white sun sails where it was reassuringly difficult to get a table. Klipspringer had called ahead to ensure privacy but despite the pre-planning, Gatsby had been stopped several times on the way to our table for head-tilted selfies with those insensitive enough to invade her space. She walked between the rippling tablecloths as though on a catwalk, fully aware that covert, angled shots of her were being shared the minute she sat down. She knew all the staff and introduced me as though I was a beloved sibling. She pressed the manager to bring off-menu drinks with a milk-white smile and covered my hand with her own, leaning over the table to whisper low about another famous person sitting in a discreet corner table, sunglasses on and head bowed. And, when the drinks had been served, about Danny.

He had taken her to Coney Island a few days earlier, a romantic nod to their shared past on the boardwalk in Santa Cruz. She had clung to him as he gunned his motorbike to Lunar Park, pressing her cheek against his warm back and tightening her fingers on his waist. Sure that no one they knew would have driven so far south from Williamsburg, they had parked in the dusty parking lot surrounded by a sagging chain-link fence, and walked along the shabby boardwalk, dodging shrieking seagulls dive-bombing overflowing trash cans and dropped ice creams puddling in the heat. She had worn large sunglasses and a baseball hat pulled low over her face to prevent recognition, but the crowds spilling off the subway and grappling beach equipment did not notice her in their midst on an ordinary Monday morning, and she dared to touch his fingers as they strolled. Despite the confetti of white paper napkins buffeted by the brisk shore wind, the drug deals in progress outside the sand-blown restrooms and the chipped paint of unloved rides, Gatsby had found it charming that Danny wanted to reset their romance to a moment in their past, had adored that he bought bronzed corn dogs for old time's sake.

The smell of the batter as it soaked the paper tray with grease had transported her back to Santa Cruz. Even more than when, emboldened by anonymity, she held her palm briefly to his face as they sat opposite each other on a splintered picnic table outside Nathan's drinking lurid slushy-machine margaritas. He was capable of growing more facial hair now he was older, she felt it against her hand, and golden down could be seen where his shirt unbuttoned as he leaned forward chasing dripping mustard with his tongue.

When he paid for four revolutions on the Wonder Wheel so they could repeatedly kiss in the privacy of the car at the top, swinging forwards and backwards and looking down on the toy town pleasure park, she felt no time had passed at all. I reflected her smile, amused that she considered a trip that I knew Danny quite frequently took as a grand romantic gesture. He had been known to give in to childlike want and ride the clackety wooden roller coaster solo, enjoying the swoop of his stomach and the weightless sensation. An endearing aspect of his Peter Pan existence. I didn't tell her. The happiness radiated off her until she switched to talking about current online criticism of her personal brand, wrinkling her nose. As we drank sharp citrus concoctions and she pushed a bowl of slick olives across the table at me, I cleared my throat and allowed myself to question her for the first time.

'Where do these stories keep coming from?' I asked, recalling T's accusations, and also for self-serving reasons. Lily Shield had been relentless in trying to convince me to talk to her friend, a commissioning editor on an upscale subscriber-email outlet who longed for a piece on Gatsby, told from the perspective of an insider. The kudos of the outlet and Lily's assurance that I could write in defence of Gatsby – counter negativity with my words – had momentarily tempted me. I had repeatedly said no, but hearing Gatsby's pain now at the accusations thrown at her I wondered if I couldn't be a good friend to her through my prose. Could I be her voice for her?

'Why don't they go away? Why don't you fight back?' I asked.

She removed her sunglasses. 'Darling,' she sighed in that clipped manner. 'What do they say? "Never complain, never explain." No one's interested in the truth anyway.'

She looked across the sparkling water and pouted. The warmth had drained from her. She was silent. I drank and waited. She squinted in the light dancing off the waves.

'You've watched *The Wizard Of Oz*, right?' she asked suddenly.

'Yes,' I laughed, somewhat surprised at the bluntness of the allegory. 'Is this where you tell me that every wizard is just a regular man behind the velvet curtain?'

She laughed too.

'No, I'm saying that people love the rumour that you can see a stagehand who committed suicide on that film, that you might be able to see that tragedy in the background. A hanged man in the trees behind the dancing characters. That in the middle of the beauty, there's something sinister, secret. You've heard this?'

I nodded, aware of the movie myth. Also aware that the

swaying shadow in the trees behind the yellow brick road was actually a large bird silhouetted, stretching its wings. The murky grain of the film stock and the light play creating an illusion, an unhappy legend. I searched my memory for the term of ascribing abstract forms with meaning. It eluded me.

'But there's no dead man dangling in the trees,' she said. 'There's a simple explanation, something pretty mundane.'

'It's just what we want it to be. We interpret shapes that align with something we know – or think we know.'

'Yes, exactly.' She smiled. 'Maybe it's just nothing more than that.'

'But is it?' She had not answered the question. 'Is it nothing more?'

'Nic.' She frowned. 'It's just shapes.'

'I didn't mean . . .' I began, but she held up a hand to suggest I should cease.

'I know,' she said re-armouring herself with her sunglasses, her face now pinched, unimpressed. 'We love the darker, meaner theories, don't we? I thought you might be someone who wasn't looking for something between the lines. But I guess none of us can help it.'

The silence between us was a reprimand. She twirled her straw and, as though deciding to, switched her mood.

She grinned, companionable again. 'As a friend, I'd like to tell you all my secrets. But they're not the ones you're reading about on your phone.'

'Tell me the real story,' I said.

She looked at the sea again, pushed her sunglasses up her nose and opened her mouth to speak, but stopped herself.

'What do you want to know?' she asked.

There were so many questions, but I knew where my fascination coalesced. I wanted to understand a consuming love, not just a physiological response and attraction. Wanted to know what it was like to yearn, connect emotionally, to be his absolute focus. What did it feel like?

'What is it about Danny? He's a sweetheart, but why wait all this time for him?'

* * *

In their versions of events, neither Jordan nor Danny had ever given much airtime to the reason Gatsby had left the throes of white-hot love in Northern California. At the height of their addiction to each other, Gatsby had received bad news from the UK. Her father was gravely ill and the pain of it sat like a stone in her gut; hard, heavy. It was nothing to rush home for yet, her father had insisted, so she had waited a few days for more conclusive tests to be completed before making a decision about whether to cross the ocean.

Danny had tried to comfort her but none of his caresses had soothed the panicked feeling of loss that dried her mouth and stung the corners of her eyes. He'd felt helpless, she said sympathetically. He didn't understand a problem he couldn't throw money at. Looking at her distraught face had seemingly anguished him and so he'd stopped asking how he could help, instead borrowing a friend's jeep and bundling her into it. She'd watched him take the route south on Highway 1, trained her eyes on the yellow line as the sinuous road ran through Monterey and Carmel, became single lane and precarious over soaring bridges clinging to rock above the coastline.

They'd said very little until he turned off the road in Big Sur, guiding the car down a narrow, steep track to a ford over the tumbling river. He left her in the car as he entered a rust-coloured campground general store and returned with a key dangling from a piece of wood with the words 'redwood cabin' scorched into it in wobbly capitals. There was a taste of firewood in the air when he tugged her towards the porch light among the trees and told her she needed to be somewhere away from the familiar. Needed the quiet of a deep forest, the rage of a boiling sea smashing onto rocks. They wouldn't talk about it, they wouldn't talk at all if she didn't want to. For three days they would only think about putting one foot in front of the other on trails from the campground, wait for hunger to return and when it did, eat; lie entwined under the plaid comforter on the spartan bed and listen to the night calls of the wildlife. The care in his eyes and voice made her cry, but not from sadness. And she'd submitted fully to the stolen weekend.

'We hiked and hiked . . .' she recalled, remembering the damp redwoods, the walking routes that ended on breath-snatching views, the air that curled her hair, made her cheeks dewy and fed the succulents that lined cliff-top paths so narrow they had to walk them like tightropes. They ate ambrosia burgers and drank dark pinot noir at Nepenthe as mist coiled against the coast, the restaurant fire warming their backs. He told her that this spot had originally been a meagre shack that had fuelled the writing of Henry Miller, before it caught the eye of Orson Welles and Rita Hayworth as they drove back from selling war bonds in 1944 San Francisco. Consumed by love and the romanticism of the place, the stars had bought the hut, an emblem of their marriage and a refuge from a critical world. Then later Richard Burton and Elizabeth Taylor arrived to film *The Sandpiper*, a year into their torrid first marriage and fused as partners for life. He told her that even after two divorces and days from death,

Burton had written Taylor a love letter calling her 'home', mailing it to Los Angeles where she found it waiting for her after attending his London funeral. Danny intimated that Gatsby and he were now those desperate lovers, and the way he looked, touched and cared for her, like tending an injured bird, was healing to her.

She couldn't imagine feeling so connected to another. And in this moment of the pull of paternal versus that of partner, she felt torn. As important a man, if not more so, than the one lying in a hospital bed letting her go. Danny felt like family, her intended, the one the universe had granted her.

He'd turned his face towards her as they snuggled close on the bench table teetering over the sheer drop of the cliffs, and nudged her with his shoulder, making the wine in her glass tremble.

'I'd marry you,' he'd said quietly.

'Are you asking?' she replied, squeezing his knee.

'If you need to stay . . .' He smiled, alluding to her immigration status. She worried she'd scared him, but his open face didn't seem perturbed.

'I'd marry you if you actually asked,' she told him.

He leaned towards her. 'I don't feel like I did that right,' he whispered. His lashes lowered. 'I'll do better next time . . .'

When he kissed her, licking the seam of her mouth, he tasted like a promise. She thought they were sealing an agreement.

'But he didn't ask?' I interjected and Gatsby almost jumped, still mentally clasping a glass of red and watching hummingbirds dart over the lavender and sage brush slopes of the continent's end.

'Not yet,' she said dreamily as her phone rang. She looked at the screen and then at me, asking permission.

'Take it,' I instructed her. 'But I want to hear the rest . . .'

She put the phone to her ear as she slid from the stool and walked towards the bar. A member of staff positioned himself between her and other patrons, discouraging approaches. My eyes were one of many sets on her as I thought about her whimsical recollection. Danny had said that he would, not that he wanted to marry her, and I knew it wasn't just syntax that differentiated those two things. As she curved her palm around the phone, covering her mouth as she spoke, I wondered at her ability to hold on to a sentiment expressed over the rim of a wine glass so long ago. She did not lack self-awareness; that much was evident in the way she marketed and commodified herself. She appeared a realist in business and optics. But her blinkered view of this chapter of her life seemed almost absurd. The ideal of marriage must have been sullied by her recent experience with Cody, and then I considered that perhaps that was exactly why she'd returned and attached so fervently to a purer version of attraction, courtship, proposal. Dan Cody, and his ferocious conquering attitude, his predatory predilection, might have made the nostalgic idea of romantic Danny all the more beautiful to her.

Her phone call was brief. She reappeared a few minutes later, just as a plate of oysters arrived at the table. Her cheeks were rosy, her lipstick reapplied.

'Tell me more,' I said, but she changed the subject and urged me to eat, deflecting my question until I lost sight of it. She was happy and she glowed with it. I wanted that for her and she for me as we tipped back our heads to allow the oysters to slide into our mouths and told each other silly secrets. She revealed her and Danny's pet names for each other; I confessed to stealing Jordan's sweater so I could inhale the scent of him when I lay alone. A limited edition gifted by the designer, he had been searching for it, perplexed. She laughed and told me I'd got it bad. Then she talked of famous people who populated gossip websites, insider observations and revelations that she would only discuss in trusted company. I cherished each secret like a gem. I might have entered her orbit because of my proximity to Danny, but that wasn't all that kept us together now. I had become the person she could talk honestly to. To answer T's snide question, it had felt like we were real friends. And why shouldn't we be?

I didn't express any of this in T's dining room. I was rudely summoned back from the warmth of the memory to the Buchanans' cool lunch table by my host clicking her fingers exasperatedly across the linen at me. It felt like waking.

'Hey!' she snapped. 'Are you listening?'

I apologised, asked her to repeat what she'd said.

'Never mind,' she huffed.

'Please.'

'I'm just saying,' she sneered, 'I don't think anyone wants that kind of friend.'

She stabbed the fish with the silver serving fork as though harpooning it.

'Why?'

'Oh, *you* know.'

I did know. But I considered myself honest in my dealings with my neighbour, my thoughts about her unclouded by social hierarchy.

'You might like her if you gave her a chance,' I told T. 'When you come to the party, you'll see.'

She looked at me curiously and leaned forward. I caught the muskiness of her in my nostrils.

'Nic,' she teased. 'Are you on her payroll?'

I laughed and leaned away from her. 'I just give people a chance,' I said as I heard Danny call out in the hall, returning from somewhere, possibly even Gatsby's bed.

'In here!' T replied.

He burst through the door like a bouncing puppy, a wide smile on his face, and stood behind T, his hands falling to her shoulders, his thumbs pressing insistently into her muscles.

'Good ride?' he asked her, his eyes on me, suspicious. 'What are you two plotting?'

T squirmed under his ministrations, wiggling on the seat as his hands moved, and she tilted her chin to look up at him.

'Talking about this dumb party on Saturday,' she told him.

'Oh?' he asked, mouth hardening. 'What about it?'

He glanced at his spouse and then back at me.

'Just that we're going,' I told him. 'That Gatsby isn't . . .' I didn't want to repeat the distain that T had articulated. 'She's a surprise. She's . . . well, I think she's kinda seductive.'

Danny's eyebrows raised slightly out of sight of T, who was now looking at me curiously.

'Jesus, someone has a crush.' She snorted, reaching up to her shoulder, resting her fingers on Danny's. 'Who's going to tell Jordan he's got competition?'

I bristled at this, unspoken words filling my mouth like dust. I swallowed them.

'It's not like that,' I said stiffly.

'Don't be shy,' T said with amusement. 'Maybe it's time you experimented?'

I stood up and forced a smile. 'I'm not like you,' I said lightly and picked up my bag.

When I turned back to face them, both had something

unreadable in their eyes, matching blue irises watching me. For the first time in months, they looked like a couple.

'Oh, come on, Nic,' T smiled, squeezing Danny's hand, 'of course you are.'

* * *

When Jordan arrived back on the East Coast he was full of tales of extravagance – dinner with Sigourney Weaver, a super-yacht trip with sponsors and a former president, late-night TV hosts drinking to excess in seedy Florida bars. He was high on his recent tournament success and a new endorsement deal. As he paced his apartment, he talked about moments of triumph on the green and in boardrooms, of the twinge in his back that he worried was a keeper. When I tried to broach the upcoming party, he would only allow that he was curious to see Danny's two loves in a room together. When I was anxious, reminding him of how vicious T could be, he shrugged. Whether the Buchanans unravelled or not was not his kind of concern.

I tried to decipher who he championed, assuming Danny. But the more he talked, with a veneer of contempt, it became clear that all of this was simply a spectator sport. Jordan almost hoped for disaster, humiliation, downfall for any of the participants. He saw no grand romance, was not invested. When I suggested he should be more protective of his friend, he looked at me sharply and told me not to patronise him. We were on the cusp of an argument and we both knew it. I thought he cared too little for anything, he thought I cared too much about everything. Our relationship really only existed in between sheets, in night-time phone sex and parties at other people's homes. So we bit back any discussion in favour of physicality. On this, we were aligned. We lost mutual understanding when we talked, when the yawning gap between our experiences and values was more easily exposed. But if he made me giggle, if I stroked his ego, if we chased pleasure, we could avoid discussing anything real. As he lay between my legs I forgot why I thought him unkind. On Saturday afternoon, when we drove back to the boathouse from the city, my hand lay on his thigh and his laughter was back in his throat as he shouted meaningless thoughts over the roar of the engine, the wind buffeting our ears.

Chapter 16

Later that evening, as we walked through the plum-coloured August evening to Gatsby's front door with T and Danny, I felt something itchy and foreign as I approached the house. I recognised the beat thumping from the ballroom and fully anticipated the throngs, the canapés, the cocktails. Rather than an escalating excitement, giddiness even, this time our journey towards the hot ticket seemed rote. Even Jordan's hand in mine felt worn. The calluses on his palm caused by his clubs chafed me. When we passed into the vast room filled with lilies and their cloying scent I realised with dismay that these events had become familiar, pedestrian to me. The glittering gossamer thread of enchantment had been handled too often and tarnished. I had grown used to it.

As Jordan led the way through the stream of people, waving at those he knew and glancing back at me and the trailing Buchanans, I tried to gauge Danny's impressions. His head turned to take it all in, his eyes raking over the celebrities and the masses with an expression that could only be read as indifference. He habitually walked through wealthy houses, appreciated finer things. Nothing about him or what he favoured could be called loud, ostentatious, flashy. Though Gatsby's soirees had always been a cornucopia of food, drink and decoration, when my focus flitted across her gift to him I now saw the excess, the meretriciousness when viewed through his 'quiet luxury' expectations.

It seemed to me that Gatsby had tried to show her operatic feelings through greater volume, both in noise and numbers. The party to celebrate him contained monstrous cheese towers, sweating elephant ice sculptures, an oyster bar that lined an entire wall with the pulpy bivalves glazing under strobing lights, jewel-like snacks served nestling in tiny bonsai trees, glasses erupting and wafting dry ice. The Moulin Rouge theme translated into magicians leering over cards, a contortionist bending her limbs inside a human-sized champagne glass. A string of actual can-can girls swished their petticoats on the dance floor. In the grimaces of selfie-takers, I saw avarice; amid the heaving number of guests, I sensed a curious depletion, a desperation. For the first time I felt a snob.

As Danny's pale eyes travelled the rooms, his expression remained unchanged and I felt embarrassed for all my enthusiastic recounting of my hours spent in the house. His beautifully cut suit and crisp white shirt casually buttoned low to reveal his well cared-for body spoke of effortless class as he moved through the crowd. In relief, the festivities around him seemed . . . I pushed the word back from my mind but it rose again relentlessly: vulgar.

'Why Moulin Rouge?' T asked as she took a drink from a passing tray and we gathered round a table, a stuttering vermillion candle in our centre.

'Forbidden love?' Jordan shouted over the beat, a sly smile on his face and his head bobbing. 'Want to dance?' He held out his hand and made a beckoning motion. I shook my head.

'I need a drink first,' I told him and tried to shoot him a warning glance to prevent him from saying anything else that could compromise Danny.

He dropped his arm and moved into the undulating bodies alone. I turned back to T and Danny, both of whom were scanning the room.

'Who *are* all these people?' T asked and drained her glass.

The remnants of the sticky beverage feathered at the corners of her mouth. She wiped at them with a finger and squeezed Danny around his waist. 'I know no one,' she said witheringly.

'City people, social people,' I catalogued for her. And as I looked into the corner of the room and spied a baseball hat covering a familiar head, a face mask attempting to hide features: 'Hollywood types.'

She smiled with relish. 'Oh, this will be fun,' she said, her lip curling almost into a snarl, snagging another drink with dangling fingers as a tray passed. Danny and I remained empty-handed, but he politely paused the waiter and took two glasses of amber, pressing one towards me with a slight bow.

'Drink, Nic?' He smiled. 'We need to catch up.'

'Where's the host?' T asked as we clinked glasses.

'She'll find us,' I assured her, wondering if even now Gatsby was poring over her CCTV, watching for Danny's arrival, trying to decipher his expression.

'What do you think?' I asked as Danny detached from T, placing a casual hand in his pocket as he watched the room over his drink.

'I'll let you know,' he replied, wincing slightly at the sweetness of the cocktail. He placed the beverage back on the table, rejected. He stole a glance at his wife and then turned to smile warmly at me. As always, he could read me, understood my anxiety. He knew I wanted him to like the party. He soothed me without saying a word. T turned from the table to grab a miniscule bowl and we both watched her use a dainty silver fork to spear a snail in its shell. When she popped it in her mouth, Danny gave her his brightest, sociable grin.

'Shall we go to the pool?' he suggested.

She groaned and discarded the bowl on the table as he turned toward the outer party.

Whether T noticed that Danny led the way through a house he purported to have never been in before I couldn't tell, but she said nothing as we moved single-file through revellers to the area outside, collecting Jordan as we went. The pool was dancing with floating lights, a glittering, twinkling windmill towering over it and wait staff fluttering around pouring absinthe over sugar cubes on filigree silver spoons balancing over doll-sized flutes. As we crowded round a tray and watched the lurid green liquid fill the glasses, Gatsby materialised.

'Welcome,' she beamed as she stepped into our circle.

Once again she wore white, the simple lines of her dress clinging to her, her hair artfully falling over one shoulder. Her eyes lingered on Danny's as he turned to her, an intimate smile playing on his lips before he rearranged his features.

'I'm so glad you could pop over,' Gatsby gushed.

T snorted into her glass at the English expression, then lifted her face to her host. Gatsby stood above her, thanks to towering heels, and I knew that this would displease T. She and Danny were usually the two most statuesque people at any gathering, meant for each other in feet and inches. She rarely looked up to anyone.

'I'm so glad we could make it,' T said like a threat. Gatsby returned it with a genuine laugh of delight.

'Thanks for the invite, Jay,' Danny smiled, radiating her joy back at her.

'Did you look over the house?' she asked, and put a hand lightly on his forearm. 'I seem to recall you like books?'

'Comic books,' T said. 'Only if they have pictures, right, baby?'

Danny shot her a disgruntled look, his forehead furrowed.

'We've spent time in the library,' I said quickly, wanting to dilute whatever I could sense in the air, moving my hand between myself and Jordan. 'It's a great space.'

All eyes travelled towards me. 'Not just comic books,' I gabbled.

'I want you all to have fun,' Gatsby stressed, her hand remaining on Danny's body. He didn't react as he watched her perform in front of his wife. 'I throw these things to see everyone having a blast. I'm something of a wallflower myself.'

'I don't know how you afford it,' T said.

Danny moved his hand back in his pocket, making it impossible for Gatsby to maintain physical contact, her fingers sliding from him. She turned to give T her full attention and shook her head.

'Oh, it's worth it.'

'Worth what?' T asked sweetly.

Gatsby simply smiled brightly at her and then turned to me and Jordan. 'You two . . .' she cooed. 'Quite the romance.'

I blushed.

'Oh, let's not get carried away,' Jordan said, oblivious to my discomfort at his quenching of the sentiment.

'I want you to,' she whispered between us, leaning in to kiss my cheek fleetingly.

I slipped my hand in Jordan's and hoped he'd squeeze it with reassurance. He did not. Instead Gatsby put a hand on my shoulder as she continued to look at me with softness. 'Darling Nic,' she purred. Her affection was clearly an offence to T. When I glanced at her she watched our host with a puckered mouth and hardening eyes. The song changed and Gatsby looked towards her dancing guests with pleasure. She smiled opaquely and I wondered if this was a song she and Danny shared.

'Anyone want to get in there?' she asked the group, but it was a question only for Danny.

He held his hand out in an overly courteous manner. 'Sure!' He nodded.

'Oh, *now* he wants to dance,' tutted Jordan and he crushed my fingers, tugging me towards the moving bodies.

I resisted long enough to put down my glass and looked apologetically at T before Danny and Jordan turned away from the group, towing me and Gatsby after them like water-skiers behind boats.

'Staying here?' I asked her as my arm pulled taut in Jordan's grip.

'She'll be fine,' Danny called over his shoulder as he walked away. 'She'll make new friends. She always does.'

The Buchanans exchanged a loaded look, before we were consumed by the rippling bodies. Jordan locked his hips to mine, with a view over his shoulder of Gatsby and Danny as they moved together. She draped a languid arm around his neck as he swayed, their golden heads together as he whispered into her ear. His cheek pressed to hers and she smiled to the heavens. Always a tactile person, his hand on her waist could be forgiven as friendly unless one observed the bliss in his partner's eyes.

The longing emanating from her made me concentrate more fully on Jordan, surrender to his touch, the music and the noise surrounding us. When the song switched to a slower beat and Jordan clammily clutched me closer, I rested my cheek against his shoulder and realised they had gone. I peered towards our table where two well-known actors were now huddled, one jabbing his finger towards the crowd as he conveyed urgent information, the other sucking on a vape as he nodded, his cheekbones becoming even more pronounced than on his coffee ads. Like the lovers, T had gone her own way, neither party in need of the other and certainly in no need of us.

I pulled away from Jordan and was bumped hard from behind. A jostle, a stumble and then the rapidly spreading damp feeling travelled from my shoulder down my dress. Jordan yanked me away from the culprit, a woozy model I recognised as shilling a designer scent on pop-up ads. She staggered even as she stood still, holding a now empty glass, her eyes and mouth both wide.

'Hey!' Jordan and I exclaimed in unison, as he drew me alongside him and pawed ineffectually at the red stain on my pale dress. It was sticky, scented with strawberry. His hand glistened.

'Sorry, sorry, sorry,' the model muttered, clattering backwards into another reveller. He pushed her roughly away so she danced on the spot in front of us. 'I'll pay . . .' she drawled vaguely even while walking away, her weight on her heels, shoulders back, her eyeline on a spot across the room, as though descending the gang plank of a boat.

I looked down at the mess, a pink continent bleeding across my chest and sticking my bra to my skin beneath. It was irrevocable. Jordan swore.

'I have to change,' I snapped.

'Yeah, let's go,' he nodded, his empathy uncharacteristic. We were both annoyed to a similar level; the drunk guest tiresome, the unanticipated pause to return to the boathouse an unnecessary chore. Neither of us wanted reality or mundanity at this point. He took my hand.

Across the lawn was still the quickest route home. As we passed the pool a girl jumped in fully dressed and shrieking, the splash from her entrance loud and ungainly. The tidal wave she created extinguished many of the bobbing lights and slapped against the sides of the pool. As she came up for air, mouth gaping and make-up running, others rushed to join her, toeing off their shoes, eager to compete. One man – an ox built for land not sea – was first in, smashing the water and erupting out of it like a kraken, shouting to encourage others. They bombed and churned the water, sinking the lanterns, tipping cocktails into the blue depths and leaving broken glass drifting in currents near the filters. The girl who had started the thrashing waded to the pool steps grimacing, holding a dripping purse above her head. 'My fucking phone!' she wailed as she slipped on the tiles. Jordan and I walked in step out of view of the pool, down the stairs and toward the dark grass below, the lamp in my window a lighthouse ahead.

We might have created an awkward moment except that, as Jordan's foot hit my first step, I noticed Gatsby's grass-stained vertiginous white shoes and Danny's Savile Row boots slung on the top stair. I pulled Jordan to a halt, pointing and pursing my lips in a silent approximation of shushing. We wobbled together, the forward and backward motion of our opposing movements threatening to topple us. Danny had clearly made use of the key I had left in the jar on the windowsill. I had boasted to him of this rudimentary hiding place as a demonstration of the safety of my neighbourhood when I'd first moved in. Had we continued we might have disturbed their vulnerable, undulating bodies.

Jordan uttered an expletive under his breath as we looked at each other and at the door. Before I could hear or see anything, I turned back towards Gatsby's house, tugging Jordan with me, hyper-aware of the gravel crunching beneath my feet with the briskness of our stride. As we made it back onto the plush quiet of the lawn, I looked at my phone and saw a message from Danny. *Don't let T come back to yours. X*

'What the hell? Does he want to get caught?' I hissed at Jordan, the phone screen lighting up his face in the darkness as I turned it towards him.

'I don't know what he wants.' He sighed. He was riled – with me or them, I couldn't decide. 'Kinda over this whole thing.'

We stopped on the grass. 'What whole thing?'

'This—' He waved towards the party. 'This neighbourhood, these people . . .'

'These people?'

'No wonder Danny doesn't want to stay in that house, full of . . .' he let the sentence die on his tongue.

I suspected they didn't leave because of elitism, rather it was nostalgia that drove them from Gatsby's well-appointed mansion. Two people who enjoyed living in their past, they were likely chasing the spark of their first reunion on the shabby floorboards of my boathouse with the lazy fan overhead. I wondered that Jordan didn't know his best friend better than I did.

'This,' Jordan said, pointing to my dress, 'is like everything over here. It's fine to dabble, Nic, but then it gets messy.'

'Who are you talking about?' I heard a brittle note in my voice. 'Me? Danny?'

He laughed and put his hands on my shoulders, a calming move which only irritated more.

'They're just playing. She'll move on and so will he. And so will we.'

Together? I wanted to qualify, but my name was being shouted from the pool area and when I squinted through the blue shadows I could discern T waving. I waved back and looked at Jordan.

'Wait here,' I instructed him, 'in case I need to stop her going further.'

I turned my back on him and returned to the steps, meeting T halfway. She pulsed with hot energy, her lipstick smudged. Her eyes widened as she took in my spoilt dress.

'What happened to you?' she asked immediately.

'This, which is just great,' I snapped. 'I'm changing and coming back.'

When she asked where our group was, I lied. When she told me about the people she had done coke with in one of Gatsby's many bathrooms, I nodded. And when she informed me she was heading to the mobile creperie in the courtyard and she would let me know before she decided to leave, I was surprised. This was a courtesy she'd never given before. The amount of times we had arrived at an event together, and she had abandoned me for better company, only thinking to message me her movements the next morning when my indignation had thawed into concern.

She returned, hips swaying, to a young man who had been watching our conversation from the top of the steps. She looped her arm through his and urged him back into the party. I turned back to look at Jordan and beyond to my home. There, the lone light source split in two as the door opened and the lovers slipped back into the night, their silhouettes rippling on the doorstep against the beam of my writer's lamp.

* * *

Later, as I lay in my bed with my ear over Jordan's heartbeat, I watched the dawn blush across my windowpane and thought of Gatsby and Danny in our place. I wished their emotional desperation for each other could be transferred to my relationship, just as the trace of Danny's cologne had lingered on my pillow. Their connection remained despite the years and other people passing through their lives, something Gatsby had been so sure of as she constructed a universe around the memory of him. All of her garnered wealth and influence had been leading to that moment in my kitchen. Even marriage to another man seemed an act of devotion, a step on the climb back to him. It was a wonder he could withstand the expectation; that anything good could have come from such fixation and hope. But here she was, enthralled by optimistic love, operating within the most cynical of worlds that was devoid of nuance, compassion. Manifesting the life she had envisaged, praying it into existence, despite it resulting in a partner that wasn't hers in the way she wanted and who couldn't expunge the years he'd been without her. Despite its obvious fragility, it was as great a romance as I had known.

I could almost hear T's snort in my head at the sentimentality of my thoughts when my phone screen lit up, demanding my attention. I intended to simply turn it over, ignore it, but my deceitful lizard brain instructed otherwise, my hand tilting it towards me to read the notifications coming in from T.

Where's the money really coming from? Weren't her ex's assets seized?

Honestly, she's not even English.

Her shoes were so wrong for that dress.

I opened the app and saw another string of missives from Gatsby, sent earlier in the night. She wrote that she had waved Danny off as he sneaked up my driveway to meet the town car he'd ordered to take him back around the bay. He had left both his wife and mistress at the event thrown for him.

He hated the whole thing, didn't he? she wrote. Then a series of long disjointed passages about how she should have made it a surf party to ellicit their past, that he must have forgotten that their younger selves had talked of visiting Paris together. She voiced her insecurities to me in a way she hadn't done before and the grasping for validation made me wonder if she'd violated her self-imposed sobriety. Both women wanted me to make something true for them: T demanded proof of Gatsby's failure, Gatsby nagged for assurance that she was Danny's priority. I could satisfy neither.

Instead, I elected to be selfish. I shut my phone off and turned my face towards the pillow, slipping a leg around Jordan and moving against him in a way that would stir him. Rather than imagining someone else's kisses from a moonlit past, I wanted his mouth against mine. I wanted to think only about the body I could feel warm under my fingers.

Chapter 17

Once, on a road trip in Arizona, I experienced a peculiar sensation in a supposedly haunted hotel, a former sanatorium looming over a mining ghost town. It may have been the wine I'd drunk out of plastic cups in the bathroom before bed, a suggestive imagination or the true paranormal. I never decided. All I knew was that I had awoken gasping into the night with the sensation of being pressed physically into the mattress. The tangible weight felt malevolent in a way I couldn't explain. It terrified me to silent inertia and I willed myself unconscious, choosing the escape of sleep rather than face whatever laid heavy on me. The next morning when I mentioned it to breakfast staff, they exchanged looks and suggested the resident ghost was not a fan of female guests.

This was a feeling I recalled in the days after the party as I lay in clammy sheets watching my ceiling fan as the summer heat became increasingly unbearable. During the day the boathouse transformed into a terrarium under cloudless skies, all surfaces feeling tacky to the touch, the air stifling as though being sucked through a damp cloth. In my bed on those late August nights I felt a similar discomfort and oppression to that I felt at the Jerome Grand Hotel – a feeling of something dank and mean hiding in the room. In my torpor I slept little, worked less and swam in salt water and chlorine whenever I could, my bathing suit sun-drying ever more faded with each use.

Part of my restlessness at night was likely caused by guilt. Lily Shield had been successful in her campaign of flattery. The day after the party when fashion sites cruelly criticised Gatsby's look as bridal, Lily managed to catch me when I felt angry on my friend's behalf and intersected that with a handsome third-party offer from the newly formed platform run by a former glossy magazine editor. Celebrated essayists contributed insightful pages for an elegant site and newsletter, and Lily suggested my writing should be seen by a wider audience than it currently served. 'Gatsby might even like it,' she'd suggested.

Once again I declined but I sat down to write a first-person article, purely to see if I could. Writing about Gatsby came more easily than I imagined; I had been fair, dispassionate and kept our private conversations off the page. I championed her as a girlboss, an independent spirit, a warm soul. And then, when the cursor blinked at the bottom of one thousand effortless words, I wondered what she might think of it. To write it at all was surely treachery, I had become another of the vampires that surrounded her. I closed the laptop, but did not delete it.

When I re-read it again the next morning, I liked it. I could imagine it popping into my inbox, the black type on white space, chiding the reader on judging those they do not know. It was a hymnal to her. She might be bashful about it but I couldn't imagine her angry. I repeatedly tried to envisage our conversation after she'd seen it and I could only picture sweetness and possibly even gratitude. She had never asked me to fight for her, but she had never asked me not to.

After hovering over the 'send' button for hours, I dispatched the piece to the contact Lily had given me and accepted the fee. I was immediately thrilled with the idea of having written something that absolutely corresponded to the subjects I had told Danny and Jordan I was interested in at the beginning of the summer. I had progressed. I didn't think that I regretted it. But the relief I felt when, days later, I received an apologetic email telling me they couldn't use the story was immense. I realised I felt released. I didn't attempt a rewrite or to sell it to another outlet. It remained in my folders marked 'Gatsby'.

I gave myself a break from the ménage à trois at the centre of the Moulin Rouge party and instead concentrated on my friendships further afield, feeling refreshed enough to accept an invitation to visit Danny and T in their robustly cooled home over the Labor Day weekend. My influencer neighbour had mentioned the get-together during a flurry of messages before either of the Buchanans reached out. She was attending and asked if I'd be there. While Gatsby and Danny's insistence on dangling their affair in front of T perplexed me, the idea that Gatsby would want to see inside Danny's new life did not. I had heard the roar of his Triumph along the lane numerous times and noted that Gatsby's social calendar had dramatically dropped to minimal as she presumably poured her passion more directly at the object of her affection.

Standards had changed at her home, closed blinds in the windows and a lack of fresh towels and refreshments at the pool when I went over. I was abashed by my peevish thoughts as I exited from a swim and was forced to walk home wet. Her social feed ceased to fill with celebratory pictures of her posing like a stork, one leg kicking backwards in demonstrative gaiety, as she leaned into a group of shouting people. Instead, she posted portraits of her hand on a tanned male back, contemplative quotes, a snippet of Ryan Adams's version of 'This Love' soundtracking the video of a blurred vista from a speeding motorbike, plus the never-ending views across the sound. The gossip sites presumed that this was evidence of her flirtation with one of the Hollywood actors I'd seen at her party and she didn't care to dissuade them, even liking some of their speculative posts herself. But I recognised the laugh that she sometimes caught in the background of her reels. I knew whose feet she snapped on the parquet flooring of her private rooms. The more she posted, the more I wondered if Danny was even aware of his appearance in the feeds of 19.4 million people; if they, or she, hoped for discovery. T would not follow Gatsby on principle but one of her friends might have recognised the scrapbook portrait of her husband, served up as romantic content.

Gatsby wasn't the only one to withdraw from the fever pitch she'd operated at earlier in the summer. Jordan disappeared to play his one true love on the emerald greens of top golf clubs. Danny's check-ins faltered and T's sneering takedown of Gatsby had simmered to sending me an occasional link to a gossip item or tweet that chimed with her beliefs.

This breathing space meant that by the time I entered the Buchanans' reception room that first weekend of September and saw Gatsby standing there dressed in soft pink like the velvet interior of a rose, her eyes flitting around the room, landing on different items as though cataloguing them, my fatigue with the set-up had been replaced by fresh allurement. And when I looked at Danny, watching her with dancing eyes, seemingly enjoying the titillation of his secret life overlapping with his marital existence, I experienced the creeping feeling that perhaps I didn't know him at all. He seemed cocky, cavalier, inviting disaster.

Why has he invited Gatsby? I had messaged Jordan on the ride over to the house.

He said it was T's idea, he'd replied, as though this made better sense. *Meet you there.*

Now he and Danny lay supine, sprawled, at either end of the enormous cream sofa exchanging coded glances, half-drunk beer cans dangling from their careless fingers.

'There's no *breeze,*' Danny complained listlessly. 'It's too still.'

The Buchanans' house felt delightfully chilly to me after a ride in an Uber with the windows down, the standard practice of drivers conserving gas.

'I'd get you a drink, Nic,' Danny sighed in surrender, 'but I just can't. Help yourself.'

'Grab me another,' Jordan ordered, gulping down the contents of his can. He had managed to crane his neck upward to give me a greeting peck, but any further movement seemed beyond him. I turned to Danny's guest, marooned in the centre of the room, and did her the courtesy they did not, asking if she wanted a beer as I moved to the door. She shook her head briskly.

'Where's T?' I asked.

'Work phone call.' Danny eye-rolled, making quotation marks with his bent fingers.

'Booty call,' Jordan chuckled, and Gatsby visibly stiffened. She probably wondered, as I did, if they talked in such disposable terms about us. Danny seemed uninterested in the now open secret that T was conducting an affair, his own transgression perhaps softening the rage he'd previously displayed. Though Jordan had told me Danny suspected T's betrayal, I was not aware that he was certain of it. Something must have changed in the last few weeks that Jordan had neglected to report. Had Danny found proof? Had it exempted his own unfaithfulness? He certainly seemed as carefree as ever. If anything, he appeared to relax even more, his spreading arms pulling his starched blue shirt open further.

'C'mere,' he growled at Gatsby, his eyes darkening.

He made a lazy beckoning motion with his hand and she moved towards him like a kite on a string. When she stood between his legs he tugged at her hand, then grasped the back of her head, manoeuvring her closer for a greedy kiss. I saw the glint of his tongue as he dipped into her compliant mouth.

'Dude!' Jordan exclaimed, admiration tingeing his admonishment.

I felt the sting of impropriety. There was every chance T could join the audience already observing his jaw working against hers. Though I'd imagined their kisses, I'd never seen it and I felt strangely affronted by the display as he smiled against her lips. I turned away, opening the door and walking towards the family kitchen at the end of the house. Even here at the core of the property, though the AC groaned, there was a vibration of the external heat in the air.

T leaned against the large silver refrigerator, head dipped to her phone, thumbs tapping fast as she chewed at her lip. She didn't look up as I entered the room and only responded with a grunt when I said her name.

'Can you believe it, Nic?' she asked in exasperation, eyes

not leaving the screen. 'He wants to move to LA. What a cliché.'

I didn't need to ask who as she slung her phone onto the counter with a huff and banged her head backwards on the metal of the fridge. She pushed her chin to the ceiling, exposing her neck. I thought of the way Miguel had suckled there.

'He's all but blackmailing me.'

'Miguel?'

She looked down at me through her lashes. 'Yeah, Miguel. His bitch wife suspects, she's refusing to work and insisting they move to be with her family. And he's actually considering it.'

'Well, California is only a plane ride . . .'

'He's telling me they need cash because she's about to lose them their job. Says that if she knew about us, she'd be distraught. It would destroy her.'

'Well, that's understandable, isn't it?' I said, thinking of the woman's heart breaking.

'Jesus, Nic, it's just manipulation. He says he'd leave her, if I give him a commitment.'

Before I could question what kind of commitment, she began to pace.

'I'm not bankrolling him, sponsoring him or any of that shit. And saying that Danny needs protecting from the same kind of hurt his wife is feeling . . . well, I get it. I know what he's saying. Maybe I just report him, and his sister.'

She turned, opened the fridge and grabbed a beer, slamming it shut in frustration. 'He doesn't know Danny, doesn't know where we live, has no way of contacting him.'

I thought of mentioning the calls Catalina had sniggered over, that Miguel had the house number in his phone. Had she forgotten giving it to him? I wondered if this was why Danny was playing so fast and loose in the other room. Maybe he had picked the phone off the cradle before Miguel had had a chance to hang up, had understood.

'What can he do, really?' she continued. 'I've been careful so . . .'

Careful wasn't the word I was thinking as I watched her rip the ring-pull so that a froth of beer erupted over her newly polished nails.

'So . . . Danny knows?'

'No, Danny doesn't know,' she snapped. 'He's just happily inviting *people,*' this word laced with spite, 'over for lunch.'

'Come on,' I said. 'Be nice. And I thought it was your idea.'

She took a step closer in confidence. 'Because he knows the influencer from before, he felt we should return the invitation after that basic party of hers. Such a people pleaser. I didn't want her coming to a proper get-together here.'

She swigged from the can as I realised I had only been invited over to the house outside of the Buchanans' feted lawn parties and charity galas. Neither Gatsby or I were suitable for 'proper' company. T finished the beer and moved back to the fridge, asking if I wanted one as though just registering my presence. I nodded and she reopened the cooler, sighing with frustration into its pale light; telling me that she wasn't about to have cooking going on in this heat, even in the chef's kitchen, that she'd ordered lunch in from Daphne's. She handed me a frosty can and pulled the rest of the pack out to take to her husband.

'I suppose we better be sociable,' she grimaced. 'I can make this entertaining.'

When we entered the room, Gatsby was sitting demurely in a chair far away from Danny, as flushed as her dress.

He made a show of applauding our arrival, his eyes fixed obediently on T as he complained again about the temperature outside.

'The south shore will be cooler,' T noted, handing out beers. 'After we eat we could drive down there.'

'To bake on Jones Beach?' Danny shuddered. 'It'll be packed. And we have a beach here.'

The doorbell rang far away, signalling that lunch had arrived. T cocked her head like a guard dog and then handed a beer to Gatsby.

'We're slumming it with brewskis,' she said.

Gatsby took the beer but didn't open it. Though she drank occasionally, I suspected she didn't enjoy alcohol but wasn't about to ask for something different. She seemed fascinated by T, eyes clamped to her, travelling down to observe her shoes and up again to watch her hold court.

'Let's eat and work out what to do,' T said and motioned we should follow her. As we walked behind her like a school party to the shaded patio, Danny allowed his hand to brush Gatsby's. I gulped down my disapproval. T's heart might have been deceitful, but her displays of indiscretion were limited to third-party spaces. When we stepped out into the suffocating heat, the patio was dazzlingly bright, white shards of the sun glinting off the water.

As we approached the table, I looked towards Danny, anticipating him being upset by the spread on the white plates – the paper napkins, already almost damp, clearly stating the provenance of the seafood rolls, coleslaw, salads and wilting fries.

'Goddamn, it's hot,' he moaned instead, pulling out a chair for Gatsby. 'When will it break?'

I wondered why T had chosen to eat outside and could

only surmise a need to make her new guest feel itchy, warm, uncomfortable. And to demonstrate the choice location of her headland house on the correct side of the bay.

Jordan and I settled opposite Danny and Gatsby with T in her usual spot facing the water. The awnings stretched overhead seemed to groan under the weight of the sun, the scent of hot canvas mixing with the broiled rosemary in the garden and the softening, slipping batter in the rolls. Two beading bottles of chilled white wine sank incrementally into ice buckets in the centre of the table. T instructed Danny to open them, which he did, standing to regale us with a college tale of him and Jordan attempting to prise open a beer keg with various inappropriate tools. His musical baritone made an essentially eventless story amusing. When he sat down, his hand went without thought to Gatsby's shoulder in a touch of assurance, and she smiled at him with such fondness that I looked at T to see if she had noticed.

It was hard to tell. Though she seemed unusually alert to the twosome, she showed no sign of annoyance. Danny continued to entertain, talking about camping trips as he tossed flaccid fries into his mouth and topped up glasses, evangelising about the thrill of big skies, self-sufficiency and getting off-grid. He recalled a desert hot spring that offered nothing but warm, sulphur-smelling waters, a cold standpipe and an enclosed pit as a bathroom; a national forest campsite where nocturnal bears had prised the door of a parked car like a sardine can to get to a stashed tube of toothpaste; a hike through a rock tunnel to a jagged bay where he stayed overnight in a dewy sleeping bag. I thought of him and Gatsby watching those waves together. She looked down at her lap.

'We never camp now,' he sulked.

'Now you don't need to,' I pointed out.

'But I do,' he said earnestly.

'Ah, Danny – all for rustic escapes,' T nodded, pushing her plate away, her food barely touched. 'You never met a silent retreat or a "no-tech" cabin you didn't like.'

'A sign that says "no Wi-Fi and no devices" is talking my love language.' He smiled.

'Honey, that's great when you don't need to work,' T said lightly, but I was unsure even in replaying it immediately in my head whether she emphasised 'you' or 'need' in the sentence. Either way, she was gearing up to belittle him. The lobster roll was soggy when I bit into it.

'Danny has this dream about a bay house,' she informed the table. 'You know about these?'

I looked at Jordan and we both indicated no. Gatsby remained impassive.

'These crappy little cabins on stilts, built into mud,' she said, her face settling into a formation of disgust. 'Fishing, duck-hunting huts, no heat, no AC, can only get to them by boat . . .'

'Exactly!' Danny countered. 'Can only get to them by boat. Only thing you can get out there is a couple of bars of service.'

'But you can't get out there, can you?' T said sweetly. 'They're tied up in red tape, only local people can own them, no buy-ups, they're never for sale.'

'Absolute catnip then,' Jordan chuckled. 'Tell anyone you can't have something and they'll want it.'

'But that's not why,' Danny insisted. 'It's the getting away from it all. And they're historic buildings, charming, just hovering on the marshland. It's a simpler life – hey, you want to go?'

T groaned and Danny threw a frustrated hand towards her; 'You said the south shore would be cooler.'

'And I give you . . . Danny's latest project.' She laughed.

He leaned across the table towards us, his eyes shining.

'I know a guy, had to get in via the preservation society,' he enthused, his words speeding up. 'He's not supposed to rent out but we have an agreement. You want to go? It'll be like camping, it's a forty-five-minute drive, we could take a picnic, stay the night if you want, sleep under the stars . . .'

Jordan halted his assault. 'Danny, we get it.'

'It sounds absolutely idyllic,' Gatsby's clear voice floated over the table.

Danny turned back to her.

'You'd love it,' he nodded and the low tone of his affirmation was so familiar, so patently affectionate that T put her wine glass down with a bang. She stared at the two of them, their heads fractionally too close, recognised an understanding passing between them, downloaded the dynamic. She realised that a transference had occurred from herself to the woman from the house across the bay.

'Something you'll get bored with,' she said sharply. 'You always do.'

Danny turned his head towards his wife without decreasing the space between him and Gatsby.

'You'd love it,' he repeated to T, a deliberate flatness now in his delivery.

'You know I would not,' she replied, eyes locked with him.

The long pause before anyone spoke skittered towards the periphery of revelation. I expected an accusation, an outburst from T. It seemed to be a burning point. Instead she dampened the ignition.

'Maybe we should go,' she said, matching the expressionless cadence of her spouse. 'Why not? Call your guy.'

Danny was fluent in T's language and understood.

'You want to do this?' he asked her, stretching a leg beneath the table to allow him easier access to the pocket that held his phone.

Gatsby fixed on Danny with a look of hope on her face that made me pity her. The ice creaked in the bucket.

'What do *you* want, Jay?' T asked.

Gatsby smiled tentatively. 'If Danny loves it, I'm sure I will.'

T nodded, her eyes like embers. 'What Danny loves . . . An adventure then? Let's see where the day takes us.'

Danny took out his phone, scrolled his contacts.

'Is it a good idea?' I asked, knowing the answer. 'We've had beer, wine . . .'

'I'm good to drive and you—' T pointed at Gatsby—'you've hardly drunk.'

She had been watching more closely than I'd thought.

'And besides,' she said with bite, 'quaint pictures of shacks on the marsh, sunsets . . . this will give you a tonne of new content. That's how you make that money, right?'

Gatsby shifted uncomfortably in her seat.

'Let's do it!' Danny whooped, leaping to his feet. With his phone to his ear, his movements were no longer soporific in the unwavering temperature. He looked cool even as I felt my tacky skin against the chair as we all stood up. An imprint of the woven seat was pressed into the backs of my thighs like a brand. Danny's fingers, unconsciously or consciously, lingered on Gatsby as he rushed past her into the house, stirring the white drapes hanging defeated in the heat. Snatches of his cheerful voice making arrangements reached us from inside the house, curling like a tendril of smoke through the doors. T rose slowly and looked at each of us as though assessing, cradling her phone with intent. I looked away from her and at the table, noting that only the wine had been consumed. I thought of the number of animals who had expired for the uneaten debris left on the plates and contemplated once again that I should attempt veganism. Or vegetarianism. I wasn't sure which I could stick to.

'I'll get supplies together,' T said and dropped her napkin onto her abandoned lunch. As soon as she'd left the table, Gatsby spoke.

'She knows,' she stated, and there was a creeping excitement in her voice.

'She might,' I agreed.

'He has to tell her,' she continued, gripping the table as though hanging off the side of a building. Her fingers were white.

'Maybe not today,' Jordan suggested. Gatsby swallowed audibly.

'I'm really not sure about this,' I began. 'Maybe we shouldn't go . . .'

'Not sure there's a choice,' Jordan sighed and turned away, his vape pen in his mouth. He had checked out.

I looked back to Gatsby, her face turned to the house, waiting for Danny to return.

'We could go another time,' I suggested.

'I want to,' she murmured without adapting her pose. 'I want to see . . .'

'Maybe I don't want to,' I pressed back, wanting to bring her to her senses.

I'd seen T like this before. I understood what would come and I didn't want Gatsby to be the recipient. I felt guilt; I had placed her in this position as much as she had herself. I had encouraged her, facilitated her. And I had done it for the same reason I'd ingratiated myself into her life. Because I was curious and there was no risk for me. I had brought her into T's arena with no real thought for the consequences of sending an unarmed combatant into the fray. Now, as I smelt blood and sawdust, I wanted to release her from a fight that she would never win.

'I just don't think it's going to be . . .' I danced around a warning. 'I don't think we should go . . .'

Any further thoughts were cut off by T sweeping back outside, a straw hat now on her head and large, dark sunglasses obscuring her eyes.

'You're not wimping out, are you, Nic?' she chided irritably. 'The more the merrier. If we're going, we should set off.'

'T, what about another day? One not quite so . . .' I struggled for a suitable word. ' . . . fraught.'

'Fraught?' she repeated, and I sensed behind the glasses she was looking between Gatsby and me. She understood I sought to protect. I sensed rage.

'It's cool, it's cool,' Jordan said soothingly.

'It patently isn't, Jordan,' T replied tartly. 'It's ninety-three degrees in the shade.'

He cackled at her attempt to joke and it set something in motion.

'Let's go,' T commanded.

I complied. I couldn't decide if it was fear that made me put one foot in front of the other, or irrational bravado given I felt as culpable as Gatsby, as though I had cheated on T myself. I felt I should chaperone, attempt to insert myself between the two women, defend, deflect. I was in the Colosseum now and I had paid for my ticket to the show, I couldn't pretend that I was unaware of the incoming cruelty and sport. And like any sad, vile, unpleasant video of tragedy I saw on my phone, I knew I could not look away despite a 'graphic content' warning. I could tell myself I wanted no part of it, but not that I didn't want to see. For that I also felt contrition.

T's phone rang and remained unanswered in her bag as we passed through the house to the front steps, where a large cooler packed by the staff waited. We all paused on the top step, awaiting Danny, when T broke the silence, pointing to the bright yellow Range Rover parked in the drive. It had an iridescent sheen that made it look like a psychedelic toy of a car, designed to be driven by a doll.

'How did you even find a car in this colour?' T asked her guest, repulsed.

'Custom,' Gatsby replied. 'It's a happy colour to me.'

'*Does* it make you happy?' T smiled. 'I'd like to try it. Let's swap for today, for fun?'

Gatsby looked confused. 'But it's a stick shift,' she protested.

'Oh, you don't have to be English to be able to drive that.' T made a grabbing motion to prompt the handover of the keys. 'I'll take the gas guzzler, the booze and Danny, you all follow us there.'

'I don't know . . .' Gatsby wavered.

'Come on, live a little,' T ordered her. 'We should all be more Danny, right? Impetuous.'

She made the beckoning motion again. As though hypnotised, Gatsby scrabbled in her bag, handing her keys over to T's outstretched hand and accepted a set in return. Mrs Buchanan stalked over the crunching gravel towards the gleaming four-by-four.

'Bring the cooler,' she called over her shoulder.

Jordan obediently lifted the box just as Danny bounded out

of the door. His step faltered as he observed T leaning against the searing metal of the banana-hued vehicle, snapping selfies in a manner that felt designed to mock Gatsby's occupation.

'All set, he'll meet us at the dock,' he announced.

'Let's go!' T shouted from the driveway, opening the car door.

Danny's jaw clenched. He disliked the situation.

'Just wait,' he said before he jogged down the steps and over to his wife.

They talked fast, T's hat brim bobbing wildly as they spoke. Danny's hands found their way to his hips, a frown creased his smooth forehead. He leaned closer, said something with a hardness I hadn't seen in him before but seemed to settle the situation. He turned from T and returned to the bottom of the steps, holding his hand out to Gatsby like a Disney prince.

'You guys and the cooler go with T, more room,' he instructed. 'Follow us. Jay, come with me.'

His designated passenger's expression was unreadable but she didn't take his hand, instead nodding sharply and descending to the drive to pass him and walk towards T's waiting car. Danny watched her go.

'What happened?' Jordan asked quietly.

'Nothing,' Danny dismissed him with a smile, putting his sunglasses on and following Gatsby. I wondered what he might have said to insist on this arrangement and considered that the power dynamic of the marriage might be more nuanced than I assumed.

'Nothing yet . . .' I noted as Jordan let the cooler slide back to the floor. It was clearly heavier than he expected. I looked at him, seeking solidarity.

'We're in it now,' he winced, just as T leaned on the horn of the Range Rover, her annoyance blasting us and the unsuspecting gardener pruning the browning roses in the front yard.

We hurried to the car. The metal of the bodywork scorched our hands as we released the trunk and loaded the cooler. We both got in the backseat like unwilling children, snapping our seat belts as Danny sped past us in the turning circle. His passing profile looked at ease. I expected T to race behind him, not allowing him out of her sight, but she sat a minute longer typing into a social app on her phone before throwing it onto the passenger seat and crunching the gears. We lurched away, the transmission screeching.

Watching her through the rear-view mirror, I wondered when, and at who, T might aim her bite. The AC bellowed through the vents as we headed south to Point Lookout; the well-watered shrubs of East Egg turning into suburban streets and then giving way to the pale highway. The surface of the road created a rhythmic percussion as we drove, too fast and in silence. Unlocking my phone, I clicked onto T's account and scrolled through the pictures she'd posted, leaning against the yellow paintwork of the car, the camera positioned to expose her cleavage, the words declaring she had a 'new ride'. Miguel had liked the post. I tilted the screen towards Jordan and he raised an eyebrow.

'Ride,' he mouthed, a smirk playing on his lips. I hit his thigh in silent rebuke.

I knew how to play T's game. I waited for the heavy quiet to be punctuated.

'Well, today has been full of surprises,' she finally said after half an hour, enunciating every word as we flew across a green bridge elevated above a channel of brackish water.

I allowed the comment to hang with no response as Jordan looked dispassionately out of the window.

'I have a couple of my own,' she promised.

There was little point in replying. My seatbelt cut too high against my neck and I tried to pull it to loosen the pressure, my jabbing inevitably trapping me tighter as the struggle incapacitated me further.

'Let's just try to have a nice time,' I appealed hopelessly as the dock came into view beyond the shimmering, silver road.

Chapter 18

When we pulled into the baking parking lot Danny and Gatsby were already on the side of the dock, their clothes rippling around them in the promised south-shore breeze. They were looking down at a man in a shallow boat who moved his battered baseball cap backwards and forwards on his head as he spoke. T parked the despised yellow car alongside her own muted vehicle at the far corner of the lot. When we joined Danny and Gatsby the man eyed us suspiciously and asked if we were 'summer people' to T's evident annoyance. Her answer didn't seem to dissuade him from his misgivings as he instructed us to get into his vessel, his accent as flat as the hull.

'Sleepin' out there?' he asked Danny, as we gingerly boarded.

Danny wobbled his head as he handed over a number of folded notes. We'd see, he said, there'd be extra for coming out late. We found space to sit on the greasy seats, the scent of fish and gasoline overpowering. An inch of dank water slopped from left to right on the floorboards, giving the impression the boat was sinking. As the man's browned arm tugged at the outboard motor, his washed-thin T-shirt rose to show a line of exposed white skin where his pants dragged down. I wondered if we might be spared this adventure as the engine failed to catch, once, twice. But just as I opened my mouth to suggest a rain check the metal casement quaked and roared with the third violent pull. The murky water behind it churned and we moved away from the concrete dock. The engine spluttered as it belched out fumes and a silver vapour, chugging us through the moored, bobbing boats towards the marshland waters. At full power the volume and register of it mercifully prevented any conversation.

I turned towards the prow and watched the emerald islands and channels that passed like a maze of neural pathways, enjoying the salty taste of the wind against my warm face. At first we passed other boats of torpid fishermen anchored to muddy banks, their lines undulating in the water as they watched for a bite. Then the mainland faded into a paint stripe between sea and sky behind us, and the marsh islands became wilder, uninhabited. We were alone.

It took twenty minutes to disconnect from the mainland, drift into the dark strait where the bay house squatted. When we arrived, it was a structure so simple it might have been transposed from a child's drawing of a home. A square, weatherbeaten wooden cabin with a sharp triangle of a roof, a central door that had once been red, and two windows either side; it had a deck surrounding it and a gangplank half submerged in the water that bobbed on the waves as we drew alongside. A sun-bleached star-spangled banner flapped heavily as though exhausted on a flagpole; faded chairs and a blackened grill were scattered across the splintered desk. The boatman killed the engine, and we floated queasily alongside the mooring as he tied off on a sturdy telegraph pole submerged in the mud. He turned back to us and motioned for us to exit as the water slapped against the bow.

'Is there power?' Jordan asked doubtfully, his athletic grace deserting him as he stumbled in the boat, trying to disembark.

'Generator,' our captain barked. 'Enough to keep your beer cold.'

After Jordan and Danny had made the leap and teetered together as they pulled the cooler from the boatman's mahogany fist, we three followed. I clambered from the shifting vessel to the moving gangplank and hurried to the deck after T, leaving a wavering, wet footprint trail behind me. Gatsby, her rose-coloured dress tucked up high to give her better mobility, managed the manoeuvre with poise. She held her arms away from her body as if walking a balance beam, her step sure. She joined the group on the relative stability of the deck which felt like safety even as it creaked under our weight. Our skipper was speeding back the way we'd come before I even turned to wave goodbye. We all stood and surveyed the shack, shading eyes from the sun, still fierce even as it dropped.

'Rustic,' T spat as Danny jiggled the lock, trying to find the sweet spot as he half-turned the key and lifted the door with the worn handle.

He looked warm for the first time today as he struggled, cursing under his breath, employing the pressure of his toe against the warped wood. When he found the bite and the key turned, he whooped and allowed the door to swing open wonkily on its jamb. He turned to us and spread his arms wide in triumph.

'Off the grid!' he enthused, grabbing the cooler from Jordan and entering.

As we remained on the deck, the windows on either side of the door slid up with a slam and the mosquito whir of a fan began inside. The group filed gingerly inside but I delayed stepping into the shadows behind them. On all sides of the house there was nothing but marsh grass, the only sign of humanity the distant drone of traffic on the highway bridge. There was a kiss of a breeze, not much but more than at the Buchanan estate. Everything outside the house was chipped and mismatched: the wood bleached pale by the elements, a life ring so battered it would surely help no poor soul in difficulty.

When I entered the hut all four were slouched in assorted chairs, breathing shallow breaths, as though attempting to use as little energy as possible. The fan in the corner clattered as it oscillated weakly. I sank onto the arm of the shabby chintz armchair that Jordan was almost lying in, careful not to touch his body; it was too hot to tolerate. Gatsby sat on one end of a small, stained sofa, while T melted at the other. Only Danny moved, loading the ancient refrigerator and talking about the origins of the house, the fishermen who'd harvested the grasses for hay when they weren't clamming or fishing, the way the properties could only be handed down to family. Gatsby and T watched him as he flitted round the room, throwing bags of chips on the scratched table, pressing beers and bourbon chasers in cloudy glasses into our feeble hands. He paused to lean against the open door, gulping the outside air in a satisfied way. He was a dark shape against the yellow light.

'You like?' he asked over his shoulder, and swallowed his measure of bourbon.

He clearly expected a response from either Gatsby or T, but neither spoke.

'I don't see the point,' I responded honestly, knowing this would prick him. I couldn't understand the allure of a grubby shack with fewer amenities than the ramshackle cabin at the bottom of his lawn used only by the gardener for compost and sneaky cigarettes. He could have easily built his own version of this on his beach in East Egg rather than rent by the hour from a man who transparently thought him a wealthy fool. 'What do you do out here that you can't do at home? You don't fish.'

Danny pouted slightly. He was used to me as an ally and I heard in my tone the cynicism of T. I grinned at him to make clear that I meant no spite. T laughed at him and Jordan sighed. Gatsby remained silent, her long legs crossed, her body alert. She pushed her glass of spirits onto the table untouched.

'It's real,' Danny appealed. 'It forces you to be present. Just you and nature. It . . . makes you honest.'

'Well, some of us are in trouble then,' T said and I had to agree. None of us were honest. 'And,' she sniffed, reaching out to stroke the lopsided sideboard with an appraising finger, 'I prefer my reality a little more hygienic.'

'I love it,' Danny insisted.

'It's fine,' Jordan attempted to mollify.

'I get it,' Gatsby smiled radiantly, looking at Danny.

He held her eyes before he looked down for a guilty moment to break the connection, but then snapped his focus back to her as though he couldn't stop himself. He smiled back.

'What's your plan, Danny?' T asked, forcing him to look at her.

Her legs lolled apart, pulling her skirt taut against her thighs. She wiped her upper lip with the back of her hand

and her impressive engagement ring flashed. He gave her his easy smile too.

'Hang out, stay off our phones . . .' He looked back out across the dazzling water. 'Guys, come out here and get into it,' he entreated.

Jordan pulled himself to his feet, grabbed the liquor bottle from the table and threw a brotherly arm round Danny's neck. They moved outside; their confident voices and the buzz of their chatter lured us to join them. Gatsby and I drifted out into the oven temperature and sat on the scorching boards dangling our feet into the cool water, her tanned knee bumping against mine. She bowed her head towards me and told me she appreciated the remoteness of the house because she would not be photographed, recognised, observed, then she looked up at Danny as though he had gifted her the power of invisibility. T stayed inside, but as the heat blunted, she followed and pulled the loungers in a more orderly line. She watched unmoved as Danny and Jordan boisterously stripped to their underwear and took turns scaling a rickety rail to jump into the depths, enjoying the splashes they forced onto the deck and us. As they clambered back up, slippery with salt, they chugged shots and egged each other on to more extravagant bombs, somersaults and dives like sugar-rush children.

'Be careful!' Gatsby called, pointlessly, as they dunked each other and wrestled, thrashing the water like a shark attack. They enjoyed the audience.

As the sun dipped further, they calmed and dried on the deck. We passed bottles, chips and soda back and forth. Alcohol had blurred the awkwardness of earlier and, for me, made the hut appear more – to use Gatsby's word – idyllic.

It felt like an escape. I now hardly cared how stained the lounger I lay on was.

'The sunsets are magnificent,' Danny assured us, pointing towards the apricot horizon where the sliver of a silver moon already hung. He circled the group refilling glasses with bourbon.

'To friends?' he suggested, holding up his glass, before throwing back the bronze liquid. We all followed suit, the burn sliding down my throat prompting a cough, but the increasingly pliant feeling it induced made me hold out my glass for more. Danny readily refilled.

'Bottoms up!' Gatsby said effusively but didn't drink.

'Oh, chin chin!' T mimicked Gatsby, curling her tongue around the mockery of an English accent. She looked at her spouse. 'Sit down, Danny,' she ordered and when he didn't, she patted the bench she was sitting on. 'Honey,' she said more sternly.

He looked at her with a frown and disobeyed, unfolding his long limbs into the lounge chair next to Gatsby instead. He tipped the chair back to almost lying and wriggled slightly as though settling in a feather bed.

'And relax . . .' he drawled, a trace of teasing in his voice.

Ordinarily, it would be appealing, but his insouciant tone seemed a gamble given the circumstances. It felt like bait. I monitored T's response. 'Okay,' she said. She reached out to grab the bottle and poured herself a large measure.

'So where did you and Jay meet again? I'm a little hazy,' she asked, pushing her sunglasses up her nose.

'School, baby,' Danny murmured vaguely, closing his eyes.

T turned to Gatsby.

'And you were there from England. I love London. But where are you from? Exactly?'

The tone of it sounded convivial but my heart sank. I had been optimistic to think this was an absconsion; it was a trap. Gatsby smiled at her and leaned forward.

'Oh, a little town you won't have heard of,' she replied with a shake of her head. Danny stirred and looked at her too tenderly, his chin down, his eyes soft.

'Try me,' T said encouragingly, sitting back in her chair, removing her sunglasses to better observe her rival. 'I travel a lot for work.'

'Well, not from any one place, really,' Gatsby shrugged. 'Lived all over the home counties.'

'And Oxbridge you said?'

'Oxford, yes . . .'

'But which college?' T prodded.

'Who cares which college?' I asked and shot a look at Danny to urge him to a rescue, but he continued to loll, his admiring gaze on Gatsby.

'Because I have friends who went there and they might recall you,' T explained. 'But maybe not. You were not this,' she added a minute pause, '*celebrity* then.'

'Magdalen,' Gatsby replied quickly. 'But it wasn't for me. I transferred out.'

'To Santa Cruz,' T nodded. 'To major in?'

Gatsby's smile widened, she put down her glass. It slopped slightly, glazing her fingers. She wiped them against her skirt leaving damp fingermarks.

'Listen, this is all on my Wiki page,' she replied coolly. 'What do you really want to know?'

T leaned forward too, her eyes glittered.

'I only want to get to know you better,' she purred.

'Because you're quite the enigma. I did read your page but the press doesn't seem satisfied by that.'

'They're always writing crap, right?' I said quickly.

Gatsby looked at me and nodded.

'A journalist friend of mine is very conscientious. She's like a dog with a bone. And when she checked she could find no record of you studying at either Oxford or Santa Cruz. In fact, it's hard to find evidence of you anywhere you say you've been.'

Danny craned his neck, suddenly alert. 'So?'

Gatsby took a sip from her cracked glass. It felt out of character, but she was attempting to match T's energy.

'Oh, I'm afraid there wouldn't be,' she said evenly. 'I didn't complete at Oxford. I was an exchange student at Santa Cruz. I was only there five months so . . .' She looked back up at T. 'But education doesn't really matter in real life, does it?'

'Only if you don't finish anything you start,' T smiled. She sat back as though that closed the conversation. I waited for a rush of relief but it didn't come.

'Hey, does anyone want anything to eat?' Danny asked, his attention now back on his wife, his eyes serious.

'Or shall we play a game? I think I saw cards inside,' I asked.

'We don't need cards,' T dismissed our diversion tactics. 'We can make our own games.'

Danny leaned up on his elbows. 'T,' he said quietly.

'Danny, I just want to get to know your friend,' she told him without shifting her concentration from Gatsby.

'I want that too,' Gatsby cooed.

'Danny tells me so little about you, so I had to go, well, digging . . .'

'Oh gosh, you can just ask,' Gatsby said, but there was a quiver in her voice.

'I'm just doing due diligence, sweetie. I need to crunch the data, do the analysis, before I invest . . .'

'This isn't the stock market,' I snapped, my scalp prickly with cooling sweat despite the temperature. 'This isn't about money.'

'Don't be disingenuous – everything is about money,' T scolded. 'Gatsby can attest to that. Can't you?'

'What money?' Gatsby asked.

Danny sat up in his lounger. 'T,' he implored, 'come on . . .'

'Come on?' she repeated. 'You want to know about the money. I know you do.'

'T, stop it!' I interjected. 'Everybody has secrets.'

T She looked at me, malice in her eyes. 'Don't they, Nic. Quite the summer you've been having.'

The cold rush of discovery washed over me. I feared that she would now choose to unleash her ferocious displeasure for my having known about Danny. And when I looked quickly at him, I thought of his disappointment in me if he knew all the confidences I had kept; for her, for Miguel. She watched me sink back in my chair, triumphant. I was too cowardly to say more.

Danny breathed through his nose and shook his head.

'I just want to have a good time,' he sighed.

'And that's the problem with you, Danny, you only ever want a good time. You never think about the fallout, the consequences, the shame . . .'

'Shame!' He was out of his chair now, his still-damp underwear clinging to him, his hair slick and his eyes blazing. 'You want to talk about shame? Want to talk about the guy in the city? A broker? Your assistant? Who is it?'

'And what about *her*?' T's withering cool counterweighted Danny's heat. 'Couldn't she find her type on Bumble?'

Jordan raised calming hands. 'Hey, hey, hey! We don't need to get into it. This should be a private conversation between you guys.'

'I don't know how it's private when everyone here seems to be involved,' T snipped.

I avoided her eyes. My silence and Jordan's confirmed everything. I looked instead at Gatsby – her chin was up and her eyes narrow. I had never seen her look this way. She shook her hair behind her shoulders and sat up straighter. The hint of a smile played across her lips as she reached for her glass again.

'So now you know,' she said, satisfied. The secret she had wanted out was now exposed, wriggling on the deck between us all.

T laughed. A bark. The short cruel one.

'Oh, I do know. I know everything about you.' She pulled the bottle of whiskey towards her across the table, making an unpleasant sound.

'I'm sure you think you do,' Gatsby said. 'We can all scroll through Twitter.'

'Mmm hmm,' T hummed. She watched Gatsby try to engage Danny in her most luminous eye contact. He did not look her way.

'Let's just take a break on this,' Danny suggested evenly. 'We didn't come out here to talk shit, right?'

'Does Danny know?' T asked, fixing on Gatsby's face. Even though she addressed her husband next, she didn't stop looking at his mistress. 'Dan, do you know everything about your friend?'

Danny groaned her name again but T was not to be dissuaded.

'Remember Lucille McKee?' T asked and Gatsby seemed physically to shrink.

I couldn't tell if she was nervous, anxious or something else. A shard of disappointment pierced me. I wanted her to be magnificent in this moment.

'I've been talking to my friend at the *New Yorker* about a story they're currently putting together. About a social media star who trades on her love of the sisterhood and her British charm but has, well, neither of those things.'

'Tom!' Danny snapped. 'Enough!'

Gatsby clasped her glass in front of her like a chalice. She didn't respond, but she blinked quickly.

'Not from England at all, correct? A US army brat from—' T paused and made her next words as contemptuous as possible '– the Midwest.'

Gatsby licked her lips. 'Like I said, I lived all over the place,' she said steadily.

'Not British, not an Oxford grad, not a Santa Cruz student. Just a flyover-states girl with a fake accent.'

'Wait, you're not British?' I heard myself say. A scattered puzzle started to come together in my brain. I thought about Gatsby's idiolect and old-fashioned way of speaking. It sounded learnt. She looked at me, her expression unreadable.

'Does it matter?' Danny asked urgently. I wondered if this was news to him.

'That stuff? Not really. Not the first to fake a past,' T shrugged. 'I mean the followers and the sponcon might not like it. But the victim procurement and cover-up for the predator husband? Well, that's career-ending.'

'I didn't . . .' Gatsby protested.

'You knew all about what he did, didn't you?' T continued, swilling her alcohol in her glass in a lazy tidal wave. 'Two of the women Dan Cody attacked were your assistants, a detail you paid very generously to keep between you and the victims. One assistant being abused was bad enough, the access he had to her because of you. But to then appoint a second girl without changing a thing? Well, Lucille McKee has decided to say fuck you to your NDA.'

Gatsby stood, her dress fluttering against her in the hint of a breeze. 'I don't need to justify myself,' she said quietly.

'You might after the weekend, sweetie,' T replied with relish. She didn't move, just tilted her chin to Gatsby. 'And you might find you can't afford that big house without the sponsors, the partners. But then, you don't own the house or anything in it. Just like the products you promise to send to your disappointed followers, it's all a bit of an illusion, isn't it? I probably shouldn't give you the benefit of a heads up, but I suspect you don't have the funds to brief a legal team anyway.'

'We've had shipping issues,' Gatsby hit back. 'And I own plenty.' She looked at Danny imploringly. 'I own plenty.'

'You *owe* plenty, that's for sure,' T laughed.

Danny moved to stand then. He was clumsy getting up and manoeuvring himself in front of Gatsby, attempting to shield her from his wife's unwavering, unsympathetic stare. 'T, enough,' he said weakly.

She smiled pityingly. 'Awwww, that's sweet. And look, if we're all bringing our side action to this camp-out, maybe I'll ask a friend of mine to join too.'

'Shit,' Jordan hissed as though he'd just witnessed a game-changing shot on the golf course. I gave him a disapproving look. It glanced off him.

'Come on,' I interjected. 'Let's calm this down . . .'

'What are you doing?' Danny asked, trying for disgust in

his tone but sounding more akin to desperate. 'T, what are you doing?'

'Guys . . .' Jordan began, rising from his seat.

'Shhh,' T hissed at him, putting a mocking finger to her lips. 'You can sit down, Jordan.'

I should have tried to stop it but when she was like this, T was impressive, potent. Jordan didn't sit, but he said no more. We were not protagonists or even a Greek chorus; the intention was that we remained the audience.

'What are we doing?' Danny repeated, his hand now rubbing the back of his neck. And I saw his nerve evaporate.

'I don't know, Danny, what's the plan here?' T raised herself to her full height, her shoulders back, matching her husband physically. It was the same question she'd asked earlier but now it pricked. 'Is it just for the summer? Or just for tonight?'

Gatsby's hand grasped Danny's shoulder. She moved closer behind him and said his name like a prayer.

'It's not like that . . .' he began. He didn't sound convinced.

'It always is,' T insisted. 'Whatever the distraction.'

'I'm not a distraction,' Gatsby snapped, stepping out to one side. 'If anything, you are.'

'I'm his wife,' T smirked.

'And he's been in love with me since Santa Cruz,' Gatsby said with defiance. Her accent flattened on the town name, no longer making the 't' distinct. It was jarring. She pressed her body back against Danny, her jaw jutted out. She was intransigent, crackling with a new energy that seemed to erupt from deep within her.

'You're the distraction,' she stated. 'You're the one who might have to rethink after the weekend.'

'Oh darling,' said T consdescendingly, employing one of Gatsby's favoured expressions. 'I don't think so.'

Gatsby whipped around to face Danny. His head was already lowered.

'Tell her,' she entreated him.

He shook his head, mouth moving as he sought the words.

'Tell her that you're leaving her. Tell her you were always in love with me.'

'I was . . .' He looked like he might be on the verge of tears.

'And you never loved her,' Gatsby prompted.

'Baby,' he exhaled and looked up at the darkening sky. She squeezed his arm, tried to connect to his eyes, but he went back to staring at the floor again.

'She's nothing. We're everything,' she urged, her accent continuing to migrate, her eyes filling. It was like watching a nature documentary and knowing the outcome was sure. A strong predator, an injured animal. Prey.

'Jesus Christ, this isn't *The Notebook*,' T snorted. 'Well, Danny? You want to throw everything away for someone who will be cancelled by Monday?'

I hated to admit it, but T had a point. Whatever he felt for Gatsby the wave of disapproval heading for her would be difficult to ride out if the *New Yorker* article was real. He was not a man who tried hard at anything. And commitment to her in the wake of such an exposé would be life-changing. I could hardly imagine him being allowed to work with his beloved kids in Queens if he was with someone who was accused of protecting a sex offender. He would struggle to walk into the drawing rooms and gardens of the East Egg community with the same easy grace he did now.

'Can we leave this?' I asked, straining for reason. 'We're all hot and . . .'

'It's not going to be a good look for you, Danny,' T cautioned him as though she sympathised.

He looked pained and his chest goose-fleshed as Gatsby's grip tightened on his bicep.

'You can't believe her,' Gatsby insisted.

But it was clear in the way his Adam's apple bobbed as he swallowed and the clenched way he stood, his muscles contracted as if he was withstanding a strong current, that he did believe T. He could envisage the consequences.

'I can explain everything,' Gatsby pleaded, her voice raspy with unshed tears. 'Danny . . .'

She tried to turn his face to her, her palm against his cheek but his eyes found T even as Gatsby bent his jaw to hers.

'I think,' he said, finding his way through the sentence and only glancing at Gatsby. The gentle attention he'd given her earlier now seemed sharp, cursory. 'I think we need to go home.'

'To which home?' T asked.

He looked at her, stricken. 'Please . . .' he whispered and I couldn't tell if he was asking forgiveness or mercy. His face was painted gold as he looked away towards the sun, a fat yolk on the edge of the sea, about to slip into oblivion.

'Poor Danny hates confrontation,' T said scornfully. 'But he forgets that I fucking thrive on it.'

'I want to go too,' Gatsby said decisively, tugging at Danny's inert arm. 'Danny, let's go.'

He looked from his wife to his lover, cheeks pink, his two different lives fluctuating before him. Gatsby tried to captivate him with shining eyes, a tear on her lashes. She groped for that past moment of certainty, hoped to see a pledge in his countenance. His eyes were fight-or-flight navy and ambivalent.

'Go,' T invited him.

I couldn't help but marvel at Mrs Buchanan's belief in herself and her world. Even now, with her husband in another's arms, she was convinced of the outcome. And with a feeling of sadness, so was I. He could not, would not take the risk. Whatever promises had been made would not be honoured. I felt pain for Gatsby even as she glimmered with hope. There was nothing to be done. T knew it too. Turning to the water, she threw her glass high in the sky, the convex surface catching the light momentarily before plunging into the now dark channel. It disappeared with a plop, barely a splash.

'That's not ours,' Danny said dolefully.

'Buy a new set,' T snapped. 'They need them.'

She walked to the other side of the deck, leaned against the railing and withdrew. She had inflicted enough injury.

'Call the boat guy,' Gatsby begged, turning Danny away from Jordan and me. He was rigid in her grasp.

'We should all go,' I offered, moving towards them and putting a hand on her shoulder. She was clammy through the silk.

'Let them go first,' T called, overruling me.

This was her final humiliation. A victor's mercy in allowing them to spend the journey back together, never to travel the same road again after tonight. Danny looked over his shoulder at his wife. I saw what Gatsby seemed unwilling to. That he may leave with her, but that he was not leaving.

'Call him,' Gatsby appealed, her lips grazing his ear, the request meaning more than the words she said. She might as well have begged 'choose me'. It seemed to anger him.

He pulled away from her, snatched his clothes from the chair and thrust his hand in a pocket feeling for his phone. Once located he grabbed her roughly by her arm.

'Inside,' he ordered, pushing her towards the door. Gatsby's elegance was gone as she tripped ahead of him.

'You wanted raw and real,' T crowed as Gatsby disappeared inside. 'You got it.'

Danny paused in the doorway.

'You spoiled everything,' he said quietly, a furious catch in his voice, his eyes burning.

'I have spoiled nothing.'

When he had gone inside the cabin, I turned to T, my hands spread to denote exasperation.

'This place stinks,' she sniffed, 'I don't know what he gets out of it.'

She slapped her shin sharply, killing one of the many twilight bugs that now began to bite.

'Did you really invite Miguel?' I asked in a hushed tone.

Surely even T wouldn't want more drama than this. She looked at me with uninterested eyes.

'I have questions too,' she said. 'Nice of you to tell me about this.'

'I didn't know how.'

She nodded. 'Right.'

'We were in an impossible position …'

'No. You two were watching the show. Enjoy it?'

I shook my head. Jordan remained silent. The deck light flickered on and off above, a stuttering beacon responding to the blanket of dusk. For a moment she seemed like an early film reel, every other second of her movement illuminated as she stretched her arms above her head like a waking cat.

Eventually the light stayed constant, a wan yellow beam casting shadows. Nightfall had come.

'I hope she fucking drowns on the way back,' T muttered.

'You don't need to be so cruel.'

'Oh Nic,' she said with contempt, 'I know you're in love with both of them, but shut the fuck up.'

Both Jordan and I knew better than to parry with her at this juncture. She hadn't even used her sharpest arsenal to puncture Gatsby and I knew once she had a taste for it, she would be sliding through cool waters looking for more blood. The lovers remained inside, their voices humming through the open window as they talked quietly and desperately. The three of us outside stared at the horizon, now a golden sliver between sky and sea, a pinprick of light bobbing on the waves towards us.

'He's coming,' Jordan said.

I reached for the bottle on the table. I filled my glass, unsure of how accurate I was being in the half light, handing the bottle on to Jordan. He took an anaesthetising pull.

'Should we go in?' I whispered in his ear as he gulped again.

He caught my chin between his thumb and forefinger as though he would kiss me, held my head steady so I took in the reply.

'Absolutely not.'

Instead, we sat watching the light of the boat approaching, waited for our personal Charon to arrive at the dock and usher two souls away. When the man's voice called out through the darkness, T rapped against the wooden wall, summoning the inhabitants back to the deck.

'Can't we all go together?' I asked T, my desire to leave

overriding the uncomfortable half hour we would have to spend in the boat with Gatsby's heart shattering.

'He needs to finish it alone,' she said. 'I can't do everything for him.'

Danny's hair was dishevelled now as he exited. He carried a half-drunk bottle of vodka in one hand and held his lover's pale fingers in the other. Gatsby looked aghast. Without acknowledging any of us, he towed her to the gangplank, a steadying hand on her hips as she entered the boat, his mouth a grimace.

T called his name and he looked at her expectantly. Perhaps he hoped for reprieve. She dangled Gatsby's set of car keys.

'I'm not driving this home,' she said with venom.

He cursed under his breath and stepped back out of the boat, stomping on the wooden deck planks, snatching the keys from her fingers. He threw T's back at her. She caught them without effort.

'Have her drop you off at home,' she called as he climbed back aboard, smashing his shin on the side. He swore again.

'Just us,' he told the man, his voice rough, wobbling slightly as the boat turned away, its guiding light now pointed towards the shore. We watched them be enveloped by the dark, Gatsby and Danny sitting on either side of the boat, weighing it evenly.

Now that they were out of earshot and the whiskey had made me braver, I felt more comfortable asking questions with more hurtful answers.

'Was that true?' I asked T as she watched the boat diminish.

'Which part?'

'All of it.'

'That she's an army brat from North Dakota? That she affects an English persona? Yes.' T shrugged. 'That she knew about the vile husband? Maybe. How would I know.'

'That she'll be ruined? They're really doing an exposé?'

She tore her focus from the water. 'It's one of the stories they're working on. She'll get twenty-four hours to respond. But she probably won't – well, not in a way that will matter anyway.'

'She never categorically said she was British, she just probably picked up a bit of an accent from living there,' I reasoned, feeling like a child arguing for the existence of Santa. 'People do.'

A patronising smile curled across T's lips. 'Or, y'know, maybe she's just another con artist about to get a Netflix documentary.'

Part of me wondered if Danny hadn't dangled Gatsby in front of his haughty wife like a shiny penny to prompt her jealousy, that this might be a pattern in their displays of affection. My next question escaped my mouth almost before I was actively aware of forming it.

'Has this happened before?'

I felt a queasiness as T turned to me. I'd never seen hurt settle on her features, but she looked pinched.

'Danny's something of a . . .' She looked away. 'An omnivore.'

She must have read the dismay on my face.

'So what?' Her voice carried through the dark, her sneering tone back.

'This has been wild, T,' Jordan said, attempting to close the conversation down and I realised, as I should have before, that he already knew. 'We should get the stuff together.'

'Just leave it here,' T said. 'They might have use of it.'

I was surprised by her act of generosity until she added, 'Besides it'll just bring the stink home.'

In the distance, the boat light had been lost in the braille of the shore illuminations as the darkening air grew thick with insects. Jordan batted them away, but T sat almost immobile except for her thumb, pushing the blue light of her phone screen through a series of messages. The deathly pall of the light on her face made her seem ghostly. Aware I was watching her, she looked up, leaned over and grabbed the whiskey bottle from me, glugging from it.

I suddenly wanted nothing more than to be alone, away even from Jordan. I felt that I could trust none of the people I'd ridden in the boat with – each had disappointed me. I disliked seeing cruelty, but cowardice (including my own) left a more acrid taste. I wanted to draw a line under everything that had been said, the inevitable ending that we'd witnessed. We scanned the indigo shadows over the water for our deliverance, waiting to return to the shore.

Chapter 19

We saw the flashing blue emergency lights on the dock from some distance out. Our captain was none the wiser about what calamity had happened as he was chugging towards his bay house for the third time in a handful of hours. When we finally sloshed alongside the dock and climbed the slimy ladder, it was clear from the white sheet tent in the parking lot and the orange evidence triangles dotted in a line towards the exit that a loss of life had occurred.

As the boatman tied off our vessel a stranger approached, giddy with excitement, his shorts riding up between his chafing thighs, worn sandals slapping the ground with each hasty step. He hailed his compatriot in a gurgling fountain of words in his eagerness to convey knowledge.

'He's drunk,' the boatman chuckled.

We stood on the jetty, sea legs and alcohol slowing our grasp of solid ground, and tried to understand the man's chatter. We gathered there'd been some sort of hit-and-run near the parking lot egress, the victim's arm nearly torn from his body in the collision, his neck twisted in a grotesque fashion. When a passerby had run to the victim's aid on hearing the crunch of bone and metal, he'd been unable to help. He knelt in blood, attempting to close the dead man's surprised eyes.

'Didn't even slow,' the inebriated man babbled as we stood with our backs to the water, watching cops set up lights. 'Drunk driver,' he nodded sagely, 'hasta be.'

'Let's get out of here,' I suggested, disliking the faces of the onlookers who strained against each other to impart information to two officers, their eyes and camera phones on the tent and a dark stain on the asphalt that was labelled with a triangle identifying it as number 5 in a series of tiny tragedies.

'Who was killed?' Jordan asked the man. 'Do they know?'

'Not local,' he said.

'Jesus,' T groaned, 'Can we even get our car out of here?'

She set off towards an officer, her posture erect, projecting sober, upright citizenship. As she approached him, she pointed to her marooned car in the furthest corner of the lot. The officer turned his head to speak with her, his annoyance with the rubberneckers replaced with a courteous smile for the tall, wealthy woman breezing in from a boat trip.

The cop nodded and pointed to the outer edge of the parking lot, swiping his arm across as he detailed the route she should take to leave and avoid the carnage. T nodded and was about to turn back when she froze.

'Come on, T,' Jordan grumbled, 'let's go. We can watch this crap on the news.'

He wasn't observing her like I was. I felt the black-feathered shadow of intuition when she turned to face us, the beginnings of panic rising in her features. She moved away and caught the arm of a bystander who was gesticulating to other gawkers, one hand mimicking a speeding vehicle, his other an inverted victory sign denoting a person. She spoke to him urgently and Jordan yawned beside me. The man pointed to another car in the lot, a battered Trans Am parked a few spaces away. Its side mirror was duct-taped to the body of the car, its roof mottled and dimpled. As she looked, T's face changed to the sort of distraught expression I might have expected her to wear on learning her husband was in love with someone else. She looked uncharacteristically out of control, stepping backwards from the man as though she'd been winded. She beckoned us towards her, away from the boatman.

'Are you okay?' I asked as we approached.

'We can leave,' she said stiffly. 'We're good.'

She stalked ahead of us, leading us across the parking area, the sound of a helicopter approaching accompanying our walk to the car. T was striding now, she was hurrying.

'What's wrong?' I asked, taking her elbow, feeling for the first time today that she was truly vulnerable.

I realised, like a panicked child observing a scared parent, that I relied on her strength. That I could not understand her any other way. She swore low under her breath, snatched her arm away and unlocked the car. We slammed the doors shut on the misfortune across the lot. Just as we had travelled there in Gatsby's car, we assumed our seats again; Jordan and I in the back, T in the driving position. I didn't dare ask anything further as she sat focusing on her phone with shaky hands, deleting pictures and posts, her breathing ragged. When the interior light automatically dimmed, Jordan leaned forward between the front seats.

'What?' he asked warily. She continued her task.

'What has happened?' I pushed, feeling this, whatever it was, involved all of us. 'T, please tell us?'

'Miguel. It's Miguel,' she hissed.

'Miguel who?' Jordan asked, but there was a falling sensation in my gut before he reached the end of his question. The sense of foreboding that began the minute we stepped back on land consolidated.

'The guy under the sheet,' she said bitterly.

'What?' I gasped, even as I understood entirely that Miguel had been felled. He lay still haemorrhaging on the asphalt across the lot. I suddenly recalled one of the tattoos on his forearm with adrenaline-fuelled clarity.

'Who's Miguel?' Jordan asked with increasing annoyance. I put a stalling hand on his knee.

'How do you know?' I asked urgently. 'You don't know that.'

She pointed at the car in the centre of the investigation, police tape radiating from it like a maypole.

'I told him where we were. I didn't know he'd come,' she explained. 'That's his. He came.'

'This is a friend of yours?' Jordan asked, and I saw realisation cross his face. I nodded at him.

'Oh T, I'm so . . .' I began, but she spat her next piece of information.

'Run down. Killed.' She took a shaky breath in. 'By a yellow SUV.'

'You know that?' I asked.

'The ambulance chaser said as much.'

Jordan and I swore simultaneously. Hyperarousal spiked in me as I thought of Gatsby's car. How blood would show up against the paint job. Knowing T's rash spending habits and wealth, had Miguel assumed the luridly-painted Range Rover in her most recent post to be her actual new ride? Had he been lured by her teasing trail of texts to a meeting place she'd mentioned and, arriving, attempted to flag down that car as it exited the lot? Had Gatsby, devastated about the implosion of her romance, been driving furiously? Her distress pressing the accelerator hard, her tears blinding her to a figure on the road ahead?

'She didn't even stop,' T growled.

She angrily slapped a tear from her cheekbone with an open palm. She started the engine, shaking her hair back off her face, determination settling in her jaw. I don't think I had seen her cry before. 'Poor Danny,' she whispered.

'Look, we don't know it was Gatsby,' I gabbled, not wanting to believe it. 'There's more than one yellow car in the world. And we don't know it's Miguel, a friend could have borrowed his car . . .'

She looked at me incredulously, halting my scattergun theorising before she rolled slowly out of the parking space, her driving atypically careful under the watch of the officers. She turned the steering wheel with clamped, white hands.

'She wasn't even wasted,' she hissed.

'We've all been drinking . . .' I pointed out, suddenly keenly aware that T wasn't perhaps best placed to pilot us. We were all compromised. 'Should we leave the car? Get a taxi?'

'Just don't get pulled,' Jordan said and it occurred to me that he had never worried about temperance while driving in the time I'd known him. His careful driving in view of police vehicles had never been through fear of a curbside sobriety test. I had pardoned this in the moment when he held a car door open for me, but now that we were passing still-glossy blood I tasted disgust.

'We're getting home,' T said, creeping through the exit, increasing her speed as she turned onto the street, the news helicopter already circling the dock overhead. 'We just need to be smart about this.'

'None of this was smart,' Jordan grouched. 'I really don't need this shit right now.'

'Shall we call them?' I asked, palming my phone, unsure of whether to dial Danny or Gatsby. I wondered about the conversation they might have had in the canary-coloured car's dark interior. Whether sharp words were exchanged, if they wept, if they were already caught.

'Don't complicate it,' T ordered. 'Keep it clean.'

She chewed the inside of her cheek as she drove, but her fingers had relaxed on the wheel. She was working through options.

'Who else knew about this thing between her and Danny?' she asked suddenly.

Jordan and I looked at each other, the road lights strobing our faces as T picked up more speed, taking the bridge too fast.

'No one but us,' he replied uncomfortably. 'They kept it tight.'

'He better have,' she grimaced. 'He's a fool.'

'How about you?' Jordan retorted. 'You keep it discreet on your end, T?'

She didn't reply and I itched to speak to either one of the riders of the yellow car.

'Don't you want to know what actually happened?' I asked both of them.

'It doesn't matter what happened,' T told the road ahead. 'But it's going to look really bad for her.'

'You could be wrong. It might have nothing to do with her.'

'I can fix it,' she snapped, gunning the car now that we were on the highway.

'How can you fix *this*? What is there to fix?'

T suddenly veered to the side of the road, bumping the car in the long grass there and grabbed her phone on the seat. She furiously jabbed at the screen, dispatching a message and then, just as quickly, yanked the steering wheel to pull us back onto the highway. Her screen lit her face briefly before fading to black.

'I just hope that she's not dumb enough to be at my house when I get there,' she snarled.

A tear spilled again from her eye, dropping into her lap as she stared at the road being sucked under the car as we barrelled north. It was solitary; no more followed.

'T, you're shocked and this is so sad for you,' I said low, as though calming a spooked animal.

She snapped her head in my direction.

'I'm not crying for Miguel,' she huffed and looked back at her path forward. 'And we're lucky that no one else will either.'

I thought of his tiny sister, of his ambitions, of his hard-grafting wife. Of the immaculate restroom at the garage. T's warrior heart ached over the mess, not the man.

'I looked around and couldn't see CCTV at the dock parking lot,' she said. 'So I'm going to assume that the only person who knows Danny was with her tonight is that boat guy who looks like he needs money.'

I silently understood the assumption T had made about us both: that we would close like a flower in the dark. I considered what that said about me and I didn't like it. I had felt assured of my integrity, but as the highway thundered under the wheels, I knew that in that moment I had none – and I was dismayed.

I allowed other uncomfortable feelings to take up space

inside me as we silently sped towards East Egg: guilt, mortification, abashment. The headlights picked out the start of the suburban sprawl when we rounded a corner and I realised as we came to a stop sign that I had to make a decision. Watching Jordan close his eyes and relax back on the headrest, and seeing T's shoulders loosen the closer we got to the lights of mansion houses, the further away from them I felt. Soon we were within the enclave that would envelop them behind its high-security gates and lawn sprinklers, private roads and acreage. The idea of that embrace felt suffocating.

'Let me out here,' I asked lightly, 'I'll take the bus back.'

'Don't be ridiculous,' T replied almost sweetly.

'An Uber then.'

'Come to ours, we'll talk, we'll have dinner.'

'You want to eat?' I asked incredulously, just as Jordan murmured his hunger. He cracked open an eyelid, sensing new conflict.

'You want to eat?' I repeated, looking at him.

'Nic,' he drawled. 'Come on, we have to be on the same page.'

In the darkness he reached for my hand but I moved away, the first time I had retreated from his touch. As I leaned against the door to put space between us, my phone alerts began to chime. I glanced down at the screen to see Gatsby's name in overlapping social notification squares that popped in front of one another, jostling for priority, and a message all in capital letters from Lily Shield asking if I knew anything about Gatsby being responsible for a hit-and-run.

'They're already talking about Gatsby,' I gasped. 'It's out. How?'

'They took their time,' T said with some satisfaction as she drove through the avenues of white houses and their baize lawns. 'Someone must have seen her.'

The Buchanan house came into view ahead. All the lights blazed in the windows, like a pretty jack-o'-lantern perched on the contour of the sea. There was no other vehicle waiting in the drive. We stopped with an unceremonious jolt.

'Everyone, inside,' T said roughly as she snatched the keys from the ignition.

I didn't want to be commanded by anyone, let alone her, so I remained in the backseat as she and Jordan exited, tapping on my Instagram to look at Gatsby's feed. It was wiped, leaving only the blankness of a white page, a broken mirror of her pixelated life; all pictures and yearning hearts erased. The actions of a person in hiding or about to regenerate. I turned the phone off and looked towards the house as Danny came out of the front door, striding into T's arms with an exhalation, his clothes changed, his beautiful facade restored. His fingers pressed into her back as they stood under the porch light and she talked urgently into the curve of his neck. Jordan stood alongside, rubbed his friend's shoulder encouragingly. They were united. I got out of the car and walked towards them.

'What the hell happened?' I asked, sounding calmer than I felt. 'Where's Gatsby?'

T swivelled in Danny's arms and shushed me furiously. All three faces regarded me suspiciously from the top step. I said Danny's name firmly. Though he looked serious, his colour had returned to his face and his hand was casually in his pocket like any other evening. He looked almost well rested.

'It's best you don't know,' he said, moving smoothly down the steps. His arm reached out towards me and, as though standing outside of myself, I noted that I didn't want to rush to him.

'I'm not a child,' I said, the simmering rage that had built in the car on the way home now bubbling, fizzing. He tried to take my elbow, guide me. I ripped my arm away.

'Then don't act like one, Nicole,' he hissed.

I felt as though I'd been slapped. I had never known him to use this tone, to show his canines, to spit. He registered my surprise and reset his face.

'Just come inside,' he whispered, trying again to move me towards the house. I resisted him. 'Let's not fucking do this out here,' he snapped.

'Where is she? Where's the car?' I demanded.

He held me close, as though in an embrace, his voice low, almost sensual, in my ear. Gatsby had left, he didn't know what she was going to do, he didn't want me dragged into it. I could almost believe he wanted to protect me, save me from unpleasantness. I shook him off and he stood a step back. He regarded me with narrowed eyes.

'Listen, I want to go home,' I said.

'We need to talk first,' T said firmly.

'You talk and then tell me what the party line is,' I said, feeling a chill dance over me despite the still sweltering temperature. 'I haven't done anything wrong.'

'You think so?' T asked, her voice low. And then conciliatory: 'Come in and wait.'

I ignored her, instead turning away and hailing a Prius on my app that was minutes away dropping another passenger. I did not expect Jordan to come with me, nor did I want him to. As I watched the tiny car move along the street towards me on the screen, I heard the trio agree to retreat behind the heritage front door. After telling me that I could come and join them if I changed my mind, they moved inside, closing the door softly, leaving the moths batting senselessly around the porch light bulb. I felt an acute homesickness for my parents that almost made me sob as I stood awaiting the headlights turning into the drive. I had hardly thought of them throughout the summer, often forgetting to call to check in, exasperated when my mom FaceTimed me at an inopportune moment. Now I craved them, wanted to regress, needing their comfort. But as I got in the car and confirmed my name, I knew I couldn't tell them about this day without revealing my own disgrace.

Chapter 20

I made my way down the driveway to the boathouse after being dropped at the turning circle, my phone lying heavy in my pocket, silenced but trembling with unread news as it bumped against my leg. I saw her glimmering in the shadows of my front door as I walked down the slope. Gatsby leaned against the wooden wall, her pink dress now almost white in the moonlight.

'Nic,' she whispered, her voice cracking.

'Are you hiding?' I asked, anger rising immediately. 'You know he died?'

'I thought that likely,' she admitted, head low.

'You thought that likely? You didn't think of stopping?'

'I tried to.'

'Not very hard,' I scoffed.

'I did, Nic, but he wouldn't,' she said sorrowfully, cupping either elbow with her hands, hugging herself. 'He'd been drinking, he knew what that meant.'

I thought of Danny's shower-fresh face, of his white shirt, so pressed and starched that it looked brand new. Of course he had been driving.

'What?' I coughed.

'They'll assume it was me,' Gatsby nodded. 'My car, so I was driving.'

'But you weren't?'

'I won't say otherwise.' She smiled weakly.

I closed the distance between us and shook her.

'Why would you do that?' I demanded. Danny had promised her nothing, we had all seen it.

'You know why,' she shrugged.

'This is crazy!' I insisted.

'It's not DUI if it's me. He has so much to lose . . .'

'And you don't? Why did you let him drive?'

'He wanted to clear his head,' she replied, and I saw the grief flit over her face. I realised that she had hoped he might think differently about their relationship if she gave him the opportunity to untangle his thoughts behind the wheel. Perhaps she thought pledging to shield him bound them together anew.

She went on to tell me how Danny had skidded to a halt between two clapboard buildings further down the street, desperately urging her to swap seats, his face terrified. She hadn't hesitated. She ran around the front of the car through the headlights, her shadow concertinaing on the wall, not looking at the fender. She climbed back into the driver's seat as he slid to the passenger side and away from responsibility. The gratitude in his eyes as she reversed back to the street fast was enough to make her determined.

'I don't know what else to do but protect him,' she whispered, and paused, looked down and then admitted with some chagrin; 'Everything's for him.'

'He's not even worth it,' I replied quickly, and in enunciating it I knew it to be true.

She looked at me as though she didn't recognise me, her pupils dilated and darting between mine. She said nothing as I took her hand. I thought of Danny's lips on hers earlier today, the way she had made the tiniest sigh into his mouth when he connected with her. I was as close to her as he had been then. I moved backwards, let go of her. I repeated my statement, this time feeling it galvanise on my tongue. Danny, in his white shirt, calm, cleansed; a liar, a coward.

'The guy just jumped out,' she implored. 'I'm not sure I could have stopped either, and I honestly didn't know if he was trying something.'

'Trying what?'

'I don't know, a carjack?' The way the sentence rose at the end suggested an uncertainty.

'Oh, come on,' I snapped.

'It was impossible to stop . . .'

'Was it?' I asked. And her chin trembled, puckered.

'It happened so fast,' she whispered.

Her desperate allegiance to Danny, and his comparative lack of it, punctured my anger. Pity and exhaustion were beginning to replace it.

'He thought you were someone else,' I sighed, sinking onto the doorstep.

It seemed like too much energy was required to even open the door. I felt that I could fall asleep right there, my head against the planter.

'He thought you were T. You need representation. Don't you have someone on staff who can help you with this? That Klipspringer woman?'

Gatsby shook her head and nudged at a stone with her toe.

'I let them go, so that Danny and I could meet without anyone knowing.'

'Isn't that what NDAs are for?' There was an edge in my voice that I knew was unkind even as I heard it out of my mouth.

I was affronted, sad – but a gnawing suspicion was also growing like cancer in me. That I wasn't incandescent about injustice or loss of life, I was upset that Gatsby and Danny had let me down. That their fairytale was only that.

'They'll come for you,' I warned her. 'They *are* coming for you.'

'I know,' she said softly and sat down next to me, our thighs aligned, feet neatly side by side. I rested my chin on my knee and tipped my head to look at her profile. Her face was tilted high, obstinate. I realised I still adored her, despite the lies. I had never been in love in my life, but this must be akin to that undeniable compulsion.

'Why did you say you were from England?' I asked.

She continued staring straight ahead.

'I didn't,' she answered simply. 'I spent a lot of time there.'

'Did Danny know?'

'He must have known . . .'

'I think you may be giving him too much credit,' I said, noting my bitter tone. 'Didn't we all?'

'Oh Nic, don't . . .' she whispered.

'Did you know about Cody? What he was doing?'

She shook her head.

'I really didn't. I agreed on a settlement to protect those women's identities. Not to protect mine.'

'Is there money?'

She turned her head and looked at me, smiling wryly. 'It's complicated.'

'That sounds like an admission.'

She blinked, her focus skittering away. 'I've made money,

like a lot of people. And a lot of people have made money off me. It's not straightforward.'

'It's illegal?'

'It's hard to explain.'

I nodded and we fell silent. I realised my queries were fuelled by the concerns of a wider digital community. Her parasocial relationships, the public tastemakers, hot-takers and op-eds would find a socially acceptable stance on her affairs and either cast her aside or forgive her. I was also assessing the damage to see whether I should turn my back, protecting myself in my probing. Would Gatsby take me down with her if I didn't? Though I'd voiced concerns about her business affairs, I hadn't asked the gnawing question, burrowed most deeply in me. The most personal aspect of this unmasking that I couldn't bear to also be a fallacy. I hesitated to form the words, afraid that the answer could unravel everything I believed to be true about myself, as well as her. I still felt that we were so similar despite our situations: imposters, romantics, idealists.

'Were we really friends?'

She breathed out and placed both her hands over mine on my knee.

'Yes.'

'Yes?'

I wanted to feel the way I had in her house the first night. It felt far away, indistinct.

'Yes,' she repeated, squeezing my fingers.

She smiled at me, willing me to remain in her specific cult. I turned my head away and looked across at her property, at her house, its windows dark, the lawn beginning to look less than pristine now that I realised I hadn't heard the mower recently. It seemed that even as I watched, nature had begun reclaiming her home just as her celebrity was eroded by furious fingers on keyboards.

'It can't have all been for him,' I insisted, looking back at her and watching her throat contract as she swallowed.

She rested her head against her forearms and whispered the truth to me as time ran out.

* * *

She had grown up having to fit into different schools, different military bases, different countries and she never felt close to anybody. The ability to sponge up the cultural currency of each new place and replicate it began young. It was a survival strategy that became a skill and then muscle memory; the magic trick of mimicking those she envied no longer becoming a conscious decision. It was reflection, not deception. In her father's last post before she'd be able to leave, she'd been in England, near Oxford, her elongated vowels sharpening almost immediately and her vocabulary expanding to accommodate local slang. It helped her navigate through a world that often didn't trust or like her based on her provenance. No longer feeling she was from anywhere in particular, she had decided to return to the States when she turned nineteen in the hope that after a peripatetic upbringing it might feel like home. She didn't return to her father, working her way from East Coast to West, via cleaning jobs, waitressing, contract work, moving constantly in search of something that clicked.

When she got to the extremity of the country in California it felt like the ground had stopped moving beneath her, even in a place where earthquakes shivered into early mornings, wobbling glasses on shelves and bringing a primordial howl as tectonic plates shifted. She'd arrived in Santa Cruz for the seasonal work on the heritage boardwalk, standing for long hours at the corn dog stand under the gondola ride where unnerving fibreglass figures sat in the chairs alongside paying humans, as the spitting, scorching oil freckled her forearms. The students from the campus nestling in the redwoods on the hill flooded the boardwalk in the last week of September for the school's orientation week, crowding the space with their moneyed, untroubled smiles.

'So rich they cry diamonds' was the summation of her grease-stained colleague as they watched them over the warm counter. It was certainly true that this UC campus attracted a certain demographic. When Gatsby was at work she was invisible to them, but when she socialised in the local bars she allowed the assumption that she too was studying, even donning a hoodie emblazoned with the school's mascot slug occasionally to move more fluidly through town. She reasoned that she was pursuing an education of sorts, she just didn't need classes and textbooks to do it.

By the time she met Danny as he pushed an idle hand through his salt-bleached hair, she was skilled in allowing others to fill in the blanks about her. He presumed her financial security matched his as they shared breakfast that morning. The student style, the school banana slug sticker on her notebook and the confident way she talked allowed the assumption to be made, and she admitted that she hadn't ever cared to correct him. It wasn't that she deceived him, but she didn't volunteer the truth either.

We moved inside the boathouse as she continued to expand on memories of their West Coast love affair, finding some vodka in my freezer and some chips in the back of my woefully bare cupboards. There was no doubt an interruption from the cops would be imminent, but she was preternaturally relaxed as she sat at the table and I reclined in the window seat. She picked at the chips, licking the salt from her fingers as she talked, but left me the vodka to preserve her legal equilibrium when they inevitably arrived.

By fall they were toggling between the large Victorian clapboard house he rented with a couple of friends and her cramped beachside motel room with a revolving door of drifters who worked the mini golf, the roller coaster, the vintage carousel. He had swept her away to Kauai, to the family timeshare on an organic farm on the south coast where lizards climbed the windows at night, their delicate bellies pressed to the glass, their innards visible, glowing and pulsating. They hiked the Nā Pali coast path to beaches where they had to shout to each other over the crashing surf, and cycled to restaurants where the owners knew his name and asked after his parents while pressing free desserts on them. The bed they lay in during that week looked over the neat rows of salad growing in rich organic soil and a view of the ocean. They paid for nothing, their stay and transportation a gift from his family.

She couldn't return the generosity, aside from whisking him onto the rickety wooden boardwalk Giant Dipper at Santa Cruz that she could ride for free when her friend manned the turnstile. She recalled never being happier than when the ride hit its fastest drop, the wooden rails clacking like a playing card in the wheel of a bike. And when she looked at him, laughing beside her, she sensed possibility in him, despite all the ex-girlfriends she'd met around town. He boasted that he stayed friends with all his previous loves, but she recognised the look in their eyes as they were introduced, especially the girl who she had replaced. She was cordial, warm even, but Gatsby knew they both sensed an overlap; that Danny had decided on the status of his relationships before communicating it to his partners. His flirtatiousness with all women – the way he leaned close when listening, his assuring hands on shoulders and elbows, the dip of his voice – made her worry about the declarations of eternity he drowsily murmured before sleep. As did the number of girls who looked at her like an opponent and him like a challenge. She blushed as she admitted that despite herself, it made him even more desirable to her. A prize.

When she left for England, Danny had driven her to the airport, thinking he was delivering her back to the sort of family security he knew. She was too proud to admit how enormous the airfare had been in the context of her savings. He did pine, she assured me. Constantly messaging her while she sat on a hard plastic seat watching clear liquid sinking down her remaining parent's prescribed drip. He would call her as he watched for sets of waves from the West Cliff Drive overlook, huskily telling her what he missed about her, his intensity crossing the ocean to comfort her.

She admitted she knew it couldn't last. Danny was a social creature who couldn't stay in his room moping. He was soon missing agreed call times, the background thump of a DJ making late-hour scrambled conversations abortive; his need to be somewhere else putting time constraints on a connection that required nurturing. When he changed schools she mourned the loss of her California dream but reasoned that he was geographically moving nearer to her. She was wrong and she knew it, unable to afford an immediate return airfare and unwilling to leave her father's bedside as he slowly recovered. By the time her dad was fully out of danger, Facebook informed her that a woman Danny had mentioned in passing was now assigned a permanent title – one that shattered her hopes and her heart. She was Danny's 'girlfriend' and she smiled in photos wearing his jacket. Not knowing how to comfort herself she flew to New York on the last of her cash, wanting the city to devour her.

'And you met Dan Cody,' I prompted.

Cody was decisive, entering the kitchen and taking the serving platter out of her hand while assuring her of their immediate future together. His chauffeured car waited on the street below the rooftop party, offering her transport away from other people's empty glasses to a life of crystal and cashmere. Gatsby admitted to pragmatically opening herself up to the experience; deciding, as Cody described his yacht and the places they might go together, that she was about to step onto a new page. Within a year she was picking out a cream lace dress and calling Danny while drunk on the excellent white wine from the cellar of a New York townhouse she now called home. He had not, she noted, changed his number – as though he wanted to be traced.

The marriage, she confessed, had not been what anyone dreamed of; but her fast ascent to fame meant the opportunity to build a personal brand. Her opulent life mixing with famous people was available to view for all who clicked, and as the millions of eyes on her increased, so did her desire for the 'like' of one particular person. She had initially felt she wasn't good enough for Danny but as her lifestyle and collateral expanded, she realised that his erroneous idea of her was now aligning with reality. They hadn't been ready for each other before because she was raw and unformed, but the closer she got to him in social strata and capital, the more certain she became of a second chance. As she talked she got that far away look again, evangelical in conviction. I looked away, unable to bear the impossible hope that still rose in her like a flare from the ocean.

She told me that even before she received news of an imminent, catastrophic exposé on her husband by a prominent East Coast publication, she had been thinking of how to reach Danny, hoping to impress. So when the savaging of Cody began she had immediately distanced herself from him physically, mentally, legally. Her first call was to her publicist, the second, her lawyer. She called Cody only after she'd changed the locks on their Palm Springs home and destroyed all the ways he could contact her. She dropped him faster than his own management, production company and the streaming service about to begin filming a multi-series drama built around him. She watched me expectantly as I swigged the vodka. My head swam.

'But did you know?' I asked, circling back to T's claim about Cody's victims again.

'I thought he was a bully, the way so many of those men are,' she replied, rubbing a scratch on my table with a finger. 'He was toxic, yes. But I didn't know about everything else they accused him of. He made my assistant cry, but she never told me what it was about. He made me cry too.' She looked up at me. 'But as soon as I heard, I had nothing more to do with him. You have to believe me.'

I didn't have to, and I still wasn't sure I did.

'That's the least of your problems right now,' I said. 'It's hard to come out on the other side of two accusations like this. Someone died tonight, Jay.'

'I know.' She lowered her chin to her chest and expelled a heavy breath.

'And Danny did that.' The truth of it stuck in my throat,

sore like a sob. 'Even if you can find a way through this, how would the two of you work out? How could you be together?'

'We're perfect for each other now,' she said with another expectant glance at her phone. 'The same life experiences, a first marriage each, equals.'

'Where will you go?'

'Back to California.'

I lay on the bench seat in the window and looked up at the moon in the clear sky. The simplicity of her belief was equal parts foolhardy and impressive. The way she clearly thought he would call, reach out, choose her – that she believed he thought they were peers seemed a perverse act of bravery.

'But everything that happened today . . .' I reminded her again, turning my head to look at her sitting at my shabby table, seemingly still pressed and perfect in pink. She folded the chip packet into a tiny square, her eyes watching her fingers work.

'We've waited so long, we can wait longer,' she replied as though reciting a mantra.

'What will be left?' I asked cautiously.

I didn't precisely know what I meant but had visions of courtrooms, public ridicule, hatred, jail.

'This will ruin you,' I told her.

'We'll see,' she mumbled.

I sat up. 'Jay, you need to think clearly.'

She watched me for a moment and then stood, smoothed her hands over her dress. There was now an oily fingermark from the chips on her skirt.

'I am thinking clearly,' she said firmly. 'I should go.'

I stood too. We stared at each other.

'They wouldn't do the same for you,' I told her.

She looked down, that hair falling over her face so once

again I couldn't tell if she was smiling or grimacing. And then she looked back up.

'You've been kind,' she said, dipping slightly at the knees before moving towards me, arms outstretched. Her hug was full-bodied, her hands rubbing my back as she squeezed. I grasped at her. She smelt heavenly while I was conscious of my own stale body odour.

'You're better than all of this,' I said as she walked out.

She didn't respond or look back. The heat was still oppressive as she slipped through the darkness and across the lawn like a pale wraith. I followed and waited on the step, watching her go. She walked across the lawn as she had the first time I'd seen her. At the time I thought I observed her progress from sisterly consideration, tracing her path as she put a foot on the bottom of her marble steps and turning to wave, her smile travelling the distance. But perhaps there was also an atavistic sense that more darkness was coming, creeping towards us, sticky like tar. When she got to the top step, she paused for a second and glanced over her shoulder, not at me, but for a long moment towards the water and beyond. I doubted anyone on the opposite shore was gazing back.

When she'd disappeared into the dark house, I sank down to sit on my doorstep and pulled out my silenced phone. Our little world was changing inexorably. Brutal threads, gleeful notifications. Gatsby was a punchline and a pariah. My own friends had messaged me, their morbid fascination dressed as concern for me. Poring over their phrasing, I knew I would have written the same missives had our roles been reversed.

I had followed Gatsby hashtags in my early days of obsessively cataloguing her, now a tidal wave of gloating, outrage, trolling and supposition flooded the touchstone in my hand. She had been an intoxication then. But, as with a surfeit of any mood-altering crutch, I was now beginning to hurt from over exposure. Her name was all over different platforms, the whisperings of gossips and ghouls as to whether she had been involved in an accident, her own posts of the lemony SUV screen-grabbed and served up alongside early police reports, diametrically opposed commentators suggesting she had done something, nothing. The swirl of opinion and factual report was indistinguishable. It bruised me to read any of it.

I wondered if she was also following her own downfall in the darkness of her house. While her pool lights cast a queasy chlorine ripple over the exterior and the studded illuminations to the beach remained on, the property was otherwise gloomy.

I went back inside, found the number of Klipspringer and sent her a message, asking if she could assist Gatsby as she needed help but was refusing to reach out herself.

'She has no one,' I typed.

Klipspringer replied immediately: 'She has the housekeeper and you. Peace out.'

I had a flurry of cryptic WhatsApp messages from T, all conveying the official story she wished to be told without putting specifics into writing. Jordan tried calling, but I cancelled every attempt and ignored his messages. When he messaged asking if I was ghosting him, I found myself making an instinctual decision.

We're done, I typed, and blocked his number.

From Gatsby there was nothing. At some point I slept on the window seat, perhaps half an hour, my face pressed to the glass. My brain wanted an escape from sorrow. I was woken by a single, muffled firework going off somewhere nearby. A bang but no explosive light. I assumed one of the mansion brats had procured a stash of Fourth of July rockets for dumb fun on their perfectly appointed grounds.

Then I heard the thin wail of police sirens, carried on the breeze from the highway. I returned to my doorstep to look across the teal lawn. I knew they would be heading here and the metallic tang of panic rose in me, crystallising a decision. Her plan to lie for him was a mistake, and I wanted to try to dissuade her. Barefoot, I ran.

I knew that to go over to the house was reckless if officers were about to spill through the doors. But the need to see Gatsby trumped rational thought, and I took the stairs to the house two at a time, dread drying my mouth and clenching my fingers. As I passed the pool I noticed that a couple of the expensive deck chairs were in the water, as though one of the parties had only just ended, a forlorn leg sticking out of the waterline. I called into the house for Gatsby. There was a sharp bang from what seemed to be deep within the mansion, like a door slamming hard or the backfire of an exhaust. The two-tone clarion call of sirens crept ever closer. I called again, but there was no response.

The house felt enormous. I knew the layout, could have easily found my way through the rooms in the dark. But something made me look towards the pool again and I saw gentle movement in the deep end. There, near the floor tiles, a pink billowing form like an undulating jellyfish, the seaweed sway of gold. She was being buffeted by the eddy of the filter, a prone form at a submerged angle, toes nudging the floor.

As I entered the water I heard cries for help so anguished I didn't recognise my own voice. The cold tore the sounds from my throat as I gasped, struggling to slice through the distance, fighting the buoyancy of my clothes. I scrabbled below the surface as I grabbed for the blush of Gatsby's dress, fingers slipping, legs thrashing. She can't swim, I thought on a terrified loop as I grabbed at her pale arm, pulling the weight of her upwards, breaking the surface with my upturned face, hers still kissing the water. I forgot all life-saving instructions learnt over the years at summer camp, floundering desperately towards the side, kicking her yielding body, tugging as her dress slid from her shoulder. I screamed for help, choking on chlorine. Gatsby sank with each stroke. Her face dipped and rolled in the waves I was making. Even as I fought I couldn't stop looking at her. Then my clawing fingers finally touched the side.

The housekeeper ran out to meet me at the pool lip, kneeling with her hand outstretched, shouting unheard commands as I pulled and pushed the weight of my limp neighbour. We clumsily heaved her from the pool, scraping her delicate skin over the edge, her dress riding up, her face covered in snaking, soaked tendrils of hair. As the housekeeper wept and rolled her awkwardly on her back, I scrambled out. Far away there were wood-splintering crashes and shouts within the house. The police had broken in and I willed them closer. I crawled to Gatsby, tearing the nest of suffocating hair away with shaking hands to find her face – her open mouth revealing a throat filled with water.

As I yanked her onto her side to empty her I tried to soothe her, telling her she'd be fine and pressing a momentary kiss to her marble cheek. Panicking, I pushed her on her back to begin CPR just as police officers appeared from around the side of the house and spilled through the patio doors. Their flashlights criss-crossed like the sky-searching beams of a movie premiere, their demands rough. We didn't know what they had found on entering the property. I put up my hands in surrender because I was terrified of the guns aimed at me and because I could see I could not save my friend. The water had hidden it, but as I knelt dripping into a puddle, another formed under Gatsby, blooming around her as scarlet as her nails.

As the housekeeper and I cowered and conveyed the information asked of us, a news helicopter roared over the house, casting a bleaching light over all of us surrounding Gatsby and showing all live-feed spectators the violent red end of influence. There was no need for the ambulance or the medics that were being screamed for; the pressure that first responders applied to the wound in her chest would not stem the life force that had already trickled out of her. She was as blank and as broken as the phone that lay at the bottom of the pool.

Chapter 21

Gatsby was not the only one with dreams. Both close friends and commentators told the media afterwards that Miguel's wife, Georgina, also nursed an immaculate image of her future. Miguel had been the great love of her youth and then, when they moved to New York, she buried herself in work, incrementally building up modest funds to give the couple a better life. She knew Miguel was handsome, charming and lazy but she believed in the vows of marriage. She accepted his mendacious tales of winning bets or of new, perfectly tailored clothes being thrift store finds. She had no reason to suspect that the days he left her working at the gas station alone were anything more than the business meetings he told her he was attending, despite nothing tangible coming from any of them. She sweated over windshields, shivered in the spartan office, withstood punishing rain to fill cars, swallowed the abuse from customers knowing that this period of her life was finite. There was a plan for Georgina, there was California.

Though he had family nearby, she wanted the comfort of her own blood and the magnetic tug of the West began early that summer. But, as she told her sister in Eagle Rock,

Miguel's plans were not aligned; he resisted. He grew angry, resentful, began to find fault and stay away from their bed. She was truly afraid that she would lose him to whatever temptation was guiding him off their shared course. She made an ultimatum of being in LA for Thanksgiving which he bristled at, and, knowing she could not cage him, she strove instead to understand him.

She began following the media figures and social accounts he did, lurking close by digitally in a way she increasingly struggled to at home. She began to see a pattern in his likes and his movements, suspected an affair but found no evidence. She stayed attentive through the summer, hoping he might return to her. And when he told her he was leaving early one evening of the Labor Day weekend as they wilted in the garage forecourt heat, she wasn't sure if he meant for a matter of hours, days or permanently. She stood in the office door to try to physically prevent him from departing, but he easily prised her fingers from the flaking wood. CCTV shows she followed him to the car, tried to climb in the passenger seat, but he locked her out. He sped away, his arm trailing from the window in a half salute.

She immediately triggered the finder app on his cell phone, following his progress to Long Island. He stopped at a place by the water that neither of them had been before. She knew not to call him so she watched as the dot remained in the same spot, relaying his departure and her findings to her friend who worked at the nearby bodega. She bought alcohol from there for the first time in months, anxiety in her voice, her hand trembling slightly as she handed over crumpled notes. It wasn't until later, when her Greek neighbour, Michaelis, banged on her door and told her to turn on the news, that she understood everything had changed.

Wasn't that Miguel's car on TV? he asked. Could she call him? Check that all was well? 'Look, Georgina, look . . .' Michaelis tapped the screen with a finger, rewinding the report to show the footage again. TJ Eckleburg narrated the view in her high-energy voice as the news helicopter circled and weaved, the camera zooming in on the group of bystanders, the white tent, the abandoned vehicle that would never be reclaimed.

Fatality, she heard as she crept closer to the screen. The camera did not pan away, the picture unblinking as Eckleburg provided new information, any information, refusing to turn from human tragedy. 'We're live . . .' she stressed as the helicopter hovered over a victim who very much wasn't. Georgina touched the screen where the mottled roof of his car was, as though feeling for the real thing.

Michaelis asked her to sit and drink water, but she told him that she needed to run. The authorities would discover Miguel's status and, when they then found her, she would have worked for nothing. Michaelis nodded, listened, told her fleeing wasn't necessary. He tried to soothe her sadness. But Georgina was enraged rather than in mourning; she wanted to find who had done this. The injustice of being unseen in a society until violence made her and her husband a statistic must have infuriated her.

As Michaelis later told the news crews who gathered on the stoop, she had abruptly seemed certain of something, resolute. She was such a quiet woman, he'd insisted, head lowered so his mouth grazed the scratchy foam of a microphone. She had turned to her phone and begun to search virtual rooms and tribes on social media, looking for the answers to her questions. One thread led to another, the truth of the situation trapped in a bell jar where it shrank under inspection, a clear narrative taking shape via double screen-taps and re-shares. Georgina followed the clues, hooked on a theory that calcified to reality as it was repeated, passed on – uncensored, unchecked.

The woman who had stolen her husband and his executioner must have conflated as she scrolled. All of the indignities suffered at the hands of those more affluent than her seemed to have beaded together into a piercing point. She read the mournful stories of others in threads, the hostile experiences of undocumented workers, law enforcement racial profiling, the myth of the criminal immigrant. There would be no day in court, no jail time for the person who killed Miguel Ortiz, she was told across social platforms. Especially a prosperous denizen of Long Island, who would wriggle from justice one hourly lawyer fee at a time. Those with benign-sounding social handles suggested what they might do in her situation, spelled out graphic pictures of brutality over 280 characters. Made her see only one path to finding justice for her husband. It seemed she felt she had no choice in what she must do next.

Georgina set off from her home leaving everything behind – the money saved in a duffel bag at the bottom of their sparse shared wardrobe, the house she cleaned on Sundays with the ferociousness of a ward nurse, the photos stuck to the fridge of her and Miguel in front of various New York tourist attractions. She documented her journey as she travelled, the comfort of a handheld witness to her actions. With her phone clutched in her furious fist, she drove east from Corona to Long Island in Michaelis's borrowed car. She talked to an audience she knew would later watch, her eyes moist, her voice rising with alternating grief and rage. She addressed the families of all poorly investigated deaths chalked up to the activities of minority communities, illegal acts and profiling. She asked her own family for forgiveness, and she talked to the spectre of Miguel, promising him deliverance and peace. Following my own first steps from the bus when I arrived in West Egg, she abandoned the car on the grass verge and followed her glowing map on foot to where Twitter had told her the odyssey could end. She found herself at the turning circle that offered gates to several properties, including Gatsby's.

We later discovered that Gatsby had turned many of her security cameras off weeks earlier to protect the secret she welcomed into her bed. That night she had no way of knowing that, as she stood on the patio casting her eyes between her screen and the winking green light across the water, Georgina had climbed the metal gates. Then, within the compound, her backpack heavy with cold metal, she had crunched down the drive towards the front door as so many party guests had before her. The size of the house and the perfect symmetry of the garden must have added insult to her injury. With her phone still tilted up to her damp face, she found her way to the stately front door, letting out a frustrated wail on discovering it locked. Guided by nothing more than bitter grief, she stumbled further around the side of the house, through the grounds and towards the pool's wide white steps, mucus trailing from her nose. She ascended, glimpsing Gatsby through the balustrade, her pink defenseless back turned towards her.

Here Georgina's video becomes even more shaky as she shrugs the bag from her back, her hand delving into the black depths of the canvas to find the gun she'd taken from Miguel's bedside drawer. I haven't been able to watch further than this point myself but millions have. It was shared widely, edited for sensitivity, certain elements blurred out so that it was suitable for breakfast news packages and the top story carousel on websites. The full video, with all its bodily fluids and Georgina's desperate keening cry before her final act, remains easy to find online for anyone who wants to watch two broken people lose their lives.

From what I understand, Georgina then flips the camera to allow all voyeurs her point of view, extending a quaking hand towards the woman in front of her. Gatsby is seemingly so immersed in her thoughts, likely oblivious to any sound around her that wasn't the specific notification chime she had assigned Danny on her phone, that she doesn't hear Georgina's sneaker-clad feet on the flags, or the click of the safety being snapped off.

I cling to the belief that she understood nothing of what was about to happen, that she was still floating in optimism, her heart full with promise, her constructed fantasy still a possibility to her. Georgina pulled the trigger, her phone wobbling with the effort, and Gatsby crumpled into the water with a splash. The bullet entered her back, leaving barely a trace externally, before ripping through her internal organs to exit her sternum, fraying the silk dress. I had hoped her thoughts were eradicated immediately, though the post-mortem suggested otherwise. She sank.

Georgina's twinned fury and sorrow drove her to push the pool furniture into the water too, her howling muffled by the scraping of chair legs and the splashes as Gatsby's earthly possessions joined her in the depths. When I arrived, the dark hour had prevented me from noticing that my friend had turned the pool water rosy, merged with it, already distributed to the elements. I did not realise that anyone else was within the boundaries of the house: but as I had walked up the exterior stairs, Georgina stalked the building inside, moaning with misery, finding her way to the front door and the way out. Perhaps she heard me call through the house. The housekeeper, watching an action movie on her headphones, heard none of the activities until the end credits prompted her to rejoin the world and hear my wet screams.

Of course, Georgina had no exit. She would have considered her life over in every respect and she resolved to have her own agency in the finale. With her eyes closed and a request to the heavens on her lips, she pushed the muzzle to her temple and pulled the trigger a second time. Her mission was complete. West Egg rather than the West Coast was where she ended up, discovered by police on the gravel and neatly solving the Buchanans' inconvenient problem.

Chapter 22

My parents told me when they arrived to comfort me at the police station that it was a shame the Buchanans or I had been involved in such a thing. What a way to end the summer, my mom said with a shake of her head, as though the weather had changed. But there was no other shame mentioned.

In the aftermath, I was questioned by the authorities but it was easy for them, the public, the documentary makers to make the shattered pieces make sense. Three people had died and, despite performative out-pourings, they merely served to illustrate election debates already mid-flow, to justify jingoism, ciphers for gossip and chatter. Gatsby's complicated relationship to Miguel via Danny and T was bent to a simpler, more digestible narrative: Georgina had believed Gatsby to be both lover and killer of her husband. The influencer's wealth matched the circumstantial clues that showed he had been financially cared for over the summer. Gatsby's secrecy and romantic social posts were ascribed to Miguel. It was easier and more profitable for all to paint her this way, serving the hastily thrown-together exposés, the crime podcasts, the later Netflix dramatisation where she was played with cold calculation by a wide-eyed English actress in a conspicuous peroxide wig.

The citizens of East Egg welcomed the Buchanans back to their fundraisers, cocktail parties and dinners just days later according to T's new Instagram, changed to only be accessible by close, chosen friends. She might have liked to exclude me from this coterie, block me from her social media, but she understood the political optics as much as she did the looks from Long Island wives that were a combination of impressed and appalled.

As far I could tell, Miguel's sister remained silent and hidden, unaccounted for by the state and subsumed into a community who safeguarded her. She would have likely known that her account of who Miguel's real lover was would be disassembled by T's protectors, her very existence mauled by hysterical patriots. Danny, picked up on CCTV highway cameras as a prone passenger and witness, was easily forgiven for his professed lack of action on account of his extreme intoxication (proved by toxicology tests at the time when police arrived at his house). I imagine that he had consumed the contents of his well-stocked liquor cabinet to smudge his results; I never asked and didn't wish to know. Of the night, he could apparently recall very little, dropping his phone accidentally into the toilet as he stumbled around his home before passing out, undressed, on a lawn chair in the garden.

While Gatsby's progress home was tracked by cameras, Danny's luck protected him in the parking lot. The lone camera tilted at the entrance and exit had been vandalised days before the incident, repair work scheduled for after the holiday weekend. No one had seen him start the engine, or a woman in the right-hand seat beside him wearing a dress the colour of a conch shell interior.

He displayed public remorse for not being conscious of the crime, not having stopped his wayward acquaintance as she drove. Gatsby's role in his life was reduced by all of us to a mere neighbour, not someone any of us knew well. T's expensive attorney ensured that the couple, traumatised by the whole sorry event, were not unduly bothered beyond initial statements. They engaged in no conversations with the media and I did the same, advised by their ferocious legal team to not complicate things further.

Gatsby, powerless and entombed in a police autopsy refrigeration unit, could do nothing to counter public appetite for disgrace. It transpired she had debts, her house was a business agreement with a real estate agency, she was as erratic as her state of mind. Her failures in business and love were examined and debated, her culpability in Miguel's death judged less of a horrible accident and more of an example of her bad character; symptomatic of her elitism.

Her real background was picked apart, laughed at and disparaged, her accent mimicked, the photos in her posts raked over for deeper meanings. Women at round tables on TV shows discussed her while pictures of her on army bases as a youth projected on a screen behind them. She joined the pantheon of heroes and villains who had breathed their last in hot tubs and pools, a particular celebrity trope of tawdry tragedy that spoke of a particular negligent privilege. Anyone who had interacted with her in the weeks leading up to the accident offered their thoughts to whoever might listen, reading new aggressions into her words and deeds. Even her ex-husband offered comment from his exile. So many believed she had got what was coming to her, that special brutalism reserved for women who made mistakes. I wanted to speak up for her but didn't, terrified of being dragged into the maelstrom of public opinion, of judgement and sentencing. Of this, I remain remorseful.

Advised to stay remote until the unfortunate affair was forgotten, I swore off social media and trained myself to put nothing in writing, not to muddy the waters by speaking to the Buchanans or Baker. Hoping for some sort of closure, I tried to call Danny once many months after I'd left Long Island and Gatsby behind; but his number was no longer in use, and he had not furnished me with another. I could have asked my family, but I knew there was no point trying to contact either him or his wife. I had seen them in their most fundamental state. They had pulled up the drawbridge and I was now just another peasant waving and shouting on the edge of the moat.

The incident created a schism in the family. My parents felt that Danny and T should have taken better care of me and were appalled that our family name was connected to sensationalist newspaper stories and gossip websites as my third-act attempt to save Gatsby was reported. They feared that Gatsby's grotesque cancelling might infect my own standing, and subsequently theirs. Even my landlady, initially fascinated by the proximity to macabre celebrity, soon tired of the paparazzi boats bobbing offshore, their long lenses trained on Gatsby's property. She could not expose her children to the circus I was connected to. It felt morbidly fitting that she should require my departure by Halloween.

My parents begged me to return home too, but I felt I had to stay on the East Coast for Gatsby who, it turned out, had very few true friends among the hundreds of faces that had paraded along her driveway. I had not served her well in the end and I wanted to assuage the guilt that pierced me daily. Gatsby's house remained empty, the realtor uncharacteristically sensitive – though I suspected, rather than compassion, it was an attempt to time when exactly the disgust with Gatsby would tip into notoriety and make the place desirable. I wanted to contact her father, but knew no way of finding him. The authorities would have been in touch with him to convey the news no parent wishes to hear even if the noise of it hadn't reached him by other means, but I wanted him to see the house that represented her tooth-and-claw climb to a social and financial summit before it was closed, disinfected, repurposed.

Klipspringer wanted nothing to do with the admin required after her former boss' body was released. She chuckled darkly when I called, saying that she had 'dodged a bullet in every way' by leaving when she did. She suggested I contact Gatsby's former publicist May Wolfsheim, who had crisis-managed the Cody situation and prevented various other indiscretions from ever coming to light. Wolfsheim, she promised, could 'make chicken soup out of chicken shit'.

Her offices were on an elegant block off the park but she asked to meet in a bar near Wall Street. I sat in a corner nursing a scotch at midday, watching the door, waiting for the middle-aged woman who slipped in wearing the black uniform of a publicist, her statement jewellery conveying her success. She saw me straight away, no doubt recognising my face from the pained shots taken of me leaving the police precinct or ripped from my social feeds to illustrate opinion pieces. She shook hands in an insincere double clasp as she sat down, waving the waiter over without looking at him, placing her phone on the table between us so she could monitor incoming communication. She tersely ordered a cocktail and immediately asked for the check.

'I no longer represent Gatsby,' she announced.

I waited. From my recent experiences, I had learnt to pause rather than offer information. I sipped my drink, watched her sigh and push her glossy red hair behind her ears.

'Look,' she continued, 'I get that you were friends, and it's terrible what's happened . . .' She glanced at her phone. 'A tragedy, really,' she nodded. 'But . . .'

She silenced herself as the waiter slid her drink across the table.

'I can't be seen to help on something so problematic.'

'I thought problematic was your skill set,' I countered.

She smiled tightly. 'I can bring you through a divorce and distance you from predatory behaviour; I can fix your borderline illegal activities; I can ensure problems go away. But I cannot fix this. Who will stand up for her?'

I was about to answer when she did it for me. 'I know you think you will, but you're compromised too.'

'I don't think compromised is the right word,' I snapped.

'Of course,' she said. 'I forget you're the writer.'

'She told you about me?' I asked, and the thought of Gatsby's soft-eyed support caused my vision to blur.

'Of course,' Wolfsheim purred. 'Who do you think spiked your essay on living next door to her?' She leaned a little closer so her large gold bracelet rattled against the table. 'You should be grateful. Imagine the mileage they'd get out of that now if I hadn't.'

I flushed, recalling the feature I'd written, the pride I'd felt in it being published, the later panic in hoping it wasn't.

'Why did you?' I asked.

'Why do you think?' She frowned. 'She asked me to.'

'Gatsby did?' I sounded incredulous.

'Sweetie, Jay and I were aligned on brand, she didn't want that out there.' She regarded me as though contemplating whether to utter the next remark. 'And honestly, I should tell you – she liked to keep people, collaborators, *friends*, at a bit of a disadvantage.'

She watched my face and nodded. 'She knew how to play the game.'

I understood it to be true, but it still smarted. Wolfsheim could tell.

'It's just business,' she said a little more gently.

I finished my drink in one swallow. Gatsby had always been one step ahead of me. It was admirable really. And despite it, I still missed her.

'I'm not talking business, I'm talking personally,' I said. 'You could help in that capacity. Come to her funeral.'

She slowly pulled the olive off the wooden skewer in her drink. It was stuffed full of veined blue cheese. I hated that combination: the pungent cheese overwhelming the briny olive, tainting the clean taste of the martini. I judged her on her order as she popped the green sphere into her maroon mouth.

'I can't do that,' she stated, chewing.

'Then why did you meet me?' I asked, genuinely curious.

She looked at me with consternation. 'I thought you wanted representation.'

I laughed. 'I don't need a publicist.'

'Don't you?' she asked. She gulped her cocktail. 'You could make decent money from your story.'

'I would never do that,' I said, my voice neutral though my emotions were charged. 'You might have lived off her, I won't.'

She set her mouth as though stopping a smile.

'I didn't live off anyone, I built her. But it's not personal, any of this,' she whispered. 'It's contractual, transactional.'

She was already looking around the rowdy bar for the waiter, her fingers probing her bag, her shoulder tilted towards the door.

'Nic,' she said, warm, patronising. 'May I call you Nic?'

I nodded.

'My advice to you, my professional advice, is to either be part of the discourse, and let's talk options; or walk away and don't get dragged down.'

She pulled her wallet from the depths of the Birkin bag and twisted in her seat, her eyes scanning over heads.

'She has no one,' I said for the second time in as many days as the waiter arrived at our table with a credit-card machine. Wolfsheim tapped her black card against it, her body already in a position of flight. She drained her glass and looked at me with something approaching sympathy.

'And that's not either of our responsibility,' she said. She rose from the seat. 'Let it all just die.'

Chapter 23

We did just let her die, her father and I. Eventually – after Gatsby had been mauled and probed, her fingerprints taken, the contents of her stomach examined, her hair tested – her body was released to a thin man with a gaunt face who arrived in Long Island wearing his military uniform as the smartest thing he owned. He had asked to be put in touch with me when he understood all the details of her demise and it was one request in my inbox I gladly accepted. He was going to sort through her personal effects boxed at the house, asking to meet there one morning in late October. I left my own home, empty except for a packed case and a cardboard box marked for disposal, to walk a final time over the lawn to Gatsby's mansion. The grass had grown ragged and there was the promise of frost in the air as I made my way to him.

The pool was drained, and cracks in the tiles were now evident without the water. Brown leaves nestled in the hollow at the deep end. I knocked on the French doors calling out their shared surname. He appeared out of the gloom and opened the door.

'Nic?' he asked with a pained smile, his shoulders square.

'Mr Gatsby,' I nodded, holding out a hand. He grasped it firmly in his warm one.

'Gatz,' he corrected. 'Jenny never liked it much.'

Despite knowing Gatsby's real name since her full background was revealed on the news, I still hadn't been able to use it when referring to her. She would always be a single word to me. And I liked saying it, as though conjuring her back.

Her father gestured that I should come inside, and when I stepped into the house it was jarring to see the soft furnishings gone. Stripped of Gatsby's taste, the large room echoed, and Mr Gatz ushered me over to a pile of FedEx boxes in the corner. A battered flask and a worn khaki duffel bag were alongside them.

'I'm going through her things,' he explained. 'I know you were a friend, and I wondered if there was something you wanted as a keepsake.'

He unexpectedly stopped so that I bumped his shoulder.

'Thank you,' he said, his voice a growl as he tried to contain his emotions. 'For pulling her out, for being there.'

I nodded. He squatted by the nearest open box and began searching through documents, frames and office paraphernalia that must have been tipped out directly from her desk.

'I don't know what most of this is,' he said forlornly. 'Jenny was something of a stranger to me.' He looked up at me and then around the room. 'She did alright, huh?'

I smiled. 'She did alright.'

'I never told her I was proud,' he said. 'Even when she bought me the house. She was always so determined, plucky. I guess I just expected her to be successful. But I never actually told her.'

'We thought we'd have longer,' I replied.

He nodded and his eyes filled.

'Mr Gatz, do you need help with any of the arrangements?' I asked, unable to say the word funeral.

He paused in his rustling and shook his head, as much in answer as in disbelief.

'You'll come?' he asked. Clearly, there was a worry that he might be left standing alone to send her off. They were a depleted family, no siblings or close relatives. Gatsby was the last of him.

'Of course,' I assured, and I knelt alongside him. 'And I can help with this.'

Together we went through the papers, determining what could be shredded and what was personal, found photos and menus, jewellery, her passport with her original name and dog-eared school books. Much of it he wanted to keep, evidence of her existence. Her clothes he decided to donate, though he easily could have sold them. He could have converted the remains of her curated life into a robust pension, but he chose to hold her close to him, keep what remained of her private.

We spent the afternoon taping boxes shut as thunder rumbled overhead. As I slipped out of the doors and back across the lawn it began to rain and I held a Polaroid close to my chest to protect it from the large drops that painted me as I hurried. We had found it in the pages of her empty journal, a talisman that had clearly been well handled, loved. The corners were bent, the writing on the white space at the bottom in her distinctive sloping handwriting was smudged, but still legible. 'West Egg. DB.'

It was the shot that she had posted so often, in all lights and all weathers; the admittedly impressive view from her pool deck across the water. The distant view of Danny. It seemed unbearably sad and hopelessly naïve. A delicate, tender thing hidden behind Gatsby's shiny surfaces and determination. This was the part of her I wanted to keep and remember. Not her waterlogged shell at the end or the bright flash of her when we first met. Not the elegant chess player who moved me around her board to get to her destination. I wanted to hold on to her hope in the face of roadblocks; her absolute, unwavering belief in love; the way she looked when she watched the waves that divided her and Danny's worlds. I loved her sentimental fixation on the light on Danny's dock: the green representing 'go', her reinvention, her money.

I hastened inside and rummaged through the cardboard box to find the frame I'd slung there, pulling out the postcard of a piece created by an artist I had no emotional connection with but had chosen to look urbane. I placed the Polaroid behind the glass, trapping it, protecting it, and wrapped the frame in a sweater before adding it to my carry-on bag. In everything I was taking back to my own beginnings, this had become the most precious.

A few days later, I placed dollar bills in the jar for my landlady along with my key, and left West Egg for the last time. I had arranged for my suitcase to travel ahead of me and I walked the path carrying only what I needed for the journey. I would fly out of JFK that evening after attending a private – and, crucially, secret – cremation in Flushing. Mr Gatz had delayed the service to allow the news cycle to move on to their next story. He wanted to say goodbye quietly, softly, letting her go gently.

I knew before I arrived there that there would be no word from Danny. I understood from my mother that the Buchanans had fled to the West Coast earlier in October, leaving their home in East Egg for sale. They had moved into a sprawling home looking across another body of water, this time in Santa Barbara, where their neighbours were other wealthy people who had escaped unpleasantness. An easy drive away from Big Sur, Danny could indulge his passion for the outdoors, Jordan was close for much of the year in Pebble Beach and their gilded life could continue smoothly. The events of September were merely the easily unkinked knot in a silk ribbon. I considered the cruel irony of them living in a place so tied to Gatsby and Danny, where she had envisaged a future with him.

Later still I discovered that they quickly had a daughter, Pammy, a band-aid baby to adhese any remaining fissures in their union. Pregnancy absolved T of many judgements, her swollen belly a panacea against potential unkindness. The way motherhood repositioned her was the only reason I could imagine her agreeing to such a submersion of her virulent main-character syndrome. I also fancied that Danny might have appreciated the inevitable yoke it placed upon her, despite their employment of a brown-uniformed English nanny my dad referred to, admiringly, as Mary Poppins. The tow-headed infant I was shown in photographs was a beautiful distraction from any of the ugliness experienced in New York, completing the image of a tasteful nuclear family beyond reproach.

I did, with a degree of self-hate, continue to follow Jordan's socials via a fake profile, and after everything was neatly packed away I gleaned some of my cousin's activities through his friend's posts. Danny, handsome and standing by the sea, his mouth often open mid-laugh, as though his new life was a constant amusement. In the spring I discovered that Mr Baker had moved on in his romantic life. Within months of a woman appearing regularly in his photos, he posted a reel of his bended-knee proposal to her. His face seemed to have lost some of that sourness. A party of onlookers cheered as she enveloped him in her arms to agree to his offer. The commitment felt out of character for him, but I had to hope that watching a warped version of love play out through parties in the punishing heat had helped him reappraise his own emotional needs. I hadn't been the catalyst, but perhaps Danny, T or Gatsby herself had been a lesson.

It wasn't until November 2022 that I saw any of them again. I had been living in Brooklyn, ensconced in a mould-pocked studio, working a dependable copywriting job that satisfied me more than I expected. Though I'd previously dreamt of flashy bylines in storied outlets, my experience of traditional journalism in the wake of Gatsby's death had contaminated that ideal. I found productivity in writing corporate blurbs, giving me a toe-hold on my lofty ambition without dishonourable compromise. The money I made allowed me to enjoy the city without ever looking towards Long Island. When I took out-of-town visitors on the obligatory trip to the top of the Empire State Building, I averted my eyes on the east balcony, studiously avoiding looking towards the flat spur of land on the horizon. But as I prepared to return to my parents' home for Thanksgiving, I was invited to alumni drinks at the Plaza Hotel. I thought it a possibility that T might attend, but I assumed it highly unlikely. Not only because she had turned her back so thoroughly on New York, but because she had often told me how much she despised the woman organising the get-together.

I had been mindlessly partying most weekends with strangers and I found myself pining for the companionship of old friends, who I hoped would cleave to the idea of me they retained from college dorms and not one drawn from my recent scrape with fame. 'Life must go on,' my mom had repeatedly told me, and this felt like an opportunity to test myself. Could I slip back among the people I grew up with and operate in their register again?

When I arrived at the private bar area that Suki had arranged, I was surprised to see T striding towards the room from the opposite direction, her nose aloft, her shoulders back. We stopped awkwardly in the doorway together, the party already a shrieking cacophony ahead. There was no way to avoid meeting, no circumventing the moment or retreating through another door.

'Nic,' she greeted with a curt nod.

I said her name back but made no move to hug her as would be customary. She appraised me, standing tall in her heels.

'You look well,' she said, and I knew she implied weight gain.

I looked down, unnerved, at the dress Jordan had bought me once upon a time. I marvelled at her effortless ability to belittle.

'How are you?' she asked, her eyes roaming the room.

'Do you really want to know?'

She pressed her hand to her chest, a social pretence of hurt feelings or heartfelt empathy, but her face was its usual immobile hardness.

'I do, but we've been so busy,' she said.

'Oh, I'm sure,' I replied sourly.

Her eyes cooled and she squeezed my arm.

'Nic, we all lost someone that day,' she said in a low voice. 'It was nobody's fault.'

The anger that I had experienced early on in my mourning

process reared up in me again, ravenous. I pulled my arm from her fingers. 'It was all your fault.'

Her eyes darted to mine as I spat out the rage that had percolated in my gut for months. The things I had been counselled not to say, not to write. By the lawyers she'd paid for. The thoughts I couldn't voice were now tumbling out of my mouth.

'You put Miguel there, you dismissed Gatsby, you set them on course to each other . . . I wouldn't be surprised if you tipped someone off to start the whole online witch hunt.'

Something switched minutely in her, a tiny enlargement of her pupils, the slightest intake of breath and I suddenly recalled car headlights illuminating long, coarse grass at the side of the highway. Remembered her frantic thumbs pressing against a screen in the darkness. Something so urgent that she had stopped our race back home.

'Who did you message that night?' I asked, as she shook her head in denial. 'What did you do?'

She pushed away from me and laughed a little.

'Not everything is a conspiracy. I think you need to practise some self-care . . .'

She pinched the bridge of her nose and scrunched up her face, speaking in a pained, clenched way as though I was a sinus infection.

'It's so unkind of you to be like this after everything we've been through.'

Unkind. I could scarcely think of a person I knew who was less attuned to kindness.

'Even if you blame me, think of Danny,' T said, her tone hushed but firm. 'He's destroyed that he couldn't make her stop. Gatsby was a monster. Don't make his life harder. Let this go.'

I stared at her, astonished that she was still perpetuating this myth. They had laced back together the night it happened, promoting this story to all who listened. Poor sensitive Danny who was too drunk to stop a wild woman at the wheel. I had never told them that I knew. And not for the first time I wondered about telling the truth. Of pulling Danny beneath the wheels of fast-breaking news and watching him writhe. But at that point, I didn't. I understood that picking at this particular scab was something I was squeamish about and not ready for, the lesion beneath too fragile and damp to withstand exposure.

'Danny does not have a hard life,' I said, and I wished her a happy Thanksgiving before I turned away and left the hotel. I thought that I would never see her again.

* * *

On that final day in West Egg, as I had walked away from the boathouse towards the gate, the neighbouring mansion had looked almost shabby; the blinds closed in all the windows, overripe flowers sprawling beyond their borders in the gardens, the gravel drive churned up and furrowed by the numerous vehicles attending the scene that night. Gatsby truly had been more like me than I had imagined; she too was just renting on that silver shore, trying on an idea, hoping it stuck. She was more practiced than I was at projecting an image to others, but in the disorganised contents of her desk and in the moonlight when she'd decided to do a noble thing she felt more real to me than at any other time I thought of her.

I had turned away from the house and walked up the drive to the circle, pushing the code for the last time to swing the heavy gates open. I can still remember the digits. I didn't want to talk to the taxi driver waiting there for me, so as soon as I fastened my seatbelt I plugged my ears with music. I shuffled the tracks because I didn't want to choose what would soundtrack that journey. It felt too sad to pick music that would accompany me to the shattered end of a dream. As it turned out, the song that was randomly selected was a perfect, mournful match for the minutes before I arrived at the squat, unremarkable building that would burn Gatsby's mortal remains.

The greatest hits of Elvis that I had downloaded for one of my father's significant birthdays clicked into the velvet vibrato of Presley singing 'Fame and Fortune', a tinkling piano behind his fluting words craving love over fleeting renown and wealth. But the lyrics also suggested that it was love itself that ushered in that stardom too, manifesting riches via the heart. As I hurried inside the building to join Mr Gatz, I considered that this could have been true of Gatsby. Her passion for Danny drove her world-building, which in itself pulled him to her. In an environment where audience is everything, it was likely impossible for Gatsby to have had both love and fame. Fleeting is exactly how we like our gods and monsters. No one should be too happy, too successful, too anything for too long. We demanded impossible perfection from Gatsby and we punished her when she couldn't deliver. It was right that I felt self-reproach as well as sadness as I watched her simple coffin slide through the maroon curtains to an inferno beyond. There, as she buckled and crumbled, her fumes rising through the chimney, Gatsby was released.

This was one of my most naïve thoughts. Of course, she might have gone but she was not freed. Over the next couple of years the idea of her was reshaped and regurgitated. Her story was spun into new fables and permeated all forms of entertainment until I no longer knew it. The truth at the core of her cautionary tale was lost and forsaken.

It was only after Danny was killed last year that Gatsby came back more sharply into focus for me. He came off his Triumph on a perilous Highway 1 corner that he had drunk too many beers to negotiate. He'd only hurt himself this time, so when I heard the news that he'd been found ragdoll limp beside his twisted bike, his blue eyes turned opaque in an unblinking stare at the sky, I found the grief was a more linear process. I thought I'd guarded Gatsby by not speaking out, that I had kept her fierce love a secret to ensure not every aspect of her life was picked over, monetised. But in not telling the truth I had only shielded Danny. My silence didn't protect a clandestine romance, it just allowed him to continue making the same mistakes. I had tacitly condoned his carelessness. That summer had taught him nothing, and he'd ended a crumpled Icarus lying in a ditch at Salmon Creek trailhead.

Death had broken our family apart and its indiscriminate hand brought us back together. My mom could no longer give her cousin the silent treatment in the wake of losing such a beloved child, her lachrymose phone calls and discussion of tragedy now repeated daily having never traded in such terms when considering those who departed that Labor Day weekend. Danny's passing eclipsed everything that had gone before, and I was invited to his tasteful funeral in Montecito. We travelled as a family to California, arriving in the pale memorial chapel as a black huddle. I was shrouded in the flurry of hugs and tears, insulated from having to face T, who stood next to the wicker coffin covered in wildflowers, bobbing Pammy against her hip. The child bawled and

T's nose was raw from crying. Despite myself I felt some pity for her, understood her loss. I had thought the Buchanans a mismatched couple, but in the final analysis they were two sides of the same coin. She had lost her other half in every way.

I hadn't spoken to Danny since Gatsby's death, a tacit understanding on both our parts that we each thought our allegiances had been misplaced. It had been easy to stay furious with him remotely, seeing his auric life in the Golden State via Jordan's posts, disapproving of his ability to move on. But standing a few pews away from T as Pammy snivelled on her shoulder, a tiny blueprint of her father, the rageful dam I had built in me catastrophically failed. As his favourite music played, as Jordan choked reading from a book at the lectern and staggered passing the casket, I recalled Danny in technicolour as Gatsby viewed him. His warmth, the way he looked at the object of his affection, his sly smile that seemed to involve the recipient in a delicious secret. And in recalling him with fondness – if not forgiveness – on her behalf, I allowed myself the tears I hadn't shed at her mortal send-off for fear of further upsetting her father. Standing in that Central Coast chapel overlooking the ocean I cried desperately for both her and the boy she once loved; heaving, ugly sobs that disturbed the family, forcing me from the service to the silence of the graveyard.

A few weeks later, when we walked as a smaller group to the jagged-cliffed beach below the cemetery, I said goodbye to both of them as T paddled in the water and tipped the cardboard tube of ashes to the wind. They settled in a grey cloud on the surface of the sea for a moment before a wave dashed them apart, churned them in the foam. Both Gatsby and Danny returned to water, bobbing in two different oceans, at the mercy of the currents. It was done, and as my parents helped me physically back up the cliff path to our rental car, my body uncooperative with sorrow, I felt I reached a turning point.

Everything that had been muddled and twisted via media autopsy became clear again. I breathed deeply and focused on the road back to the airport, feeling a sense of emancipation. It began an unravelling in me that led, finally, to the proper self-care T had so flippantly suggested at the Plaza. That included taking proper ownership of my own failings in being Gatsby's friend. Contrition requires accountability.

I began to see myself more clearly too. I allowed myself love. Both in my own assessment of my past and in my partner. She was a librarian – a quaintly antiquated vocation in a digital world – who helped me find texts among the stacks of the New York Public Library and my way to haltingly kissing her in a bar in Soho. I found truth in the shape of her body in my hands, a sense of homecoming in the taste on her tongue. She, with her aversion to TV, her sentimentality for Pooh Bear and her active listening, gave me kindness and a grand romance like I had never known. And it was she who encouraged me to write.

I wanted to course-correct Gatsby's narrative, reposition her in recalling my own experience, put it down on paper. I wanted to reveal her particular singularity, that she was not a boilerplate rise-and-fall. I could have told the world the real story via social media, an essay, even a TV show – I probably could have made good money from it. But I wanted the permanence promised by a book. Wolfsheim ultimately helped me place my manuscript with a literary agent who found a publisher's fee that felt suitably remunerative without cashing in.

With the numerous exploitative, unqualified voices who have had a say in shaping her tale, I can provide an authoritative take. But in the writing I know I have only added to the noise. Gatsby was a black swan event, totally unexpected and yet, with the benefit of hindsight, entirely predictable. But she was a dream, both when I recall her and when I consider her quest. She wanted what any of us does; to make her real life match her imagined one. Who is truly who they say they are through reels, photos, stories, filters, posts? We are all unreliable narrators. Any of us who manage to sew our projected and actual selves together is living within Gatsby's precarious eternal hope. But she wasn't perfect. She was foolish and fooled. And she was what we all are when we return to meat, gristle and fluid: human.

Her demise only fuels my need to follow her example while I live – to keep chasing experience, stay afloat, cling to a destiny of my own design. I ascribe to Tennessee Williams's belief that we are all living in a perpetually burning building where love must be saved daily through the act of sharing. When the world is burning I choose to pluck love in all its forms from the fire.

I want to live authentically, fully present, with grace – everything I didn't do then. And I want to truly experience the world with all its savagery and wonder, sure in the knowledge that what happens outside of an algorithm, a hand-held device, a square image that demands comparison, is real life. I don't want to exist in a curated, edited, staged, filtered community. Gatsby unintentionally gave this to me, a glittering token hurled from the vortex that surrounded her. I feel more assured of that being an attainable mission, especially with the love of a girl with a Monroe silhouette and soft brown eyes who kisses me to sleep at night. She is *my* harbour, not the storm. She is also part of Gatsby's gift to me – to recognise who I truly am.

Perhaps I'm building sandcastles as vulnerable to tides as Gatsby's, but my past does not dictate my future. I can go forward with an open heart, believing as she did.

Unlike Jenny Gatz, I can, and will, swim.

Acknowledgements

First and foremost, I must thank the genius that is F. Scott Fitzgerald. 'Every author ought to write every book as if he were going to be beheaded the day he finished it,' he opined and it was with real trepidation that I began writing a reinterpretation of his novel that so enamoured me as a kid. A 1974 paperback with Redford and Farrow on the cover that my Mum had bought, it enchanted me over numerous re-readings and I fully understand the respect and reverence with which it is regarded. His words are wonderful – I offer mine in supplication at his feet.

Fitzgerald had the support and editing nous of Maurice Perkins and gratitude must also go to my very own Perkins at Borough Press. Editorial director Amy Perkins believed in *Gatsby* as a modern retelling from the minute she read it, and along with commissioning editor Jo Thompson shaped drafts and provided championing. Similarly my agent, Harry Illingworth at DHH Literary Agency, has been a partner-in-crime and shepherd in finding a home for an idea we discussed over lockdown zoom. The exacting copy-editing skills of Ed Wall were also invaluable.

I'm indebted to the early readers who gave their time and notes: Caroline Forbes, Ben Ross, Jo Monroe (and her beatsheetcoach.com skills), Dr Erica Acevedo-Ontiveros and Laura Morris, as well as the advice of my publishing Obi-Wan, Helen Whitaker. Thank you to my family and friends for putting up with the constant craning over a laptop and questions about synonyms. And a hat tip to Lana Del Rey, whose *Born To Die* was the soundtrack to *Gatsby*.

I must also thank my parents for encouraging a bookworm and a writer, and for sending me to UCSC as an exchange student. Truly, like Nic, it was a certain summer that made me.

Thanks also to my biggest cheerleader, Hal, who I hope sees that it's possible and continues to write his own stories – both on the page and in life.